Like a Panther in the Night

Sharon J Sockey

WestBow
PRESS
A DIVISION OF THOMAS NELSON

Author Credits: CD (single) Like a Panther in the Night

WestBow Press books may be ordered through booksellers or by contacting:

WestBow Press
A Division of Thomas Nelson
1663 Liberty Drive
Bloomington, IN 47403
www.westbowpress.com
1-(866) 928-1240

ISBN: 978-1-4497-1661-5 (sc)
ISBN: 978-1-4497-1662-2 (hc)
ISBN: 978-1-4497-1660-8 (e)

Library of Congress Control Number: 2011927809

Printed in the United States of America

WestBow Press rev. date: 05/11/2011

I would like to dedicate this book to Angela, Dwayne, Brian and Tamarah. The idea took place so many years ago. If time had allowed, maybe things would have been easier for us all.

But, we know, the wood had to be cut, the cows had to be fed and the table had to be set. Now, could be the best time.

Somewhere along our often rugged journey, you all got to be the kind of men and women you are.

For that I am proud and thankful.

Acknowledgments

I would like to thank family and friends who have believed in me. I can remember, as a child, Mama and Daddy made me think I could do well in school. It's amazing where encouragement can take you. I have looked back over the years and realized I was running on sheer trust instead of such a high level of intelligence. Thanks for being the kind of parents you are.

Mattie, Heather, Sarah, no matter how long it took, you never made me feel as though I couldn't finish this book. Thanks for wanting me to hurry so you could read it.

Angela and Tamarah, thanks for listening, reading and your true opinions. I knew if the two of you passed it, I had a good chance. Most of all, thanks for being excited with me.

Barbara, Kendra, Kerry, thanks for your hours of reading and your comments. I'm so glad you liked it.

Linda and Pat, you never failed to have time to listen. Thanks for being such good friends.

To all others who have ever listened to my dreams, you know who you are, and I thank you.

Life is a gift and for that, I thank God.

Chapter

1

Penny's long brown hair shone with tiny beads of water as she sat in the cool mist of rain. She couldn't help but think how easy it had been to slip away from her father tonight. Gunther Brown had been in his usual drunken stupor. Penny felt fortunate that her father had not been as violent for the last few months as he had been in the last seven years, but she knew how very easily that fury would be shown again if he knew she had slipped away to be with Brent Holbrook.

It was an exceptionally cool night for the month of May. Dark clouds covered the full moon and threatened to present a downpour of rain before the night was over. In the distance, Penny could hear the trickling of the water as it ran through the huge boulders before turning into the rushing falls. This had been one of Penny's favorite places when she was a young child. "Baby, if you don't stay away from those falls, they will surely be your destruction." Penny could almost hear her mother say the words. The glow in her huge jade-green eyes was overshadowed by the solemn, haunted look that always came when she thought of her mother.

Now, alone in the dark like so many times before, memories flooded her consciousness and took her back to the night her mother had left her, only thirteen years old, with burning tears in her eyes and a lump in her throat that felt it would choke the life from her. Julia Brown leaned forward, pressed her fingers to her daughter's lips, and pleadingly said, "Please don't tell your father I've gone. This is our only hope of starting a decent life somewhere else. When I'm able, I will be back after you. Take care, Penny."

When the people of Alder found that Penny's mother had gone, their narrow-mindedness made her life miserable. She could never forget the cutting words said about Julia, the only person in the world who had ever shown the girl any love or affection. The children told Penny that her mother had run off with a man from a big city, that everyone in Alder, Missouri, knew the truth but her. At first she had fought against them, but what was a thirteen-year-old girl against a whole town?

The crackling of a branch startled Penny back into reality. A raccoon fell to the ground from a nearby tree and skittered up another.

A brief smile played on her small but full lips; womanly, yet still so innocent. Shivering, she wrapped her shawl tighter around her shoulders. A slight breeze was beginning to blow and listening to the rustle of the tall pines, Penny succumbed to her thoughts again and drifted into her past.

"Easy little Penny, just like her tramp ma."

Penny stood barefoot and ragged in the street of Alder, her head down, wondering about and half believing the other children's accusations about her mother.

Six months before, fire would have burned in her eyes, now only ice cold hate was there. When the painful scene ended, she looked up and saw the face of a man that would be engraved in her mind for years to come.

Brent Holbrook looked down at Penny from what seemed to her a monstrous height. His dark wavy hair was as black as the shirt he wore. His bronze-colored skin was a contrast to his deep blue eyes; eyes that held no pity, no condemnation, only genuine understanding and empathy.

The straightforward, curious look Penny gave Brent made him smile, and after a few moments, a radiance filled her eyes that hadn't been there in months.

"Now, that's the way you should look at people; head up and eye to eye. When they find out they can't get you down, they'll respect you. They might not like you, but they will respect you."

Penny thought at that time she could look into Brent's blue eyes forever. It was such a relief to see something other than malice or pity in another human being.

Within a short time, Brent Holbrook had become a respected name in Alder. He was owner of one of the largest cattle spreads in those parts. No one seemed to know much about him. They all thought it was amazing that such a young man could have become so prosperous. He was a good neighbor, always ready to help others in need, but he was a loner.

It wasn't long until Brent became life itself for Penny Brown. He found ways of helping her without simply giving her handouts. On one occasion, Brent took a calf to Penny and asked her to bottle feed it for him. Its mother had died and he didn't have time to take care of it himself. Of course, in return he made sure Penny had several nice dresses to wear.

"Oh, Brent. I've never had anything like this before, not in all my life." Penny crushed the lemon-yellow dress to her as though it would vanish if she didn't hold on tight. She marveled at the thought that this tall man with such kindness in his deep, dark blue eyes could care about her.

Yes, life had changed profusely for Penny since she met Brent. She had matured quickly in the last few years from a thin, sad child to a tall, high-spirited young woman. This had seemingly gone unnoticed by Brent until her birthday just a few weeks before. He had ridden out to find Penny. She had become a significant part of his life, too. He wanted to give her his mother's jade necklace as a gift for her birthday. He didn't spot her as he rode past the Brown's house, so he stepped down from the horse and walked to the mountain stream. He tied his horse at the edge of the wooded area and began to follow the trail to Penny's usual hideaway. The falls could be heard not far away. As Brent reached the clearing that held Penny's haven, he was mesmerized by what he saw. There before him was a blanket of green grass spotted with bouquets of yellow and purple wildflowers, a background of tall pines, and standing ankle-deep in the clear, cool spring water was a tall figure with long, tan legs, slim hips, and small supple breasts. Her eyes were shut, her head slightly tilted upward as if to catch the warm sunlight with her delicate feminine features.

Her slender fingers held thick, waist-length hair from her shoulders. A swift movement from the far side of the creek caught Brent's eye. With what seemed like one quick motion, he reached the water and pulled Penny onto the bank in his arms.

Penny had not seen the cottonmouth water moccasin, nor had she seen who or what had grabbed her so roughly from the cool, refreshing brook. She flung herself from the arms encumbering her, turned, and blindly swung a hand at Brent. He moved to the side and grabbed Penny again. She then saw it was him. He nodded toward the snake slithering on downstream.

"Brent, Brent ... I, I didn't know it was you." Her breathing began to slow down and Brent couldn't help but notice the slow rise and fall of her breasts. They held each others' gaze for a long moment. Penny felt loved and protected as she always did with Brent. Still looking up, and on tiptoes, she put her arms around Brent's neck. Before he knew what was happening, he was tasting the soft innocence of her lips. His hard muscles tensed as emotions began to run out of control.

Penny felt a sudden tightening of the muscles in her lower abdomen. Her heart began to race as she felt a rush of desire. Her legs were weak and she leaned against Brent. She felt Brent's big, calloused hand slide slowly up her back into the thickness of her hair. He pulled her head back ever so gently. "Not now, Penny. Not like this." Brent was trying to hold on to the thin thread of control he had left so as not to take Penny's virginity before they were married. He had only been waiting to ask her because she was so young. But, as he searched the expression of confusion on her face, he knew she was acting on natural instinct and not the knowledge of what was about to take place. She pushed her naked body against him and pressed her lips to his. Again, Brent pulled away. Penny stood looking up at Brent, her long, thick mass of hair slightly tangled, her face still flushed. He took a step back. His eyes slowly and purposefully roved over Penny's body. "Penny, you're beautiful." Brent's voice was low and husky, filled with restrained passion.

Penny knew instinctively that she should feel embarrassed and ashamed standing before Brent, but instead she felt love and a strong sense of belonging.

"Brent, hold me. Touch me. I need you." Penny felt the hardness of Brent's muscles as he lifted her from the ground.

In moments, his long strides had taken them to the shelter of an immense sycamore tree. The branches hung low and the shadows fell deep in the early morning light. He gently laid Penny on the soft, green grass. He was totally enthralled with the loveliness of the young woman as he unbuttoned his shirt and covered her with it. As he lay down beside her, he cupped her head in his hand. Leaning over her, he tenderly kissed her soft lips.

"Penny, you have so much to learn about life, about men and women. So often I've felt guilty for the feelings I've had for you. I've wanted you so much at times I've been miserable, but you're so very young."

"I know I'm young, and you've probably known lots of women who knew all that women are supposed to know, but Brent, none of them could have loved you as much as I do. I don't understand my feelings sometimes. There are times when I feel like your little girl and there are other times when I feel like your woman, but I always feel as though I belong to you." Penny looked distant. With a low and almost inaudible voice, she said,

"The frightening thing is not that I don't *want* to belong to you. I *need* to belong to you. What scares me, Brent, is that sometimes I feel you belong to me and I know what a heartrending situation it can be when you think you have someone and suddenly find out you don't."

Penny moved close to Brent, and his arms tightened around her. He brushed her hair from her face. He wanted to do right by Penny, but he wanted desperately to make her his own. His resolve faded quickly, when Penny put her arms around him and kissed him urgently. Brent lingeringly pulled his shirt from Penny. His eyes raked over her naked body, and he shuddered involuntarily. He was now aware of her misconception of his love life. He didn't tell her that he was not the experienced man she thought he was.

He fought for the control he needed to love her as he knew she deserved. As he held one hand under her head, he began to explore her soft young body with his other.

Her hands began to move over the bulging muscles in Brent's powerful arms and then onto his chest. She could feel the beat of his heart underneath her finger tips. Brent moaned as his craving for Penny heightened. He kissed her lips again, this time demanding more and receiving more as Penny's arms went around him and she automatically lifted her body toward him. He gently pushed her down as his tongue tasted the sweetness of her kiss. This time the voice heard was Penny's. Brent was, naturally, a skillful and hot blooded lover, but where Penny was concerned his love and protectiveness again over rode his own needs. He knew Penny was almost ready to be entered and within moments he had undressed. At the sight of Brent's nudeness, came Penny's first moment of overwhelming fear, but again, his tenderness and unending love had her seeking the unknown. Brent spread Penny's legs and guided her to the gratification of womanhood.

Their coming as one felt natural to both of them, but later as they lay in each others' arms, Brent felt the warmth of tears on his chest. Abruptly, he sat up. "Penny, Sweetheart, what's wrong? Have I hurt you?"

With that ever recurring innocence and trust showing in her eyes; through the blur of tears, the young girl searched her lover's face. "Mama said we all reap what we sow. Oh, Brent, I know it was wrong, but I love you so much. I'm so confused. Brent, am I a bad person?"

Gathering Penny into his arms and stroking her hair as if she were a small child, Brent felt a pang of guilt. Certainly not for all the love and goodness he felt toward her, but for letting the inevitable happen before they had married. "Penny, you're the most decent and loving person I have ever known. What has happened here today has only made me love you more. I couldn't think of spending my life with anyone but you. Will you marry me?" The answer was silent but unmistakable.

Chapter

2

A fierce slash of lightening and boom of thunder again brought Penny from the deep reverie she had been in for what seemed like hours but actually had only been minutes. She began to get an eerie feeling and wished she hadn't sneaked out to meet Brent quite so early. Penny whispered half to herself and half aloud, "I wonder what Brent's surprise is. He wouldn't have had me meet him tonight had it not been important."

She was about to get up from the low hanging branch she had been sitting on when her mouth was covered from behind with a huge hand. Without warning, she was yanked backwards from her sitting place onto the ground. Out of natural instinct Penny bit down hard on the hand still covering her mouth. She jumped to her feet and turning swiftly, as a frightened animal on the rebound, she struck out wildly with long fingernails. She felt the tearing flesh.

Behind clenched teeth and in a voice vaguely familiar, Penny's enemy spat out, "You little wild cat!"

Knowing her opponent had been taken off guard, Penny turned and ran. Being well acquainted with the area her lithe young legs carried her unhampered on through the meadow and into the woods beyond the pines. Here she had to be careful of the low hanging thorny branches of the hawthorns. The thorns seemed to reach out ripping and tearing at her clothing. Ducking and dodging, Penny made her way through the shrubbery and to the rocky area near the falls. She had hoped to hide here until the hunt was over.

Moving with long angry strides the bulky figure, in the dark, was murmuring, "I have to find the bitch and get rid of her before he gets here." Lightening clashed and thunder roared. There was a sudden down pour of rain. He made his way on through the jumble of woods and undergrowth.

Penny saw him coming and moved to try to keep out of sight. Her foot slipped causing a loose rock to tumble down the ravine and into the swirling water below.

Her enemy closed in on her like a death trap. Lightening lit the sky once again and Penny got a quick look at him. "Brent, it looked like Brent." Her mind was a mass of confusion.

The words came in a roar of anger. "Come out Miss Brown.

You have no where to go except to the falls." She was caught by the wrist with a cutting grip and thrown to the ground. This time there seemed to be no escape from the shame, humiliation and pain she was about to suffer. The man yanked the jade necklace from around her throat and slipped it into his vest pocket. He ripped the skirt of her dress half in two and threw it into the water below. He then took her slippers, tossed one onto a ledge protruding from the embankment and left the other to be found by the edge of the creek.

Making one final attempt to escape, Penny drew all her strength together, got to her feet and tried to run before an almost lethal blow to the head whirled her into a world of darkness.

Chapter
3

Drenched with rain, Brent led his horse to where he and Penny were to meet. He called out to her. There was no answer. Tying his horse's reins to a small tree he squinted and skimmed the darkness for a glimpse of her. Lightening again split the sky and his gaze fell upon a small hump on the ground. He moved forward, bent down and grasped Penny's shawl in his hand. Searching the area, he called her name over and over again. Still no answer. A feeling of dread washed over Brent. He hurriedly rode back to the Brown's house. He swung the door open without stopping to knock. All he found in the small room of the shack was Gunther sprawled on a cot still clutching a bottle of whiskey in his hand.

He tried the bedroom door. "Penny, Penny are you in there?" There was still no response. With one hard kick the door flew open. The room was empty, the shutters still open and flapping in the wind. The gut feeling he had about Penny being in danger was becoming stronger by each passing minute. Outside the torrential rain was washing away any tracks that could have been left by man or animal.

On the rough-hewn table set a burning lantern. Brent carried it with him as he walked back to the place where he had found the shawl. There were no tracks in sight. He stopped and thought to himself, "If Penny had been on her way to my house I would have met her on my way here." He made his way on down stream calling out and scanning the landscape the best he could in the darkness. The water was rapidly rising and it was becoming difficult to walk in the muddy area beside the creek. He tread on through the pines to the place where the hawthorns grew. He raised the lantern and started to push a thorny limb out of his way. A foreign object clung to the thorns. He pulled it from the tree and holding it up to the light, examined it closely. "Penny's dress," Brent whispered. He squeezed the royal blue silk material before putting it in his shirt pocket. An image of the girl he had protected for so long formed in his mind. He saw her lying in the mud, the cold rain splattering in her face and long silky hair. Brent wiped a hand over his eyes as if to clear the vision from his head.

Fear like he had never known before put a sickening hard knot in his stomach, "Oh God, help me find her." He trod on toward the falls. The creek was rising and moving swiftly. Then, the light of the lantern Brent carried hit the soft slipper lying by the edge of the gully. Again, he shined the lantern into the darkness and the sight of Penny's other slipper on the ledge below brought a tormented cry to Brent's lips. "Penny, no not my sweet, sweet Penny!"

Half crazed, Brent searched on through the night for signs that Penny might still be alive. He circled around the hillside traveling downward past the falls. He rode steadily on down stream until daylight. The sun beamed bright and warm upon the fields of green clover and wild flowers. Blue birds sang their melodious songs. Squirrels scampered on the ground and jumped from tree to tree. But the warmth of the sun didn't penetrate the cold numbness surrounding Brent nor did he hear or see the beauty of nature around him. Once again he dismounted his horse. He followed the curving creek to the tributary of the Osage River. There wedged on a large heap of debris, washed up by last night's storm, was a shredded, muddy remnant of blue silk material. Stripped of all hope of ever seeing Penny alive again or feeling life within, Brent mounted his horse and started home.

Chapter
4

Penny awoke to a throbbing headache. With great difficulty she opened her eyes. The swelling in them kept the sight of her environment to a minimum. From what she could see she was on the floor of a small dimly lit cabin. Her hands and feet were numb from being tied so tightly. A small fire burned on the opposite side of the room. It took several moments before Penny could grasp any perception of where she was or even who she was. As she began to regain more and more consciousness she was also becoming more aware of the racking pain in her body. Her mind reeled back to the obscene ordeal she had gone through hours before. A sickening sensation formed in the pit of her stomach and contracting muscles caused a series of uncontrollable retching. But, not the physical pain nor the humiliation created as much mental anguish for Penny as did the thought of her beloved Brent's betrayal.

Penny pulled herself into a sitting position. From the corner of the small room she watched the fire swirl round and round as she tried to retain her consciousness. Almost incoherently and as her tears flowed she mumbled, "What's wrong with Brent? Something has to be wrong. He wouldn't have done this if something terrible had not been wrong."

Penny again sank into unconsciousness. She awoke the second time to a cold slap in the face. Gulping and straining for air she realized she had been soaked with water. "Wake up, Miss Brown." Penny's skin crawled as she recognized the merciless voice. What sounded like a tin bucket was tossed onto the floor. The looming figure stepped back and another shorter and much smaller took its place.

Running his fingers down the upper part of Penny's dress, he held on tight to the material. Pulling her close and holding a lighted lantern near her face the man gazed at the girl several minutes before roughly shoving her back into the corner. "Surely you don't expect the full price for damaged merchandise, Holbrook."

Again the sickening sensation came to the pit of Penny's stomach.

"You said two thousand, Chandler."

"Money, he's selling me for money." The thought tore at Penny's mind.

"Fifteen hundred and that's all. From the looks of her she won't make the trip and if she does my profit can't be much with her in this condition."

"She'll be as good as new in three weeks." She's a strong little slut. She fought like a tiger last night."

"Only one night?" Penny felt like she had been tied here for days.

"Well on second thought, since I am a man of my word you'll get your money. If she does straighten out I'll get a hell of a price out of her."

The cabin door was opened and before leaving, last night's abductor turned toward Penny. A wave of hopelessness washed over her as she took one last look at him. Almost without voice Penny whispered, "Brent, oh Brent, what have you done?"

"You are a fool, Miss Brown," was his only reply.

Never before had Penny noticed the sneering smile, raspy voice or the wicked glare in his eyes, nor would she ever forget it. The next few days were horror for Penny Brown. She rode slumped on a horse barely capable of comprehending the world around her.

There were two other men with Chandler. One short, with a big belly, fat hands with pudgy fingers, collar length greasy red hair and yellow, tobacco stained teeth. He spoke loudly and often, usually in an insulting tone. The second man was huge, probably reaching a height of six foot four inches. He had curly brown hair streaked with gray that matched the color of his blue gray eyes. He seldom spoke and when he did his voice was somewhat kinder than the men with whom he traveled.

Penny thought over and over again, "I have no use to live. Why does my body go on living?"

A voice broke through her thoughts. It was the gray haired man who went by the name of Buck. "Better eat, Miss. Sure to die if you don't."

This had been the man who pulled Penny from her horse during the day to rest and had spoon fed her at meal time. "Things'll get better. In a few weeks you'll be good as new and the bell of the ball."

Penny heard his words and wondered how life could ever again throb within the empty shell she had become. "Where are you taking me?" Her voice sounded distant to her own ears.

"Don't worry about that. It won't be so bad. You might even learn to like it."

Chandler and the red haired man, Clyde, were standing several yards away saddling their horses and preparing to leave. "Come on snap it up. If we hurry we can be back to camp by night fall." Clyde yelled in a sarcastic voice.

"Man, she has to eat or she's not gonna make it."

This time Chandler yelled, "Ten more minutes and we're headin out."

"Come on, lady. You heard em. You wanta live, don't ya?"

With a sudden surge of hysteria, Penny kicked the plate from his hand and screamed, "No, I don't want to live. Why would I want to live?"

"Okay, lady, let's go. If you die, my conscience is clear."

She walked and half stumbled the short way to her horse. The huge man lifted her upon it as if she were as light as a child. Seeing the wild look still in Penny's eyes, he pulled the reins over her horse's head and mounted his own.

"Might as well avoid any temptation you might have to finish what Holbrook started."

The hot sun shined brightly. By Its direction, Penny knew they were taking her eastward. The terrain was made up largely of forests and hills. The four horses and their riders followed narrow trails winding in and out of the wooded areas. The red and white colors of the flowering dogwoods and hawthorns entwined in the green of the enormous black gum and sycamore trees were a scene of magnificent beauty.

Could time have been turned back, Penny would have been bubbling with joy at the sight. She remembered the times spent with Brent sitting by a mountain stream, running into his house to keep from getting soaked in a summer rain and the delight she felt when he gave her the first horse she had ever owned. Penny was fourteen. She had walked to his house early one Saturday morning. Brent seemed, to Penny, terribly preoccupied as he worked on his corral fence. She was beginning to feel very neglected. Walking inside the barn door she spied a young filly she had never seen before. She was tall and strong built with a long creamy white mane and tail. Her sleek coat shined like yellow gold. Penny walked over to stroke her muzzle and talked to her in a deep whispery voice. As she turned to run out and ask Brent about his new horse she was surprised by the sight of him in the doorway.

Brent had been there for the last several minutes watching Penny's excitement and tenderness as she poured out all of her attention to the filly. He was beginning to see traces of the woman Penny would someday be as the tall willowy figure walked gracefully toward him. She wore the buckskin riding skirt and leather boots he had bought for her the week before. The tan colored blouse she wore offset the dark brown luster of her hair. Standing directly in front of him, she looked up and saw a mixture of amusement and affection.

"What did you name her, Brent?"

"Oh, I haven't. I thought her new owner could do that."

A look of disappointment took the place of the excitement in Penny's voice. Well, I hope he gives her a name that is worthy of her beauty."

Turning to go, Brent laughed and said, "I'll bet you can think of something."

Trembling with delight, Penny threw her arms around Brent's neck and gave him a quick kiss on the cheek. Then, she backed up. With a great deal of maturity and earnestness about her she said, "I can't imagine how I ever lived without you or what I would do if suddenly I didn't have you anymore."

He reached out softly touching her cheek. "Let's hope you never have to find out."

As the slight stumble of the black gelding Penny rode jolted her back to the present, she reached up and slowly brushed her own fingertips over her cheek, yearning for the gentleness of the man she had so loved.

A large river valley stretched out in front of the riders. A tall hill dense with trees and shrubs set just beyond the valley.

"Won't be long now."

"Yea, no thanks to you, spoon feedin that girl like she was something special."

Chandler broke in, "All of our captives are special, Clyde, and don't you forget it. We want um alive and healthy when we get um to Orleans."

"New Orleans, a world away." Penny had read about the city while reading one of her mother's books. Julia had begun teaching her daughter to read when she was very young. She learned quickly and continued to read any sort of book that she could find.

The travelers progressed on across the river valley and up the trail leading into the depths of the forest. The passageway wound up the hill and lead the riders over a ridge that flattened out into a small open meadow. There in the meadow was what looked like several families of people. Five wagons set close together and off to the side was an odd looking wagon, a large cage on wheels.

The men dismounted, and again the largest of the three pulled Penny from her horse. Together, they walked into camp. Groups of people began to gather around them. The aura radiated by them was one of filth and malevolence. An unkempt, red haired woman more than twice Penny's age, came closer and eyed the young girl in a very brazen way. Suddenly and frighteningly she let out a boisterous laugh. "You were right Chandler. You really picked a dandy this time." The others gathered round and roared with laughter.

Penny stood with her head down until now. She hadn't even thought of how she must look to them. She lifted her hand to her hair and ran her fingers down the length of it. Clumps of dried mud fell to the ground. The swelling had not gone from her eyes and large blue and yellow bruises surrounded both of them. Her silky smooth olive complexion was one of pasty white. The long black lashes that usually emphasized her large jade green eyes were made a pale brown by the dust gathered in them. Her once beautiful blue silk dress was half torn from her body. It was as if time had been rolled back and Penny was again the ragged barefoot girl who stood in the streets of Alder.

"Head up and eye to eye. When they find out they can't get you down they'll respect you. They may not like you but they will respect you." The words hit Penny hard and she felt a rage of anger flow through her body giving her extra strength. She straightened her drooped shoulders, held her head high and slowly looked each person in the eye with utter defiance.

Chandler's voice rang out loud and clear. "One of you ladies take her to your wagon and nurse her back to health. She has to be in shape to start traveling again in a few days." The women walked away one by one.

A child, a small girl child, Penny had not seen until this time, stepped forward. "Mr. Chandler, I'll take care of her. You know I can."

Chandler looked at the girl who couldn't have been more than seven years old, and gave a nod of his head.

A small hand reached for Penny's and led her to the far side of camp. There the child made a bed of leaves and pine needles under a shabbily built shelter. It was a welcome relief to Penny. The last thing she saw before drifting off into a deep sleep was a little angel with long, silky blond hair and big blue eyes watching her admiringly.

Chapter
5

"Jake, you and Dan take the northeast corner. Steve, Ed, John take the southeast." Ben, the foreman of the Blue Mountain Ranch was giving orders on rounding up stray cattle. He and the ranch hands were standing in front of the large two story home of their boss.

"Hey, Ben I thought you said Mr. Holbrook wouldn't be out today."

The foreman turned to look in the direction of the other man's gaze. Coming from the far side of the ranch was a rider. As he came into view, Ben's bottom jaw dropped.

"Why, he can't be. I just left him in the house there not five minutes ago."

Pulling his horse to a halt as he reached the group of men was a large man with jet black hair and deep blue eyes. Ben continued to stare at the man. His mouth moved to speak but not a sound came from hs lips.

Stepping down from his horse, the man smiled at the foreman. Extending his hand he spoke, "Is Brent in?"

There was still not a word uttered by any of the men. "I'm his brother, Frank."

As if glad to know he hadn't lost his sanity, Ben gave Frank a hardy handshake. "Mr. Holbrook is in the house there. He's restin up so he can ride back out and search just one more time. Always just one more time. He's not himself since the accident."

Frank questioned. "Accident?"

Ben looked uncomfortable. "I wouldn't have said anything, but I figured you knew. It's Penny. Do you know about Penny?"

"Yes, I came in for the wedding, but what about the accident?"

"You better speak to Mr. Holbrook about that."

There was a knock at the door. Brent heard, but wished who ever was there would go away. Again, there was a knock, this time louder. Still Brent did not answer. He heard the turning of the knob, footsteps and then he heard a voice that brought him from his chair.

"Frank, Brent began, it's Penny. There has been an accident."

Frank had a look of unbelief on his face. "I'm sorry, Brent. What happened? Is she alright?"

"Last week, from all appearances, she fell from the falls. All I was able to find were some shreds of her clothes and her shoes. I have searched everywhere." Brent's eyes filled with unshed tears. He moved to the window. His huge shoulders slumped. "God forgive me. I was going to bring her here to meet you. Frank, I wanted to tell her you were coming to the wedding. I shouldn't have asked her to meet me out there."

"Do you know how it happened?"

"No, she knew those falls like the back of her hand. She had played there since she was a young child. It's so hard for me to believe it was an accident. It was obvious she was being pursued. But by what, Brent hesitated, or by who? I was expecting you to be here that night. I was going to bring her here to meet you. You would have loved her, Frank. She was the kindest person I have ever known."

Frank thought quickly, "I was detained with unexpected business. Had it been possible I would have let you know my where abouts. I'm sorry, Brent." An uncomfortable feeling swept over Frank as he thought of the stormy night. "Did Penny know why she was to meet you, Brent?"

"No, I was going to surprise her." Brent's words trailed off. "I never told her anything about you, Frank. I wanted her to be able to form her own opinion without someone else's misjudgement getting in the way."

"Brent, I don't know if I ever told you how much I appreciated you standing up for me like you did. To know someone believed in me made it possible to withstand my time in Ellsworth."

"I only wish I could have done something. To be punished for a crime you didn't commit must have been almost unbearable."

"Yea, and I know how you must feel right now. You mentioned Miss Brown often in your letters. You must have loved her from the moment you laid eyes on her."

"Frank, you would have had to meet her to know how she really was. She was the most natural and sincere human being I've ever met. When I first saw her she was just a barefoot, long legged, skinny little girl. She seemed so helpless. It didn't take long for me to see that helpless was the last thing she would ever be. She had more spunk at thirteen than most women have at twenty five. That first year she followed me around when ever she could. It gave me such a sense of satisfaction to do things for her because she was so appreciative of every small luxury. As time passed that akward, long legged, self determined little girl began turning into a gentle, sensual woman. She worked her way into my heart and mind, and when she was torn from this life, so was a part of my soul.

"In time Brent, the pain won't be so bad. Just hold on."

The men sat together until sundown recalling the past. They talked about the happy times and not so happy times of their childhood. Their father was a soldier. He began his career at a very young age. Margaret Evans was the daughter of a farmer in Illinois. Jeremy Holbrook was stationed in Illinois when the two met. Jeremy was a tall, dark haired man; with a dark complection and brown eyes. It was as close to love at first sight as could be possible. Jeremy and Margaret were married within two months of their first meeting. Margaret followed him all over the country. It was years before they had children. There couldn't have been a happier couple. Margaret had twin boys but only lived three months after they were born. Jeremy retired from the army and took the twin boys back to Illinois. He raised his two sons there on a cattle ranch. He bred short horned cattle and gained great wealth through trade brought by the Oregon Trail. He took Brent and Frank on many cattle drives. Then came their 19th birthday. It was soon after, they took their first trip to Independence without their father. They were in charge of the cattle drive that year. Jeremy, their father, was not feeling well after a prolonged illness the winter before. When the brothers returned to the farm they found that their father had passed away. In the years that followed, during the many trips through Missouri, Brent had learned to love the beauty of the land and Frank had learned to love the fast paced living of the city. Eventually, the Holbrook brothers divided, equally, the wealth accumulated by their father. Frank went to seek fortune in the city and Brent kept working and saving until he was able to buy a ranch in Missouri.

It was in the early fall, when Brent set out to look for just the right location for his ranch. He longed to live in the beautiful hills of Missouri but knew that he had to have the fertile grasslands of the valleys to continue producing the quality of cattle he was known for. After weeks of riding and searching over the land, Brent found what he had been looking for.

A large, two story, red brick home with a wide front porch set on the lower slope of a thickly wooded hill. From a distance, it had the appearance of being built into the side of the land. Off to one side of the house was a beautiful rose garden made up of many colors. There were pink, wine red, pale yellow and snow white. The rose bushes were no longer separate plants. Without care the stems had grown rampant and entwined themselves, mixing and mingling the various colors into one giant sized rose bush. As the broad stretch of land in front of the house sloped off becoming level ground it was shaded by clumps of ash leaf maple, cottonwood and mulberry trees. To the far left and right the land again rose into mountains, plentiful with cool clear mountain streams and wild life.

By standing on the steps leading to the front porch, Brent could see that the large ranch home overlooked miles of fertile grasslands. It was a dream come true. He couldn't have hoped to find a place closer to what he had imagined. After the legal transactions were completed, Brent made the long move to Missouri. By early summer of the next year his roan colored, short horned cattle grazed the green grass of the valley as he had planned for so long. But, now, the Brent Holbrook who was ordinarily selfassured, energetic and looking forward to the demands of the following day sat haggard and disillusioned.

↓

Chapter

6

The wagons reeled and rocked as they rolled over the rough ground. Penny leaned her head back and let it rest on the iron bars that encaged her and the other women. Her eyes roved over the other prisoners. There was a resemblance in all of them. Each had dark hair that varied in shades from medium brown to coal black. Penny was the only one of the captives who didn't have brown eyes, but they were all dark complected. She wondered how old the others were, where they were from, how they were captured, but sensing the hostility within the group didn't ask any questions. The only person traveling with the small band of people against her will who wasn't caged or chained was Lisa, the child who had taken care of Penny while she recovered from the brutal kidnapping. Thanks to Lisa, Penny was regaining her strength and the dark bruises around her eyes were beginning to fade.

The women were all allowed to take baths and sunbathe during the rest period in the early afternoon of each day. In fact, it was one of the requirements for the prisoners to lie naked in the sun for a short while every day. That was the only time in which they were not either caged or chained, but they were watched closely by the free women of the wagon train. With the help of time, Lisa's care, the daily baths and sunshine, Penny was again showing her unusual loveliness.

It was a warm, sunny morning in June. The thick foliage of the forest cast many shadows on the dew covered grass growing beside the narrow trail. It reminded Penny of the early spring mornings when she and her mother took long walks through the fields picking bouquets of wild flowers. Their little cabin was always cleaned and shining and filled with fresh flowers before Julia went away. Penny remembered the loving relationship she had with her mother and a wave of loneliness washed through her. She longed for her now. At the same time she needed her mother's love so badly, she hated herself for that need.

Being so deeply enthralled in thought, Penny had been unaware of the tears streaming down her cheeks until she heard a voice coming from outside the bars. "Penny look. Aren't they pretty?" Running along side the wagon was Lisa holding up a handful of violets. "I picked them for you."

Hurriedly wiping the tears from her eyes and smiling affectionately, Penny reached between the bars for the flowers. "Thank you, Lisa. They are beautiful."

"Put one in your hair, Penny. The leaves match your eyes."

Laying all but one of the flowers in her lap, Penny reached up and worked the stem of the largest violet into the thickness of her hair. "How is it, Lisa?"

"Oh, it's nice. And, Penny, don't cry. Everything will be alright." Lisa slowed to a walk and the wagon filled with the captives took the lead once again. Thinking Lisa a brave little girl, Penny gathered the flowers together and smelled the sweet fragrance. Looking up she notice the watchful eyes of one of the other women. She saw no mention of hostility in the stare only a wann look of envy. By Penny's judgement the lady must have been in her mid to late twentys. She picked up one of the violets and handed it to the woman. It was taken without reluctance.

"What is your name?"

"Emily, but everyone calls me Ema, Ema Griffith."

"I'm Penny Brown."

"What she said is not true. Things won't be alright. They'll never let us go."

Just then another spoke up. "Well, if they don't it won't be any worse than what we had before."

A woman from the far corner asked, "Where are they taking us?"

"As much time as you spend with the men, you should know."

"I can't help it if the men enjoy my company, can I?"

"Oh, is it your company they enjoy?"

Just then as Penny, Ema and the other women sat in stunned silence, the two exchanging the insulting words began a knock down drag out. They were rolling on the floor of the wagon biting, scratching and pulling hair as if they really meant to kill one another.

"You high and mighty, stinking bitch. This time I"ll teach ya."

The largest of the two women rolled the other to her back and straddled her. Breathing heavily and with her hands holding to the woman's hair she began banging her head against the floor.

Penny screamed out. "We have to stop them. They'll kill each other."

"Let them. Then, maybe the rest of us can have a little peace and quiet." A woman whom Penny had not heard before spoke.

As Penny rose to try to stop the fighting the driver of the wagon pulled the horses to a halt, unbalancing the girl and causing her to fall directly onto the winning woman's back.

At that moment the woman turned her attention to Penny who was scrambling around trying to get back to her feet. She grabbed Penny by the arm throwing her to the floor with ease.

Penny felt the hardness of the metal wagon bed as she landed flat of her back. She instantly found herself in the same predicament as the prisoner she had wanted to help. Her head was lifted and thrown back down again to bang against the floor. Just then the driver of the wagon was pulling Penny's enemy from across her. The large woman continued to kick and claw at the air as the man pulled her from the wagon.

"Alright, everybody out." He shouted.

The captives climbed out one by one. Penny was the last to step down from the wagon. By this time everyone in the small band of wandering people had pulled his wagon to a stop.

Chandler yelled from the seat of his wagon, "What's goin on back there?"

"I think these ladies need a short rest, Chandler," answered the driver.

Clyde walked up, his eyes fixed on Penny. With a sneering look and lustful gaze, he put in, "I think it'll take more than a short rest to calm these ladies down."

She understood the meaning by his malicious tone of voice. His breath smelled of tobacco and decaying teeth. Penny had to swallow hard to keep the nausea from gagging her.

Escorted by two men carrying double barrel shotguns the women walked to sit under a nearby tree. Penny was again the last in line. Ema turned to her. Seeing that she was still rubbing the egg sized knot on her head she said, "Get smart if you want to survive. That was just your first small lesson in survival."

As Ema walked away, Penny stood staring with a distant look in her eye. Remembering Brent, she said, "No, not lesson one." The words were spoken softly but with determination. But, I will survive and I will teach a few lessons of my own."

To have lived a life that would have embittered most people long ago, Penny had continued to exist as a kind natured young woman. But now, surrounded by malice and hostility, natural survival instincts were beginning to take precedence over the sweet personality that she had always possessed. She learned to be cunning and conniving in order to survive. It seemed to Penny that the only people she had ever loved and trusted had forsaken her and for no other reason but to fill her heart with misery and pain. She had no one to live for, no reason to live except to repay Brent for selling her soul and to prove to herself that she could learn to forget the pain of her mother's desertion. Penny regretted having to be a hard hearted person but she had to learn to live under the conditions she had been thrown into. She learned in time that the women held as prisoners with her had been forced into their way of life long ago and it was apparent to her that they had forgotten any way of life other than the one they were living now.

Penny hoped that she would be able to hang on to the knowledge of when and where kindness, rather than maliciousness, should be shown. She hoped that if she could ever fight her way out of the situation she was in now, she would be able to again find love and tenderness in her heart.

The last week's travel had taken Penny and her captors miles away from Alder. This was farther away from the small town than she had ever been before. The beauty of the country was magnificent. The land was a mixture of tall hills and green river valleys. Despite the situation she was in, Penny loved seeing the beauty of the land. At the moment, swimming in the cool waters, she was at peace. The rest of the women were standing in the more shallow water bathing, but every day Penny hurried with her bath and hair washing and spent the rest of her time swimming. She floated on her back, eyes closed feeling the warmth of the sun on her face. Her long hair spread out on the water, her arms rested in an outstretched position and her feet moved in short quick motions moving her gently through the water. Penny opened her eyes looking up at the baby blue sky undisturbed by any cloud. She was in deep water. The bed of the creek had narrowed and there were weeping willows growing thickly on both sides of the stream. Suddenly, becoming aware of the silence, Penny kicked pushing herself into an upright position. She, at first, became a little frightened and then had a sudden urge to jump from the water and run away to freedom. Her forehead creased in thought. Her green eyes flickered with light, as she tried to make a fast decision whether to run for freedom or not. She asked herself aloud, "Where would I go? How would I survive?" She realized she was not prepared to leave the security of the wagon train. An inner feeling of calm settled through her. She realized by this accidental happening that she did have a chance of escaping. With long strokes, Penny swam back up stream. No one had realized she was gone. The other captives still stood splashing in the shallow water and the two women guarding the prisoners seemed to be bodily present but missing in mind. One sat holding a gun across her lap. Her head rested against the trunk of a large oak tree and her eyes were fixed on a butterfly fluttering near a large bunch of honeysuckle vines. The other sat with her head turned toward the direction of the wagons.

The women began filtering out of the water to lie in the warm sunshine. Penny walked onto the grassy bank, her long brown hair shining with just a touch of an auburn red color. Her jade green eyes glowed with new found hope. Her black lashes were moist with the water from the creek. Even as she lived as prisoner to these people, she walked proudly with her shoulders back and her head held high. She tipped her face up toward the sky. Penny couldn't seem to overcome the embarrasment of nudity, but she enjoyed lying in the warmth of the sun. The memory of the hard slap in the face she had experienced the first day she refused to sunbathe made her look automatically at the redhaired woman sitting under the oak tree.

The woman was watching her intensely. Her attitude toward Penny had changed considerably since the first day the girl had walked into camp ragged and half beaten to death. Penny, although adapting to her surroundings and new life style quickly, was still very unaware of some of the cruelties of life and people. She thought the woman was looking at her with some sort of respect because Penny had proven to be a survivor. But the red head felt envy and hate toward the girl because of her youth and extreme beauty.

Penny's eyes drifted over the dark complected women lying on the ground and with a smile curving her lips thought to herself, "They could all pass for the half breed slaves I read about in one of Mother's books. What a coincidence," Penny thought. "The slaves I read about were sold in New Orleans." She shrugged the absurd idea away and went to find a nice soft place to lie in the sun.

As the days passed, Penny became less and less filled with fear. She accepted her situation for the time being and calmly planned her escape. She had worked hardily to change inner turmoil and anxiety into inner strength and ingenuity. The only obstacle between Penny and freedom was the feeling she had for Lisa. Penny sat on a short tree stump in the cool night air. Lisa sat at her feet with her small blond head leaned against Penny's knee.

The wagons had been stopped for the night. The free women slept in the privacy of their own wagons but the women held captive slept on worn blankets on the bare ground. Most of the others had already gone to sleep, but Penny sat with Lisa for a while each night trying to show the child that she did have a friend she could feel free to love and trust. She felt an obligation toward Lisa because she knew most likely she wouldn't have made it through the first week without the child's loving care. It wasn't only a feeling of obligation toward Lisa. The girl seemed to bring out a premature maternal instinct in Penny. They both sat quietly. The stars were shining a bright blue against the black sky. The crickets and bullfrogs could be heard in the distance and every now and then one of the prisoners would move in their sleep and the rattle and clanking of the chains would break the illusion of peace and quiet created by the rest of the surroundings.

Suddenly a coyote let out its eerie howl and Penny could feel the tenseness of Lisa's muscles as the child moved closer to her. Penny ran her hand down the smooth silkiness of Lisa's hair trying to soothe away the fear. She felt the wetness of tears soaking through the thin cotton dress she was wearing. It was the first time she had known Lisa to cry.

"Sometime I'm so scared, Penny." Lisa looked up with tears dripping from her face, her small chin quivering and her face contorted in a look of misery and fear. Her words came in short snubs and Penny had to listen closely to understand. "Mr. Chandler came one night. I woke up and he was fightin with Mother. She fell and didn't get up. Someone knocked on the door and then Mr. Chandler saw me. He grabbed me and ran out the back way. I never saw my mother again."

This was the first time she or any of the other captives had told what had happened during their kidnapping. Penny knew that a close bond had been built between her and Lisa or she would not have talked now. "How long has it been since it happened?"

"I don't know. It seems like a long time. I just remember Mother and I miss her. I don't like it here."

Penny and Lisa slept on the worn blanket together. She held the child in her arms until she stopped crying and fell asleep. It would be hard for her to leave Lisa trapped in the clutches of these deadly people.

Early the next mornig tin plates of food were brought to the prisoners. They ate and then had a short amount of privacy before they were again forced into the cage and headed for their destination. The hilly country had leveled off and they were now traveling through flat stretches of land. Far away, though, there could be seen, again, mountains and forests. Penny knew from the books she had read that the Mississippi River formed the eastern border of Missouri. Her captors were taking her in that direction.

The wagon wheels screeched and cracked as they rolled over the bumpy trail. The other women were unusually talkative but Penny did not indulge herself in their conversation. She sat quietly contemplating the details of her escape. She had learned many things about survival during her life as a child, especially after her mother left her alone with her drunken father. Gunther was drunk most of the time. He only worked enough to keep a little food in their house. It had been left up to Penny to care for herself and a great deal of the time she had to care for her father. She had learned to cook, sew, clean and care for herself medically. Julia had been an avid reader and had left a great number of books behind. Penny had read most of them and through self motivation, had become a very versatile young woman. Brent had taught her to ride and hunt and she had proven to be a worthy student.

She thought to herself, "If only I could manage to take a gun, I could get by on my own. But, the only time I'm free of the chains is when I'm locked in this retched cage. I can't take one into the water with me." She searched and searched for the pieces to this puzzle she had to put together.

The morning passed quickly and it was again time for the noon meal. The prisoners were herded out of the wagon and given food on their tin plates. It was during her meal that Penny noticed for the second time the intense stare of the red headed woman. This time she saw the hatred in her eyes. Penny looked away but it was long moments before she felt the relief of the resentful gaze leave her direction. Immediately after lunch the women were taken to the water for their daily baths. These were precious times for Penny and they passed all too quickly. But, even though enjoying the water and sunshine, she couldn't push the face of the red haired woman from her mind. She knew intuitively that there would be trouble between them. It didn't take long enough for the thought to become an actuality.

It was on the way back to the circle of wagons that the trouble took shape. Penny could see the red head, Mildred, standing out in the open holding onto Lisa's arm. The girl's face was set in a painful expression. Mildred was looking directly at Penny. As the prisoners drew closer, the woman began to shake Lisa roughly yelling in a hateful voice. "You never do what you're suppose to, you little brat. This time you'll pay for it with your hide. Glancing at Penny and then back to the child again, the red head struck her hard in the face. The blow would have knocked her down had she not still been holding to Lisa's arm.

Penny stopped in her tracks cringing at the force of the blow. Without warning, the woman hit Lisa for the second time. This time knocking her to the ground. Penny could almost feel the pain as she envisioned her father's fist coming toward her own face. He had only hit her once, but she remembered her mother's bruises even more. All hell broke loose when Mildred reached for Lisa the third time. Penny ran, leaving the prisoners and guards behind. She heard the firing of the shotguns and felt the sting of dirt and rock as the lead hit the ground close to her feet. She gained speed with distance and did not slow down as she tackled the woman who had looked up and was now braced for the fight. Penny hit her with a force that sent them both tumbling over and over. They fell to the ground. The young girl fought wild and hard and even though bigger and more experienced in battle the other woman didn't have a chance as years of bottled up anger were turned loose. People gathered round them cheering the fight on. Penny stood up, pulling the redhead up with her. Both were tired and panting. Penny administered one final blow knocking the woman to the ground. She stood watching Mildred. There was no movement. Penny turned slowly to walk away. Suddenly, she heard the clicking of metal. She turned back toward the woman, quickly, to face the barrel of a shotgun aimed straight at her heart. Her eyes fell to the trigger and saw Mildred start to exert pressure to fire. A shot rang out. The gun flew from the hands of the redhead. Penny thought for a moment she had been hit, but then realized the shot came from Chandler's gun, not from Mildred's. He had seen the trouble and fired, tearing the gun from the hands that in another instant would have killed Penny.

Chandler stood looking down at the terrified redhead. He yelled, "What the hell is going on, Mildred? This prisoner is very valuable."

"She's nothing but trouble. Lisa won't do anything since you brought the lady here." Mildred looked Penny up and down with a sneer.

"You have no right to keep this child as a slave," retorted Penny. She clamped her teeth together to keep from saying too much.

"Save your words. You may need them, half breed."

"Enough." Chandler gave Mildred a warning look.

Once more she glanced at Penny, grabbed Lisa, roughly, by the arm and pulled her away.

"Make sure this woman is chained tightly until she is put back in the wagon." Chandler gave the orders to the guards and turned to go.

Penny knew she had probably made things worse for Lisa and she was determined, now, to take the girl with her when she could escape these ruthless people.

"Save your words. You may need them, half breed." The memory of the words cut through her thoughts. As she was led back to her prison on wheels, with her hands chained behind her, Penny asked, silently. "Dear Lord, don't let my fear become a reality."

Chapter
7

She sat in the stagecoach only a few miles from Alder. It was almost time to leave the relay station and continue what had been a long trip back to her old home. She was dressed in a fashionable, satin, rose colored dress. She was a tall, thin woman only showing her age by the thin lines creasing the skin along the outer edges of her eyes. The man who sat beside her was short and stocky built. He too was dressed in fashionable clothing. He reached over and took the woman's hand in his own. He tried to talk Julia out of taking this long trip back to Alder, but she was determined to be with her daughter once more; even at the expense of her own health. After all, this is what she had worked for.

The night Julia had left, she had no idea where she would go or how she would ever have the money to come back after her. She only knew that she wanted a better way of life for both herself and her daughter. She could almost hear Penny's words.

"Go Mama, before he kills you."

Julia knew, if she stayed she wouldn't live to raise her daughter, but that didn't block out the guilt of leaving. She had read of the aristocrats who lived in New Orleans and hoped to get a well paying job as a seamstress there in the busy city. The first year hadn't worked out as she had planned. The only job she found was in a hotel scrubbing floors. Julia had worked everyday with only the thought of Penny keeping her going. She spent her evenings after work–and her only day off; knocking on doors of well to do families–asking for work and trying to prove herself as a seamstress. Finally, her determination began to pay off, when she was hired by one of the richest families in New Orleans. She worked and saved with the thought of going home to get Penny. During that year, she had met George, a prominent banker. Within a short time, he had asked Julia to marry him, but she would not seek a divorce from Gunther until she was again reunited with Penny. Julia's health had declined for months. She was so ill, she was unable to make the journey to Alder. She worked hard to get strong enough to make the trip and although she was still yet in a weakened condition. She finally realized there was the possibility that she might get weaker again. She made the crucial decision and planned the trip to Alder.

George had suggested Julia stay in New Orleans and let him make the trip, but she had very adamantly refused. Now, she sat nervously awaiting the reunion with her daughter. So many questions flooded her mind.

"What does she look like by now? Are her eyes as green as they were before? Is she still all legs and arms or has she matured into a young woman?" She looked down at the ivory music box she had brought all the way from New Orleans to give to Penny. As she ran her fingers slowly across the delicate carvings, she fought the urge to cry. The realization of precious years lost, swept through her mind. "George, was I right to leave her behind with no one to care for her What if she has grown to hate me? Can our new life together ever make up for the time we lost?"

"Julia, you did what you had to do. That is all we can ever do. It's a shame you had to leave your daughter behind, but just think what your hard work can do for her now. Will she not understand that you did it all for her? Did you not do what you did for the love of your child?"

"Yes, yes, I did it because I love her. For so many years we had nothing. There was no hope of ever having any better life had I not left Alder. I couldn't take her with me. I had no idea whether or not I would even have food when I got to New Orleans. At least there, she could exist until things were better."

Julia and George sat in silence for the remainder of their trip to Alder. As she looked through the stagecoach window, she began to recognize the surrounding country leading into her old home town. She tried to put fear behind her and concentrate on the loving times she and Penny had shared in years passed. She remembered the night her only child was born so many years ago and a faint smile touched her lips as she thought of the small bundle of love placed in her arms by, then, her kind, loving husband, Gunther Brown.

Penny was born with a head full of dark brown hair. Her eyes were just as green that first night as they were the night Julia left her crying in the lane near their old house. The first few years of Penny's life had been spent in a happy home, but when things started going wrong, so did Gunther. The Brown's lost their crops to a series of hard rains one year. Instead of fighting to hang on to the farm, Gunther gave up. He started drinking and beating his wife and neglecting Penny.

After the abuse started, the happy times Julia and Penny had, were only shared by the two of them. They both tried, but there was no changing Gunther. All the mother and daughter had was love, and they made the most of it. Their life was simple and so were the good times they had. Julia, eventually, tired of seeing her child live on the scrapings of life. She made her decision and hoped and prayed she was doing the right thing. Now, as the stage pulled into the small town, Julia knew only time would tell.

"Whoa." The driver of the stage pulled the team of horses to a stop in front of Murphy's Hotel. People began to come out of the surrounding buildings to meet the stage. As Julia stepped down from the stage, she recognized several faces in the crowd. She stood hoping to get a glimpse of Penny. She could see that people were beginning to recognize her, also. The faces held no friendly welcome. Their eyes swept over Julia in a very opinionated manner.

With a nod of her head, Julia acknowledged their presence with a gracious but reserved attitude. Some spoke or nodded stiffly. As the people began to walk away, she heard one of them say, "Look, how she's dressed. How could she have left that poor girl alone to survive on her own all this time? Why, it must be true what they said about her."

George took her by the arm and escorted her into the hotel. "We would like to rent two rooms, please."

The hotel owner looked first at George and then at Julia. "How many nights?" Suddenly, there was a glint of recognition in his eyes. "Julia, how are you?"

"Fine, Mr. Murphy. It's nice to see a friendly face."

"I have no reason not to be friendly, Julia. I know how much you loved Penny. Knowing your situation, I knew you must have had a good reason for leaving. I just wish you could have made it back sooner."

Julia detected a note of saddness in his voice. "Have you seen Penny?"

Not wanting to be the one to tell her the bad news, the man said, "No, Ms. Julia. Go talk to Brent Holbrook. He owns the ranch north of here. He's the one you need to talk to." He took their money for two nights and handed them the keys. As if finished with the conversation, he lowered his head and again became busy with his book work. When they walked away, Mr. Murphy looked in their direction and watched regretfully as they climbed the stairs.

When the couple reached the top of the stairs, Julia blurted out, "Something is wrong with Penny." Her voice was full of worry.

"What makes you think so?"

"Didn't you hear what Mr. Murphy said? He sounded so downcast."

"Julia, you are only tired and worn out. Lie down and rest. Later we will rent a carriage and ride out to talk to Mr. Holbrook."

"I don't want to waste another moment, but I know you're right.

I want to feel well when I see Penny." She went into her room and slipped out of her satin dress.

Chapter

8

"Frank, I just ran across two more strays up over the ridge. You take those. Jake, you head south along the river and up to Stony Mountain." Brent was again issuing orders to the men who helped him run his ranch. He took off his wide brimmed hat and wiped his brow with the back of his hand. It was not much after noon and he had already put in what most men would call a full days work. To everyone's surprise, Brent had made a complete turnaround within the last few weeks. He had gone from a man beaten and withdrawn to a steadfast worker, almost to the point of being a fanatic. He didn't expect any more than an honest days work from his men or his brother but he pushed himself unduly. He sat astride his high spirited sorrel gelding, once again, in control of his ranching business and apparently, in control of his emotions. It was apparent to all but his foreman and good friend, Ben Richards, anyway.

As the old man sat waiting for his own orders, he took great notice of the lines developing around Brent's eyes and mouth. Although the younger man was a picture of great physical stamina, his loyal friend sensed the frustration he was trying to overcome. He was old enough and wise enough to understand the need for Brent's total indulgence in his work. But, the awareness of that need didn't keep Ben from being concerned about both Brent's physical and mental health.

"Hey boss didn't you need to pick up some supplies from town? Me and the other men can handle this. Why don't you ride into Alder and we'll see you back at the ranch tomorrow afternoon. From the looks of ya, ya need a break."

"I can send Frank into town. He's the one who likes the city life. He'll be glad to go."

"Yea, but, Boss, he's not the one who needs the break, now, is he?"

Brent knew his forman didn't, necessarily, care for Frank. He didn't hold it against the old man, because he understood the conflict between Frank and the men at the ranch. Brent and his men held a love for the land and their ranch work that Frank didn't really comprehend. His love was for the city. He didn't feel the responsibility for this type of life. He never had, not even before their father passed away. It had always been Brent who had shared in the real responsibility of the business. Frank had been care free and everyone had accepted him as he was. He did his share of the work but never seemed to take anything too seriously. He spent all the time he could in the city kicking up his heels and having a good time, as he had with his share of the inheritance from their father's ranch.

Brent laughed. "You're right as usual, Ben. It's about time Frank took some real responsibility in running the ranch. He'll be disappointed, but tell him he's in charge until I get back. Have it your way, Ben, I'll spend the night in town and be back tomorrow evening."

Ben smiled as Brent rode away. He was happy that he had been able to talk his boss into leaving his work for a while.

Brent rode toward the ranch house to pick up his buckboard. He was thankful to Ben for his suggestion. He already felt some relief for having an excuse to leave his work behind for a while. He knew down deep inside what he was doing to himself but some force drove him. He felt it was the only way to keep his sanity after losing Penny. The loss had been great. She had become a part of all his future dreams. In the beginning, he had only wanted to take care of her. She had no one and he knew he could make her young life more pleasant. As time had gone by, and Penny grew into a young woman, he knew he had fallen deeply in love with her. He felt guilty in the beginning and tried to ignore his feelings. He knew how much she depended on him and didn't want her to confuse that need with love. He had wanted to know that she held the same sort of love for him as he held for her and when he knew, he had asked her to marry him. Brent's thoughts reeled back to the years he had Penny, from the first time they met until the last moment he held her in his arms. He took a deep breath. Love, hurt, loneliness and wanting all filled him. He knew that Penny loved him the same way he loved her. He held that thought deep inside and it helped him go on living. He could see his home in the distance. The home he had hoped to share with Penny. Every living thing he passed reminded him of the girl and her love for the simple things of life. He had never before met anyone who could make the ordinary seem so beautiful. He remembered the excitement and love reflected by her faithful attitude and genuine smile.

As he thought of the woman he loved, his longing to look into her stormy green eyes and touch the softness of her flesh became a hard cold ache. He shook the thought from his mind for fear if he didn't it would soon possess him and break the thin thread of control he had gained over the last few weeks. His thoughts, again, were turned to the ranch and the business to be taken care of in town.

It had been a long ride back to the ranch house for Brent. Now, as he approached, he could see Mary, his new housekeeper standing on the front porch. She was young but had led a hard life up until Frank had talked Brent into hiring her.

"You need a woman around here to keep this place in order, Brent." Frank had said in a serious tone. "You would have more time for working if you didn't cook your own meals." He laughed. "In fact, if someone else did the cooking we might feel more like working."

Brent had relented to the idea, since he had often thought of hiring someone before he met Penny.

Frank had brought Mary home late one Saturday night. After showing her to the room she was to occupy, he said to Brent, "She'll work real hard. She hasn't had an easy life and she'll be able to appreciate a job like this. I promise you won't be sorry."

"You talk like you found her in a saloon." Brent had eyed his brother suspiciously.

"Looking a little guilty, Frank had replied, "I did." He smiled sheepishly. "Aw, give her a chance, Brent. I know her. She'll work hard."

"Okay, but the first sign of any trouble and she goes. I won't have strangers running in and out of my home at all hours of the night. She'll have two days a week off and she can spend those days anywhere she wants to."

Mary had proven to be a hard worker. If she had ever seen any man, she had not let her private life interfere with her job at the ranch. Now, riding toward the porch where Mary stood, it came to Brent's mind that he had never known of her leaving the ranch at all since that first night Frank had brought her there.

In her usual respectful tone of voice, she asked, "Is there any trouble, Mr. Holbrook? You're home early."

"No Mary, I Just need to ride into town for supplies."

"Will you be eating before you leave?"

"No, I'll eat later on in town. By the way, I won't be back until tomorrow evening."

"Is there anything else I might do for you before you leave, Sir?"

"No, I'll be leaving right after I wash up and change."

"Yes, Sir." The light, quickly faded, from Mary's eyes. She turned to walk back into the house. Walking back to her room, she stayed there until Brent left. When she heard the front door close, she walked to her bedroom window. Pulling the pale yellow curtains apart, she peered out, watching the buckboard roll away. A shiver went down her spine. Mary felt far more secure when Brent was at home. She thought for long moments and then decided to clean Frank's room. Maybe he would be in a good mood if she did something really nice for him. She walked down the hallway. Twisting the knob she put her shoulder against the door and pushed her way in. Noticing the disaray gave her increased hope. She thought Frank would surely appreciate the gesture. Mary worked quickly to tidy up the room. After folding the last bit of clothing she opened the top dresser drawer. While rearranging the items, a shiny piece of jewelry caught her attention. She pushed the material from it. Mary took in a deep breath as she pulled the jade necklace from its hiding place. She recognized the unique piece of jewelry as the one Penny had worn. She had seen Brent and Penny in Alder more than once, when she use to sit on the balcony outside her own room at the saloon.

Now, Mary thought to herself, "What is Frank doing with the necklace his brother's woman wore? Maybe, this could be my way out of here." Only a few days before she had told Frank she intended to quit her job as Brent's house keeper. It was then she knew for sure she was being held prisoner. Frank told her in a way that left no doubt in her mind that she would be in grave danger if she tried to leave. She layed the necklace back in place, covered it and closed the drawer. Her heart jumped at the sound of footsteps. She gasped at the sight of Frank standing in the doorway.

"What are you doing in here?" His eyes narrowed together in barely controlled anger. Moving toward her he grabbed her by the hair at the back of her neck.

"I just came in to clean your room. I know how busy you are and I wanted to do something nice for you." She tried to hide her fear, but to no avail. It showed by each hard pulsation of the vein in her neck and quiver in her voice.

"You know very well that you are never to come in here. Didn't I make that clear?" He pulled harder on her hair.

Mary had tears in her eyes. "Please Frank, believe me. I just wanted to find something special to do for you. You can't be mad at me for that can you?" Her fear seemed to provoke the already angry man even more. Mary knew by her experience with Frank that he took some sort of pleasure in hurting her.

With the fingers of his free hand he grasped the low cut material at the top of her dress. With one yank he ripped it to her waist. He squeezed her flesh until she began to whimper. Suddenly as he dug his finger nails into her soft skin she screamed out loudly. Angered even more Frank brought his knee up hard between Mary's legs. As an animal of prey he feasted on her still, limp body.

When she awoke, she was lying sprawled on her own bed completely naked. Her tattered clothes were piled in a heap in the corner of the room. Pain shot through her when she tried to move. She took an involuntary gulp of air as a dark shadow fell across the bed. As Frank hovered over her she felt a smothering sensation. In a low sinister voice he threatened, "Don't tell anyone what happened or attempt to leave. If you do either, you may not be as lucky as Miss Brown." As he left the room Mary realized she was trapped.

Down stairs there was a knock at the door. Frank was slightly taken aback as he looked ito the eyes of the visitor.

Extending a hand, the woman said, "Hello, I'm Julia Brown. This is George. We were looking for Mr. Holbrook."

"Yes, I'm Mr. Holbrook. What can I do for you?"

Shaky and pale, Julia asked, "Is Penny here? Mr. Murphy, the owner of the hotel in Alder sent us here to you."

"May I ask who you happen to be?"

"I'm Penny's mother. She must have told you about me."

"Yes, many times," Frank left the conversation open for any information he could obtain.

"Then, I am sure she explained every thing to you. Is she here? Is my daughter here?"

An artificial look of sadness touched Frank's eyes. He explained the details of the accident, repeating as precisely as he could the words Brent had used to explain it to him.

Julia stood in shocked silence. Every ounce of color drained from her already pale face giving her a look of living death. She turned to George with a blank stare. She began to sway, and both George and Frank grabbed her.

"Bring her into the study. I'm so sorry. How could I have told her such a thing without even asking you in? How thoughtless of me. Here, lie down on the sofa. I'll get some water."

After long moments of oblivion, the distraught woman broke into relentless sobs. Although being in a questionable mental state,

Julia took an instant dislike to the man standing above her. He stood looking at her with a lifeless stare that made her shudder inside.

"I don't believe you. What have you done to Penny? Where is she? Who are you? Why was she here with you?" She screamed the words. The tears came again. This time she said, quietly. "My daughter has been familiar with those waterfalls since she was a young child. She would have known how close to the drop off she could get and still be safe."

George, put his hands on her shoulders. "Julia, listen to me. Accidents do happen. Penny's gone." His voice was firm but gentle.

With a look of defeat, Julia agreed and in a hoarse whisper said, "I need to see Gunther before we go back home."

Worried about her health and the toll this catastrophe would take on it, George reluctantly agreed. They headed for the old home place. The short trip was one without the long awaited joy. Julia sat in silence, knowing her life would never be the same. So long she had waited and worked to get back to her child. She felt as though her life had ended with those terrible and tragic words. "She fell from the falls." She was numb inside with a hollow feeling she could not have imagined before. All the time she had the aching and tumultuous remorse of leaving Penny, she had also had the hopes and dreams of being reunited with her. Now, it was all gone.

As they approached the run down house, Julia longed for the past. "I was wrong to leave Penny here, alone those years. I should have taken her with me no matter what the chances." She was numb with grief but part of her would not and could not believe her daughter was gone. The yard was strewn with empty bottles. Gunther sat on the front porch in an old wooden chair. With glazed eyes he searched the intruders faces. He stumbled as he got to his feet. Julia saw no recognition in his eyes. She couldn't help feel a pang of sorrow as she looked at his shriveled face and tossled gray hair. She called his name. There was no answer. The woman moved closer to the man. She called to him again. "Gunther, it's me, Julia. I came to talk to you about Penny."

"Penny the man mumbled. I have no money."

"Penny, our daughter, Penny." Julia said the name, loudly.

As he walked passed her, she knew the glazed look came not only from the whiskey, but from a dead heart and mind.

Chapter
9

Brent pulled his team of sorrels to a halt in front of the livery stable. In one quick movement he jumped from the buckboard. A stable hand came out and Brent handed the team over to him. "I'll be staying in town until tomorrow."

"Sure, Mr. Holbrook," the young man said. I'll take care of them." He watched enviously as Brent turned and walked toward the hotel.

The sun was still hot. People sat in front of their places of business gossiping, sipping cold drinks or just watching the lazy day go by. Two pretty young women giggled and smiled as Brent walked past them.

"Now, I wouldn't mind if he came to call on me, not one little bit." One of them said to the other.

The other wrinkled her small nose as she said, "Why, he's too old for you."

"So what if I am young. That old Penny Brown was younger than I am."

"Penny looked older, though. And she acted older too."

"Oh, you mean she was more mature."

"Yes, something like that. And she just happened to be extraordinarily beautiful. And, besides those irrelevant facts, Brent loved her."

"That's just it, loved her. She is gone and I am still here. "

"Her body is gone, but something tells me her love lives on within Brent's heart."

"You know what's wrong with you" You have no imagination."

"Yes, and you have too much of one."

"Only time will tell."

On the way to the hotel, Brent stopped and talked to several acquaintances. They expressed their condolences and somehow Brent knew they meant it. He also knew that there was no one on earth who could wish away the empty spot that Penny left behind. He sauntered on over to the hotel. As always Mr. Murphy, the hotel owner, was busy at his desk. "I'd like a room for tonight, Mr. Murphy." Brent said.

"Sure thing., Brent. How did the meeting with Miss Julia go?" Brent stood with a puzzled look on his face. "She did come out to see you didn't she?"

Brent questioned, "Julia? Who is Julia?"

"Julia Brown."

Again Brent stood puzzled.

"Didn't she come to the ranch to see you?"

"No"

"She checked in here earlier today. Asked about Penny. I told her she needed to talk to you. I sent her out to your ranch. Couldn't bare to tell her about her daughter."

"I must have missed her on the way. When she comes back, will you tell her I'd like to see her?"

"Will do, Brent."

Brent slowly climbed the stairs feeling as though this was another hurdle too high to jump. He unlocked the door at the end of the hall and stepped inside. Suddenly feeling very tired, he tossed his hat on the floor, stretched out on the bed and fell asleep. He dreamed of Penny. They were in a place only vaguely familiar. Again Penny was barefoot and in tattered clothing. But in his dream she was no longer the child she was when they first met. He was pushing his way through a crowd of people. He could see that her hands were tied. The faster he tried to move toward her the heavier his body felt and the slower he moved. Just as he was almost close enough to touch her two men pulled her away. He saw the fear in her eyes just before the crowd pushed itself between them. Brent awoke in a cold sweat. He sat up abruptly wiping his cold wet hands on his pant legs. He said aloud, "So long I loved you, Penny. I didn't tell you because you were so young, and now I feel like the lost child without you." He walked across the room, filled the wash basin with water and washed the perspiration from his hands and face. He absent mindedly ran his fingers through his black hair and put his hat back on. Brent left the dark room behind looking back as he stepped into the hall leading to the narrow stairway. His look was pathetic. Half way down the stairs, he murmered, "Excuse me, when he bumped into a woman's shoulder. He proceeded to move on without even noticing who he had run into.

Julia turned and called his name. "Mr. Holbrook." There was such a note of surprise in her voice that it brought Brent out of the daze he was in. Yes, Ma'am," he said in a slightly apologetic manner. He looked up first noticing the color of the woman's eyes. That is when he began to assume that she was Julia, Penny's mother. He couldn't have missed the similarity between the coloring of this woman's eyes and Penny's. Although, that was the only likeness. While Penny's hair had been dark brown with a warm glow of red the older woman's was ash blond. While Penny's complexion had been olive, this woman's was fair. Penny's appearance was delicate but Julia's was fragile. But, both were beautiful. Brent finally saw the expression on her face. It was one of half fear and half amazement.

"Mr. Holbrook, What are you doing here?"

"I'm spending the night in town. I came in to get some supplies. You are Julia?"

"Yes," Julia replied, looking quite perplexed.

"Is something wrong?" Brent asked.

"Yes, you look different. It's your eyes. Your eyes are different."

Suddenly knowing what the problem was, he reached out taking her by the arm. "Ma'am, you must have talked to my brother, Frank, at the ranch. I'm Brent, Brent Holbrook."

"How did you know my name?" Julia asked.

"Mr. Murphy told me you were on your way out to see me." Brent hesitated and then asked slowly. "I guess you know?"

"I know what your brother told me." She added in a tight voice. "I can't believe Penny is gone."

George walked to the bottom of the stairs. Looking at Julia and then Brent, he said. "I see the two of you have introduced yourselves. Mr. Murphy told me that you wanted to talk to Julia."

Julia introduced Brent to George and the three walked to the lobby of the hotel. They talked until late into the night. This time Julia believed the story she heard. To know that someone loved Penny as Brent did was a great consolation to her. Julia told Brent of the last two years and the events leading to her leaving Alder. He understood because he too had tried to deal with Gunther Brown concerning Penny's welfare. When asked if Penny resented her mother's leaving, Brent lied. "She knew you would come back someday, Julia." He didn't tell the bewildered woman of her daughter's confusion and feelings of being deserted. He felt that there ws no need to put Julia through any more pain than she had already had to live with. He knew there would be a life time of guilt and self doubt for her now, even though she had thought she was doing the best for her child.

After persistence from Brent, Julia and George decided to accept his offer of hospitality and stay in his home for a few days.

During the visit Julia grew to know and trust Brent more and more and to distrust his twin brother equally. She knew outer appearances were the only thing the men had in common. She knew that Brent would have made a wonderful husband for her daughter, but no matter how much she wished things had all happened differently she could not wish away the past. She gained a close relationship with Brent and he with her. They were tied spiritually by a common denominator, the unshakable memory of Penny.

The time came when Julia and George knew they had to make their way back to New Orleans. She had become a bit stronger physically and was thankful for the chance to know Brent, but nothing could replace the disappointing and shocking homecoming. She and Brent said their goodbyes, aware of the mutulal loss.

Chapter

10

"Penny, Penny."

Jade green eyes searched the shrubbery. Not seeing anyone, Penny lay back on the ground. She closed her eyes but heard the sound again.

"Penny, Penny. Over here."

She sat up again looking back over her shoulder. Her eyes lit up when she saw Lisa peeking out from behind a clump of wild plum trees.

" Please don't let Mildred know I'm here, Penny. She'll come and get me and then she'll punish me for coming to talk to you."

Penny lay back so as not to create any suspicion. She could hardly contain a low gurgle of laughter caused by the happiness of seeing Lisa again. "Where have you been, Lisa? I haven't seen you for days."

"Mildred said if I came near you she's goin to skin me alive. She's watched me so close I didn't dare come near you."

"How did you get here without her seeing you?"

" I saw her slip into Mr. Chandler's wagon. I knew she wouldn't be back out for a while. I saw her lay down beside him. They take naps together all the time.

Penny was half amused, half frightened at the child's innocence, knowing what a short time ago she would have probably believed the same thing about Chandler and red head. She suddenly became aware of what would happen to Lisa if she grew up among these people. "I can't let that happen. I won't let it happen," thought Penny with a note of finality.

"Did she hurt you any more?"

"No, she just made me work harder. Scrub her back, wash her clothes, things like that. I use to like helping Mother. But it's not the same here helping Mildred."

Penny couldn't help looking back again to give Lisa a smile and to reassure her that things were going to get better. "You and I are going to get out of here, Lisa."

"Oh Penny, they won' let us go."

"No Honey, we're going to run away from them."

The child's mouth fell open. "No! They're sure to shoot us if we try to run away!" Lisa's eyes were filled with fright.

"Don't be scared. We are going to do it when they are not looking. Do you see the mountains ahead of us? When we get there. That's when we're going to run away. There will be lots of places to hide in the mountains. Trust me, Lisa."

"I do trust you, Penny."

"I'm so glad you're alright. I was afraid Mildred had hurt you and you couldn't come to see me. You know, Lisa I always wanted a little sister. I guess I have one now.

A glow of happiness washed over Lisa's face. "You mean it, Penny? Do you really like me as much as a real sister?"

"I love you, Lisa. You better run on now, before you get caught."

Lisa jumped up to give Penny a hug but remembered the consequences if she was caught. She stopped and gave Penny a look of admiration before running in the opposite direction.

Penny looked toward the distant range of mountains. She lay back on the soft grass beneath her with a new sense of satisfaction. She had been planning her escape and planning well. She knew she must have a gun and it would be up to Lisa to get it, since she herself would be chained or caged all of the time except for times like these when she was sunning or swimming. Later, when they reached the mountains she would talk to Lisa again and explain to her what they needed to do in order to make the plan work.

As if by natural instinct, both Penny and Lisa stayed as far away from each other as possible, knowing that being seen together would only cause them problems. And by the overpowering looks of conquest the redhead had been giving Penny their instincts were right.

"You won't have a friend here by the time I get through with you half-breed," Mildred said. She walked past Penny and gouged the end of her shotgun into the young girl's ribs saying simultaneously, "Get up! It's time to get back to your cage where you belong."

Penny barely controlled her own look of victory as she walked toward the caged-in wagon. Again the wagons reeled and rocked toward the great mountainous region to the east. With each mile made, Penny was more determined to escape her wicked captors. She spent a part of each day's travel planning her vendetta against Brent, but with each vengeful thought an over powering urge to believe he was innocent of any event leading to her present situation over-whelmed her. As with the love she felt for her mother, this different kind of love she felt for Brent was just as strong and just as difficult to terminate.

Penny's head rested on the metal bars as the wagon bumped along the narrow path through the wilderness of Southeast Missouri. She was again the glowing, healthy young girl. Her already dark skin was tanned golden by the hours in the sun. Her hair was lightened enough by the sun's rays to catch every glint of light and the natural spark of fire was again reflected in her green eyes. But just as always, Penny seemed unaware of the outward beauty she possessed. Her thought were on survival. Not only did she have her own future to save, but that too of the young girl she had grown to love as a sister.

Outside the splendor of each day's scenery seemed to replicate the day before. The level ground gradually began to tilt upward and the forests became more dense by the day. She had plenty of time to plan her escape and did so to every last detail. She knew it wouldn't be long now until she and Lisa would be free.

Two days after they were far into the mountains, Lisa again found a way to avoid Mildred's presence and go to Penny. Penny was swimming alone in the deep waters of a mountain stream quite a distance from where the other women wer bathing. The woods were thick and would have been difficult for the naked eye to discriminate between a tangle of vines and a human being. Lisa called to Penny from the far side of the creek.

"How did you cross the creek without being seen, Lisa?" Penny asked, while looking at the child's wet shoes.

"There are big rocks on down the creek. I waded across."

"What if you had fallen in?"

"Oh, that wouldn't have made any difference. I can swim a little creek like this easy. I just didn't want to get all wet and let Mildred know I had been talking to you, Penny."

"You're getting to be quite the little sneak, aren't you?" Penny asked laughing at the face Lisa was making.

"When are we going to sneak away, Penny?"

"That's what I wanted to talk to you about. Everything will have to be done just right, at just the right time. I think I have a way." Penny and Lisa went over every last detail of her plan. Somehow when they finished each trusted the other without a doubt.

"I'll see you tomorrow, then."

"Okay, I'll see you, Penny."

The day passed quickly. Penny went over the procedure of the escape time and time again. Finally it was time to spread the worn blankets on the ground and sleep. "Just a few more hours and then we will be free," she thought. And then with the sudden thought of seeing Brent again, an unexpected feeling of excitement and love rushed through her. She immediately halted those feelings. "It is so unnatural to feel this way, she thought. A normal person could not love someone who had done this to her. It is so unbelievable that Brent could have done this. The man who loved and protected me for so long." Tears stung her eyes, as her chin quivered. And then the reality of what she had lost hit her and the tears overflowed. She awoke the next morning with a detached feeling.

She had to keep fighting for the will to carry out her escape. She wondered if maybe it would be best to be taken far away from the place she had always known: the home where she had learned and lost the love of her parents and Brent. "How could such as this happen?" She whispered to herself.

"Everyone up!" The ever recurring voice called out and the monotony of another day started out just as usual. "But this day will end so differently," Penny thought as she held her hands up for the guard to unlock her chains. The day began warm and still. By late morning, the air felt heavy and humid. Lunch time passed and it was time for the daily baths. More importantly this was the time for Penny and Lisa to escape. Penny entered the water just as she had many other times before. No one suspected anything when she began to swim through the water far away from the other prisoners. This had begun to be expected of her daily ritual. Only this time she swam farther and farther away until she was completely out of sight. She kicked herself up straight in the water looking all around for a glimpse of Lisa. Although she was aware of the meeting with the young child, she was startled when Lisa jumped from behind the trees.

"Hurry, Penny. I brought everything you told me to bring."

Penny swam to the bank and with one energetic movement, leaped out of the water. Knowing she had to move quickly she pulled the clothes on that Lisa had brought for her. "Where is the gun, Lisa?"

"Over there behind that tree."

Taking Lisa by the arm, Penny picked up a sack of dried meat and bread and both girls ran to the nearby tree for the gun. Handing the sack to Lisa, Penny took the shotgun in hand and checked to see if it was loaded. She smiled at the child. "Good girl, Lisa. Come on this way." They moved hurriedly through the thick forest hoping to put as much distance as possible between themselves and their captors. Both the girls were physically fit and fast runners. They put much ground behind them in a short time. After a while they both needed a break. As they sat on a fallen log, Penny noticed the clear blue of the sky, darkening with black clouds. The wind began to blow, at first only slightly, and then as the huge black cloud moved closer, the wind became stronger and stronger. Penny knew it was an absolute necessity for them to seek shelter.

Lisa began to cry. "Penny let's go back! It's a terrible storm! I'm scared! Please, let's go back!"

Penny ran her hand over the child's tangled hair. "It's too late to go back now. Things will be alright. You'll see Lisa. We'll find a shelter from the storm. It won't last long." But the wind was very strong now, and Penny wasn't too sure of her own words. She took Lisa by the hand and pulled her toward a rocky area in the distance. They made their way up a rocky trail surrounded by pine trees. Just as the trees and shrubbery were so thick that the girls had to bend over to pass through, they found themselves at the opening of a cave. Although to enter was frightening, neither of them hesitated. The wind was so strong now, they almost had to yell to hear each other's words.

Penny was first to enter the darkness. Continuing to hold the younger girl's hand, she moved deeper into the shelter until they could no longer feel the force of the strong wind pushing them. Both shivering, they sat down on the gritty surface of the ground and listened to the shrill howl of the wind outside. Lisa put her hands over her hears and cried as the storm grew in intensity. And then, as if the storm had never been at all, it ceased to be.

The quiet was almost as deafening as the storm had been until a soft moan broke the silence. Penny's heart seemed to stop as she sat waiting for the sound to come again. Her first emotion was that of fear. But as the sound came again and again she recognized it as a sound of pain and not one of rage. Next came the recognition of a human voice instead of the growl of an angry animal. Penny's mind raced. Her first and most natural instinct was to run away from the possible danger that could await her and the girl she felt so responsible for. But as the moans seemed to become more and more filled with agony, she knew her concience would not let her run away whether there be danger or not.

She firmly told Lisa to stay where she was. She stood up, and slowly began to move toward the sound. She could now see a fraction better than when she and Lisa had first entered the cave, but still was forced to move inch by inch over the uneven ground. Her heart pounded in her ears as she came closer and closer to the source of the pathetic groan. She came to a sudden halt when she almost ran face first into the wall of the cave.

She continued to move slowly along the, now narrow, pathway to her right. There was a light in the near distance. Her way became light and she entered another larger opening. To her left she saw the figure of a young boy lying on the ground by a small fire. Penny approached him slowly and carefully. When she was close enough to see his torn and bloody body clearly, her fear was quickly and completely replaced with the urgency and determination to save his life. She knew she had to move quickly. First she lit a torch by the fire the boy had somehow managed to start. She ran back to get Lisa. The child was still sitting in the exact same spot where Penny had asked her to stay.

"Lisa, come with me. A boy, he's been hurt. We have to hurry. I'm afraid he's going to bleed to death if we don't do something." Penny was beside the boy again within moments. The bleeding was heavy and the wounds were deep. Her moves were smooth and effective. In a short time, she was able to stop the severe bleeding and bandage the wounds on his arms and chest. She looked at the jagged tear on his left cheek and thought, "You will carry that mark for a life time. That is, if you are lucky enough to live through this." She looked down at her torn clothing. She had used half her dress for bandages. She suddenly laughed outloud. It was not a laugh of joy but one of a brief expulsion of hysteria. "Will there never be a time when I won't be wearing only half a dress?" Lisa looked at her curiously. Penny moved to put her arm around the girl's shoulders. Lisa layed her head against Penny as if she felt as much comfort and protection with her as she had her own mother.

Chapter
11

As the days passed, the Indian boy, Jerome, became stronger. When he was well enough to speak with any coherence, he told Penny and Lisa of his accident. He had been attacked by an old mama wildcat when he strolled too close to her den. "She could have killed me, but she only wanted to protect her young," he said.

Penny was surprised by his fluent use of her own language. "Where did you learn to speak English?" She asked.

"My grandmother was a white woman. She was captured by Black Hawk as a child. He was enemy of my grandfather. During a battle, my grandfather took her from Blackhawk's camp. He said he had found gold in her hair and heaven in the blue of her eyes."

Jerome kept his eyes on Lisa as he told his story.

Penny saw a look of trust as she watched the two young people communicate without words. She knew she must have looked at Brent in the same way many times. Her mind wondered back to another time. She felt a chill spread through her tired body. She rubbed her hands over her arms trying to rid them of the goose bumps. Tears stung her eyes and her lips quivered. A longing for Brent washed over her. She could almost feel his strong arms around her.

"No time for this," she mumbled to herself. She quickly stood up and brushed the dust from what was left of her dress. She kissed Lisa on the cheek and said, "I'll be back in a little while. I have to go check my traps."

"Be careful, Penny. You know Mr. Chandler will be looking for us."

"I'll take care." She smiled at her young friend as she left the cave. Penny knew Lisa was right. She must be careful. Chandler had paid a great deal of money to take her to New Orleans and she couldn't imagine him leaving her there in the woods. She walked, bending under the low hanging branches of the trees down the incline from the opening of the cave. She had set up rabbit traps in order to feed herself and the two young people who depended so heavily on her. She didn't dare to use the gun and take a chance on being heard and tracked down.

She looked to the west. The red-orange color of the sun was barely peeking through the trees. It would not be very long until dusk. The animals were already on their way to the creek to drink the cool water. She hurried to her traps knowing it was dangerous to be out in the wilderness after dark without the protection of a gun. What had happened to Jerome could easily happen to her. When she came to the last snare, she heard the sound of voices. Swiftly and cautiously she ducked. Looking out from behind the bushes she saw the movement of people in the clearing near her. She sat still without taking a breath until they were out of her sight. As she started to move she heard a low sinister laugh behind her. She jumped at the sight of Mildred and her deadly shotgun.

"Hey, Chandler, over here, I found her."

The others were quick to come. "Okay, let's get back to camp." Chandler said.

Mildred goosed Penny in the ribs with her gun.

"Wait, Penny said in an urgent voice. We have to go back for Lisa."

The red haired woman frowned. "We don't need that kid. The two of them together ain't nothin but trouble."

Chandler disagreed, "We'll get the girl. Leaving her here would be murder."

Penny's heart ached for Jerome, but she knew he would be better off here waiting for his people than to go with the treacherous group she and Lisa were with. She watched Chandler walk away while Mildred and the other men stayed behind. The cold barrel of the shotgun was still yet pressed into the soft skin of her back.

Mildred stood in silence, as did the others. When the leader of the pack was out of hearing range, Mildred looked at the man standing nearest. "Stay here for a while. Tell Chandler you never layed eyes on the girl again." Her lips pressed together tightly, and then spewed a brown stream of chewing tobacco on the ground at Penny's feet. "You won't ever see that girl again."

Penny knew she meant it. Her heart sank, but just before the tears welled up in her eyes, she turned her head so Mildred couldn't see the raw fear. She choked back the bile in her throat, swallowed hard and headed for camp. The walk back seemed, to Penny, far too short. It was dark and the camp fire was burning bright. Everyone was sitting, watching, waiting as if a great performance was about to begin. When Penny's eyes fell upon the two large poles standing within the circle of wagons, she realized she was to be the main attraction. Her attention came back to the present when Mildred gave her a hard push. Penny lost her footing. Stumbling forward she fell on her knees. Struggling to get up, she felt a foot against her back side. The women laughed as her face fell into the dirt. Every inch of her body wanted to stay down, but her heart told her to get up. With all her strength, she pushed herself out of the dirt, once more, and stood up straight. Before she could move, her clothes were being ripped to pieces. Her breasts were half bare, and the end of her tight fitting dress hung in jagged shredds just covering the top of her thighs. Suddenly, her arms were stretched high over her head, a wrist tied to each pole.

Mildred appeared before her again, this time with a bullwhip. She slowly swung her arm letting the whip unroll and then the sharp crackling noise broke the silence. Coming close to the younger woman's face, Mildred ran a slimy finger down Penny's cheek. At the same time she heard the words, "It would be a shame if I slipped, now wouldn't it?"

Penny could hear the crackling of the whip behind her. She knew Mildred would prolong the ordeal as long as possible. With every pop of the whip, Penny flinched, tightening every muscle in her body and expecting that time to be the time she would feel the torment of the lash.

Without warning Chandler was taking the whip from Mildred's hand. "I've changed my mind. Look at her, stretched out there. If we put her on the auction block in that getup, what a price she'll bring. I don't want a hair on her head harmed. Is that understood?" Mildred looked at him with a murderous look, but backed down just as quickly, knowing that he wouldn't have anything to lose by putting her in Penny's place.

The small band of wagons traveled on through the mountains and passed the flat stretches of land. Finally, they reached a great, wide river. Penny soon realized it was the Mississippi. Once there, she and the other prisoners were turned over to a crew of men, obviously some more of Chandler's hired hands. The women were sent on their way toward New Orleans. During the trip down the Mississippi, they were treated very well. The food was not only nourishing, but tasty. They were still expected to sunbathe, but in a private area away from the men. It turned out to be more like a pleasurable cruise for aristocrats than for women to be sold as half-breed slaves. Evidently these men knew what they were doing for by the end of the journey, the women were healthy, vibrant and beautiful.

On the day the boat docked at the port in New Orleans, crowds of people stood waiting to see the new load of half-breed slaves that were to be auctioned off that afternoon. Both men and women seemed excited. The women walked off the boat one at a time. Some of the men whistled and cheered while others, the ones with their wives, just watched with envy.

"This is the best bunch yet," one man shouted.

"What a housekeeper she'll make," another yelled.

All the women had been extravagantly dressed; all except Penny Brown. She was the last prisoner off the boat. Inside she was humiliated, but for all outer appearances she was strong and proud. A hush fell over the crowd as the young girl came into sight. Her chin was lifted high: Her eyes were flashing. She was determined not to be broken by any of these people. Instead of being dressed in fine silk as the other women were, Penny wore brown satin, the color of her hair. The dress had been cut to look exactly like the one she had worn on the night Mildred had wanted so badly to beat her. The neckline was swooped in a low cut v. The material fit snug and clung to her waist and hips. The bottom of the dress had been cut in a zig zag fashion barely covering the tops of her thighs.

The feeling came quickly. Penny was afraid. She shook with fear way down deep. She began to feel as though her knees would give way and she wanted to cry out. Thoughts ran like lightening through her mind. "Why have I met with such a fate? Mama, where are you? Why did you forsake me? Brent why did you betray me? Didn't you ever love me?" Her eyes filled with unshed tears. Her head was bowed low, her shoulders slumped. Penny was, for all appearances, the beaten young girl in the streets of Alder once more. Only this time she was far away from the familiar streets of Alder, Missouri. She had no idea that every eye in the crowd was on the green eyed girl with smooth tawny skin and long silky hair. Penny stood on the platform for all to admire, but she was oblivious to her beauty. Her hurt and shame ran deep.

"Whatda you say we start the bidding now?" A loud voice bellowed from below.

One of the guards walked up beside Penny. "Not a chance. Besides you better do your bidding on one a little more calmed down. This one is going to be rough to handle. She hasn't been tamed yet."

"So that's it," Penny thought. "I'm on display as a wild woman." The word woman entered her thoughts automatically. Somewhere along the path of her yet short lived life she had seemed to lose out on her childhood. "I'll prove them wrong. I'll tell them all that is happening here."

At that moment, the guard took her by the arm and led her down the steps and past the people to a waiting wagon. They rode only a short distance until they were again unloaded and taken into a large building. Penny assumed this was the place where all the slaves were housed until auction time. The duration of her stay was short but long enough for her to decide what she would tell the people at the auction. The building was locked and only the women prisoners were left inside. Penny went to the others. "We can tell the people here what Chandler has done to us. Surely then, they will set us free."

"Do you think they will take our word for it. You know Chandler probably had phoney papers fixed up for us." The woman ran her hand over the silk of her dress. Besides, this don't seem like such a bad deal to me. I've never been dressed up like this before."

"It's no use" another said. "Chandler is in this business. He knows what he's doing. He's done it before. They wouldn't believe us if we told them. They wouldn't want to believe it."

Penny looked at the group of women. Their eyes all seemed to say the same thing. She couldn't believe they valued their freedom, their self respect so little. She knew she would have to do this alone.

The locks on the door rattled with the turning of the key and they were on their way to the auction. This time they walked. Penny was again the last in line. The women walked single file through the streets, led by one guard and followed by another. The day grew hotter by the minute. Penny could feel the perspiration pouring down her back, her thick hair sticking to her wet skin. She looked ahead at the group of buyers and spectators standing in the streets. The heat and the fear were both stifling to Penny. Each step was mechanical now. Each breath she took was short and difficult to draw in. She thought she would smother before she reached the platform where she would lose all freedom.

Within moments the auctioneer was announcing the arrival of the women who were to be auctioned off. With an elaborate gesture of out stretched arms, he asked for the bidding to begin as the first woman was ushered to the auction block. She was sold at an excessive price. With each slave sold the crowd became more alive. It was plain to see that these people thrived on the business of buying and selling slaves. As Ema was led upon the platform, she looked back at Penny with a look of helplessness.

The young girl became aware of the beauty of Ema and the other women who had been sold. Although they all had characteristics that were the same, they all had their own unusual qualities that made them unique. Penny noticed the fullness of their figures. They all, were so womanly and probably so desirable to the men.

Penny thought for a moment, "Maybe no one will want me. Maybe they will send me on my way." She had a moment of hope before she reminded herself that it didn't take anything but a strong, young back to work in the fields. She no longer questioned Chandler's mental integrity for trying to make her the center of attention. She realized now, that he had to do something if he wanted any price at all for her. After what seemed like hours, all the other women were gone and Penny was left standing in the street alone.

The auctioneer's voice boomed out. "And now, Ladies and Gentlemen, we have our last and youngest of all, Shanda."

Penny looked around trying to see the girl called Shanda. Before she knew what was happening, the guard standing next to her had her by the arm and she was being yanked up the wooden steps toward the waiting autioneer. Penny looked out toward the crowd. Her eyes fell on some of the familiar faces of the women who had already been sold. They were now standing beside their new masters. She felt dizzy as she stared at the eager faces of the people. A floating sensation swept over her. She had planned to be so brave, but suddenly, it was just the opposite. She thought she would, at any moment, collapse and sink to the floor below her.

She found herself thinking about Brent. "I need you, Brent." She needed him to hold and comfort her. She needed him to make this nightmare go away as he had done for the last few years of her life. But, she knew this time there would be no hero to save her. She thought of her mother. She missed her so. Penny felt like a woman who needed the strength of her man and a child who needed the protection of her mother. Her head was down. Her shoulders were slumped. She thought sure, she would fall face down on the splintery planks beneath her bare feet. But, as the bidding began so did the vulgar remarks. The remarks that would have embarrassed a harlot.

Penny's head snapped up. Her temper was smoldering. She slowly drew herself up to her full height. In the air, unseen sparks were flying. For a moment, everyone was quiet, waiting. Waiting for what? No one knew.

The unique creature on the aution block held them in suspense with her sparkling gaze. Her voice was low and smooth. "My name is not Shanda, as I have been called. I am Penny Brown. I am not the one who is untamed. It is the heathens who kidnapped me from my home in Alder, Missouri. The same people who beat me and subjected me to humiliation that not even an animal should have to endure. They have done this to me, to others before me and will continue to do the same to women in the future unless this bizarre business is stopped." Still the crowd was quiet.

The auctioneer stepped up. "How about it men? Who will be the lucky one of you to own this royal, untamed wench?" Again the bidding was started. The atmosphere was now electrified more than before Penny's words. The bids went higher and higher. An outlandish price had been reached when a tall well groomed man stepped up from the crowd and offered a price which far exceeded the previous bid. "Going once, twice, sold to the man for eight thousand dollars." Penny's heart sank as she was led to a waiting buggy by her new owner.

Chapter

12

The horses hooves clattered against the street as the carriage passed the tall buildings. But, Penny did not hear the clatter or see the buildings: buildings so unlike the ones in Alder: buildings, outstanding, with their balconies laced in intricate ironwork. She felt like a lost child: so afraid of the unknown. But she was sure, that from somewhere down deep in her soul, she must find the courage to go on. The ability to keep hidden, this fear that now overwhelmed her. She swallowed, trying to fight back the bitter tears that were swimming in her eyes.

The horses didn't stop until they had reached an enormous house just on the outskirts of the city. Immediately a young black boy was in sight, ready to take the horses away. The tall man helped Penny down from the seat, took her by the arm and led her up the steps and into the his home. Penny looked around her. Every magnificent item was blurred by the tears in her eyes. The spacious room was exquisitely decorated and presented a look of splendor.

They had no more entered the room when an older black gentleman came in with a silver tray that held two fragile wine glasses. "Thank you, Jesse. That will be all." Penny's new owner set the tray on a glass table top. He filled the first glass with a maroon looking liquid. Penny did not know what it was, but as he handed her the drink, the scent of it reached her nostrils and she knew it contained some of the same intoxicating ingredients that Gunther, her father, used to drink. She had smelled that fragrance many times before in her life time and did not want any part of the effects it had on people.

She held the wine toward the man saying, "I have no use for this, Sir. I know that it does not quench one's thirst. It only creates a craving for more."

"Well, now, you don't sound much like a half breed."

"Then, you do believe me?"

Jason Reynolds, Penny's new owner, shrugged. "It really doesn't matter who you are, Miss. Fact is, you now belong to me. And, truthfully, I would rather have a slave girl who is well aware of proper etiquette."

Her eyes blazed, "White slavery is against the law." She spat the words at the man who was now holding to the back of her neck and looking down into her jade colored eyes. He gave her a lopsided grin before his lips came, roughly, down on hers.

She quickly jerked away from his grasp, knocking the glass of red wine from his hand. Falling backwards onto the hard floor, she felt a searing pain shoot through her belly. Never the less her next response was just as swift. She was up again. Taking two steps forward, she wiped the blood from her bruised lips and spat even more visiously this time, "When I am free, it will not only be the white slaves to gain their freedom."

"I can see you need some rest for now," he laughed. "We'll discuss your duties tomorrow. I believe when you begin to fullfill your purpose here, you will calm down." He picked up a bell from the table and with one ring, a neat sturdy looking black woman was at Penny's side. "Show her to her room, Celia."

"Yes Sir, Mr. Reynolds." She took the young girl by the arm shuffling her out the door and up the stairs to her room. There was nothing about the room to denote it was that of a slave girl. The lilac colored drapes covered a large window that over-looked a sloping hillside shaded by several large magnolia trees. The bed coverings were of the whitest white Penny had ever seen. They were made of satan and lace, embroidered with lilac flowers to match the drapes. One large white rug lay on the shining hardwood floor beside the bed. To the right was a large dresser. She walked so that she could see herself in the mirror. She stood for a few moments as if in a trance and then turned quickly away. She looked at Celia, her tears finally overflowing, wetting her cheeks and lips before falling to the floor. The black woman put her arms around her and gently helped her into bed. She pulled the covers up to Penny's waist and brushed the hair from the girl's forehead. Penny's last thoughts were of her own mother and the way she had tucked her into bed each night. Within moments her eyes were closed and she was asleep. Celia moved away and stepping out into the hallway closed the door behind her. She lit out down the stairway and toward the kitchen.

Jesse, the black man who served Jason Reynolds, sat at the small kitchen table. "It's just a cryin shame. Why that girl ain't no more than a baby." Celia had a scornful look on her face. " This kind a thing ought to be stopped. It's bad enough for us olda folks to be slaves, much less for a po girl like that to be stole right out of her own yard."

"You just might as well calm down and not git youself all riled up ova what you can't do nothin about. We is all slaves and that is all we'a eva gonna be. An besides, how does you know that girl ain't been a slave all of hu life just like you an me?"

"Jesse, you is knowin what goes on in this city just as well as I do. And anyhow it don't make no matter whether or not she full black, half black or plum white, ain't nobody in this whole world got the right by God Almighty to cage nobody else up and own um like they is a animal." The more angry Celia became, the more she used her black dialect. "No, someday the Lod's gonna send a angel to set us free."

"Well, if they be one on the way she sho is taken a time bout gittin hea." Jesse spoke abruptly, but when he looked at his wife, Celia, he saw she had been deeply hurt by his thoughtless words. He got up from the table and put his strong arms around Celia. "I'z be awful sorry I said them words. As many times in these last forty years that we been bought and sold, it could a only been the good Lod hisself that kept us together."

Celia replied, "Yes, we had easy lives to have been born slaves. So many others been beat, starved or worked until they dropped dead. We always been treated more like white people being paid for cleanin and waitin on folks."

"Yea, exceptin for the pay and our freedom."

Penny slept for hours but it was not a restful sleep. Every minute seemed to be filled with nightmares about her tragic life. She saw faces laughing, sneering, familiar, Julia's, Gunther's Brent's, Chandler's, Mildred's, Jason Reynolds. They were all jumbled, laughing, wicked before her. She tossed and turned in her fitful sleep. Then, they were not just faces but were whole people who encircled her, closed in on her. They were pulling at her hair, hitting her. They were hitting her hard in the stomach. The pain became intense. She began to moan. With each hard blow the pain became more and more unbearable. Her moans became even louder. Suddenly the faces changed. They were no longer laughing or scornful. They were no longer the same faces. Penny slowly began to realize that she was being awakened from a horrible nightmare. Celia, the black woman, was shaking her gently.

"Wake up, Baby. Wake up. You're havin a bad dream." Penny's eyes kept fluttering, half opened and half closed. She watched Celia and listened to what she said but she couldn't seem to control the moaning, and the pain in her belly didn't stop. As she tried to sit up and the covers fell to the floor, Celia saw the bloodstained bed. Pushing the young girl back and holding her, Celia began to call for help. "Jesse, Mr. Reynolds, someone come in hea." She called several times before Jesse appeared in the doorway. "Tell Mr. Reynolds if he don't be gittin a docta hea and quick, he gonna be losin a slave girl." Jesse left the room and in moments Jason Reynold's was standing in his place.

"Mr. Reynolds, this girl gonna be bleedin to death if'n you don't send fo a docta."

Jason Reynolds walked to the bed. He knew by the deathly pale look of the girl and the bloodstained bed clothes that the black woman knew what she was talking about. "I'll send Jesse." He turned quickly and walked from the room.

Celia was left alone to manage the sick child-woman as best she could. Her experience with tending the ill was expansive but her knowledge of medicine was limited. She hoped the doctor would be able to give Penny an injection that would help stop the bleeding. There was no way she could know for sure what was wrong with the young girl, but she suspected it was something that could be very harmful to her at this point.

"You're so young to be goin through all this, Chile. So very young." Celia left the room. Hurriedly she came back with some cloths and water. She began to wash the beads of sweat from Penny's face. Celia doubled a pillow and propped up Penny's feet. She knew that would help slow the blood flow. Their time alone seemed to linger on and on. Finally, Celia heard voices echoing from down stairs. Running half way down the hall and leaning over the banister she called, "Hurry, hurry, Docta. This girl be mighty sick. Come quick."

The old doctor, with snow white hair and spectacles moved to the top of the staircase as quickly and efficiently as if he had been right out of medical school. One look at Celia and he decided against trying to remove her from the room. She stood firm inside the doorway. Towering about two inches above him, she stood with her arms crossed and her jaw set. He understood her feelings and relented to her obvious wishes. Entering the room, he immediately took control. Celia moved quickly to his commands, more than glad to help the young girl who lay so helpless and innocent in her own pool of blood.

After his examination, the doctor opened his medical bag and took out a needle and syringe. Filling it with medicine, he motioned for Celia to help hold Penny's flailing arms. Just as suddenly as he had begun, he finished. Putting his supplies back in his bag he said to Celia, "There's nothing more I can do. If the shot doesn't work she will go ahead and lose the baby. If she begins hemorrhaging any worse, send someone after me."

"Yes Su, I sho will do that." Celia was not surprised at the doctor's words. She had seen many slave girls lose baby's because they had been forced to work too hard in the fields or simply because they were viciously, sexually abused. She suspected from the first sight of blood that Penny was with child. Pictures of bizarre events that could have caused the pregnancy swept through her mind, but she discarded those and began to wonder what would happen to the girl when Jason Reynolds found out she was carrying a child.

She could hear Mr. Reynolds and old Doc Henson talking as they walked down the hall to the stairway. After a few moments she heard the younger of the two swear loudly. With every footstep the voices faded until she could no longer hear what was being said. She turned back to the bed to tend Penny. She stayed with the girl until the evening shadows began to fall across the room. The bleeding and moans had ceased and the young girl rested peacefully. Late into the night Celia slipped away and went to her own room to sleep. But sleep did not come, for she could not erase from her mind, the probable decision Mr. Reynolds would make about the girl's further use to him as a mistress. Her contemplation turned to plot and she drifted off to sleep.

With little sleep she rose early the next morning. She had been servant to Jason Reynolds for several years and had never really been treated as a black house servant would have expected to be treated. Because of this unusual experience as his slave, she felt safe in expressing her opinion about his continuing ownership of Penny. After doing so, she found that Mr. Reynolds had ideas of his own. She also found that his ideas were nothing near her own thoughts.

"I paid an unreasonable price for the girl, Celia, and I don't intend to let a few months of latency spoil my plans for her. She's young and healthy. She should have a healthy child. That child could be sold for a moderate price. After that I shall continue with my first intentions."

As the black woman walked to the kitchen she couldn't help shudder at the thought of the child being sold away from its mother. "I'z will worry about that later," she muttered to herself.

After breakfast was prepared and Jason left the house, Celia took a tray up to Penny's room. The soft light of the early morning sun fell through the window when the lavender curtains were pulled open. Penny began to stir from her peaceful sleep as the sweet aroma of warm biscuits and honey mingled with the smoke flavored smell of ham. Suddenly and fully her green eyes popped open. She remembered where she was and the sick feeling came back to the pit of her stomach. Not noticing Celia, Penny tried to sit up. A wave of weakness hit her and she fell forward. Celia turned and grabbed her in time to keep her from falling to the floor.

"We'z not gonna have none a this, girl, lessin you be wantin to lose that little baby a yours."

"Baby? Why I don't have a baby." Penny was confused.

"Not yet. But you be goin to if'n you be careful and stay in that bed."

Penny began to remember the night before. She remembered the pain in her belly that would not go away. She remembered the nightmares. She remembered the kind and worried face of Celia looming over her. Vaguely, she remembered the doctor with white hair and spectacles. The thought came to her that she had not had a monthly period since before she was kidnapped. With all the confusion that had gone on in the past weeks she had not even thought of such a minor thing. Now, the reality of the sorrow, and tragedy of it all, hit her.

"But, I, I'm too young to have a baby." She said it matter of factly as if the statement would change things. She layed back on the bed in silence. She thought of Brent. How much she had loved and trusted him. She thought of the many times he had protected her from the world. Now, her hopes and dreams for their lives together were shattered. "I can't have a baby," she thought. "Not this one. Not Brent's. How could I love it, knowing everything he ever did, ever said to me, was a lie? How can I go on trying to believe that Brent is not the one who has done this awful thing? I saw him." She mumbled the words. She spoke, "I won't have this baby. I won't have this baby. Not this one. Not Brent's." Her words were becoming hysterical but her body was becoming weaker and weaker with each word, until finally she was left breathless and sleeping again.

Celia sat in Penny's room until she awoke again. She was determined to convince Penny that it would be best to have the baby. She had wanted a child of her own for many years but had never been able to conceive. To the kind black woman a child born was a blessing to be thankful for. She talked to Penny trying to convince the young girl she would feel differently about the baby later on. After a while it was evident to Celia that Penny could not foresee feeling differently about the baby in the future. She gave up trying to arouse Penny' motherly instincts. She told her in explicit terms just what Jason Reynolds had in store for her the moment she was physically able to comply.

Penny knew she didn't have a choice, since it was put to her that way. She knew that carrying the baby and giving birth to it would borrow some time. Something down deep inside told her she wanted the baby, but for now, her pride told her she didn't. Her conscious realization of that fact would be later to come, perhaps too late. Right now, Penny felt the only safe thing to do, was to put all love for any other human being to rest. With her jaws clamped tightly together, she said under her breath, "I won't love his child: not after what he did to me."

Celia looked at the girl with empathy and said, "There will come a time when you will wonder how you ever felt this way, Child."

Penny replied, "Mama always said we reap what we sew. I guess that is true. I'm being punished for loving Brent. I knew eventually, God would punish me."

"God never punishes us for love. He just wants us to love at the right time. Why, it's just like a mammy tryin to keep a baby's hands off the hot kettle. If he touches it, the mammy didn't cause the pain. I kinda believe that's how it is with us grown folks. It's us that punishes ourselves."

It seemed to Penny that she was seeing and hearing Celia for the first time. She was beginning to realize that this strong, black slave woman was perhaps very wise.

Chapter

13

In the following weeks, Penny found herself being catered to much the same as any rich southern girl It seemed that she had been adopted by Celia and her husband Jesse. As for Jason Reynolds, he used her for nothing but company. In fact, he was very considerate of Penny's feelings. Now, she sat watching as he finished up some paper work. He was so unlike Brent. He had blond hair and his eyes were somewhere between blue and gray. He was tall and slim and in his own way, a very nice looking man. He didn't seem to be the kind of man that would use a woman as she knew he intended to use her, but then again, she knew looks could be very deceiving.

Jason lifted his head and looked in Penny's direction. His eyes swept over her. Her condition was becoming apparent. The simple cotton dress she wore clung to her belly. Jason rose from his seat behind the large oak desk and crossed the spacious room. He looked down at the young woman who was suppose to have been his slave. Taking her hand, he pulled her up to him. Before Penny knew what was happening, his lips were on hers. They were warm and lingering. Finally, he raised his head. He seemed to feel everything and Penny felt nothing. She felt no revulsion toward him. She felt nothing. He looked into her eyes and said, "You'll feel differently later.

"Yes, everyone tells me I will feel differently later. How can someone feel good about being a slave?"

He laughed. "Slave? You have not been a slave. You have no idea what slavery is."

"Then you know I was kidnapped. You know I wasn't born a slave."

"Of course I have no way of knowing any such thing. But, yes I do believe you."

Penny asked with a pleading look in her eyes, "Then you'll let me go?"

"I didn't say that." But if you're willing to cooperate, things can be good for you."

"I'll never be used for what you want me for."

"Oh, don't worry. You wouldn't be expected to entertain guests." Then, with a mischievous look, he said, "Entertaining your master will be quite enough." He edged closer with a questioning look in his eyes, but before the words were formed on his lips, Penny's long nails slashed at his face, bringing blood. The look in his eyes turned, quickly to anger and Penny was frightened at her own spontaneous action. They stood face to face neither moving, until Jason reached up to wipe the blood from his burning wound. "You are on the wild side, aren't you? Oh well, that will be changed in a few months.

With this, Penny turned and ran upstairs to her room. She slammed the door behind her and leaned against it for several moments before walking slowly to the cream colored, velvet chair. With her legs curled under her, she sat looking out at the darkness. The summer breeze blew softly against her damp skin, helping to cool her. She reached up to wipe the tiny droplets of perspiration that had formed over her top lip. The only thing on earth that seemed to be stirring was the breeze.

At the moment Penny felt at peace and safe behind the walls of her room. She had learned to wipe the world from her mind when threats became too intense for her to handle. The full moon gave faint shadows to the trees below. She unconsciously ran her hand over the mound of her swollen belly. A fluttering sensation caught her attention. At first it was so light she wondered if she had really felt it, but it grew to be more distinguishable within the next few moments. In the beginning, she could not grasp the idea that the baby had just moved, but as the kicks became harder, she responded naturally. A slight smile curved her lips as her hand moved to find its position.

She was suddenly aware of feelings that frightened her. She felt a closeness to the small being inside her. It was a closeness, she had never quite felt before. The feeling brought tears to her eyes. This new feeling confused Penny, for with the feelings she felt for the baby, came tender thoughts of Brent Holbrook. Up until this time she had thought of the baby as something that had invaded her body. Some thing that made her feel very tired and nauseous most of the day. But, even with the feeling of fright her emotions gave her, she was held in awe by the new small wonder that was moving within her. Penny sat for hours in her peaceful aura, before crawling into bed and falling asleep.

The next morning she awoke to the small fluttering sensation she had felt the night before. Again her hand moved across her belly as she felt for the baby. She was smiling when Celia came into the room.

"Well, well don't you look like the happy mammy this morning?"

Penny was startled by Celia's familiar voice. She had been so involved with the movement of the baby she had not noticed that Celia was standing in the doorway with a big breakfast tray.

Penny tried, without success, to hide her feelings of total bliss. After all, she had sworn not too many weeks before, that she would never and could never love the child she carried. The attempt was fleeting, however, for when she looked into Celia's piercing dark eyes, she knew she had been caught. Knowing that very little, if anything could be hidden from the wise black woman, Penny let all barriers down as she said, "I feel like such a fool, loving when I never seem to get any of that love returned. I know it would be the wiser to put all my feelings away. I must be totally without pride. I've tried to forget my mother, Brent, my father and his abuse. What's wrong with me, Celia? Is it a weakness in me?"

Celia looked down into Penny's weary eyes. She knew the girl was being completely open and honest with her. "It's hard for me to tell since I don't know what these people have done that hurts ya sa bad."

Penny broke down telling Celia what seemed to be her whole life's history. She told her about Gunther, her father, about her mother and about the most painful of all, Brent. "So you see, it can't be right for me to go on loving."

Celia thought about what Penny had told her. She had expected to hear something bad but the whole story about Brent confused her. There was no reasoning what so ever behind what he had supposedly done. As far as Julia, Celia didn't agree with her actions but she very well understood them. She was also wise enough to know that the last thing Penny needed right now was someone defending the people who had hurt her so badly. She said only, "So strong a love could never be in vain. Always something good will come of love such as yours. If love was so shallow that it could never cause pain, how could it ever by very rewarding?" Penny did not answer. She knew Celia didn't want an answer. She wanted her to think about what she had said. Penny understood, but for now, there was no consolation in the words. She could see clearly, that she was destined to love the child she carried. She took a long, slow breath, and prayed a silent prayer that she would not lose the love of her child as she had lost the love of everyone else in her life.

Chapter

14

Penny and Celia walked through the busy streets of New Orleans. Penny's graceful movement had long since turned into more of a waddle than a walk. The once long hot summer days had passed and now the cool autumn air surrounded them. Penny's fear of love had been replaced by an overflowing need, to hold in her arms, the small being growing inside her. She had begun to see life differently than she had always believed it to be. It was a hard lesson to learn, but she had awakened to the assumption that there would never by a time of complete happiness in this life. She was learning to grasp every bit of happiness that came her way no matter what her circumstances were at the time. She was learning what faith really meant. She truly believed that she and her child would some day be free. It was not her belief that God would hand all of her wishes down to her, but she did believe that if she worked hard enough and leaned to the future: He would provide the stepping stones she needed.

"Oh Celia, look," she gasped as she peered into the store window admiring a delicate, pink, baby's shawl. The black woman saw delight written all over Penny's face. "Someday I'll dress my little girl in the most beautiful clothes."

"Lawzy Gal how you know it gonna be a girl? It might be the roughest boy you eva did see."

Penny shrugged her shoulders. "Could be, but I feel like I'm going to have a girl. I hope it's a girl. It would be nice to be close to my own daughter just like Mama and I were." Then with a look of saddness she said, "Anyway, close like I thought we were." She looked Celia straight in the eye. "I would never leave her, no matter what."

"I believe ya girl. I believe ya."

Celia quickly changed the subject to chatter on about the silk undergarments on display. She laughed, "Hav ya eva seen such a little bit a nothin in ya life?" Penny watched the sincere look on her face and laughed until she was embarrassed by the shaking of her own belly. They walked through the crowded streets window shopping and daydreaming.

Remembering the time, they decided to take a short cut down one of the back streets to where they were suppose to meet Celia's husband, Jesse. He was to bring the wagon around to pick them up. Penny and Celia had gone with him to get food supplies and then went window shopping while he attended to other business. They hurried down the deserted back street. Seeing Jesse at the far end, they slowed their pace. Both of the women stopped short when a wagon driven by a white man pulled into the street and momentarily blocked their way. The back of the wagon was filled with at least five black men. One of them stood up, never taking his eyes off Penny. His size alone would have intimidated her, but the bewildered look and heavy chains he wore took away any fear she could have felt. She had a feeling of kinship toward him. She knew how degrading it was to be chained like an animal. Two more white men with guns walked to the side of the wagon ordering the blacks to get out. They did as they were told and began walking away single file. Penny gasped at the sight of the disfiguring scars on the black man's back. When the wagon moved on, Celia continued to walk on toward Jesse, but Penny stood still, her thoughts lingering. She too could be carrying the scars of a bullwhip, if Mildred had had her way the night of Penny's recapture. Noticing that Celia was now waiting on her, Penny walked on. When they reached their destiny, Jesse was waiting patiently as usual. They all climbed into the wagon and Jesse headed the horses, not toward home, but toward the most expensive stores in new Orleans. "Where we goin?" Celia asked.

"Got some errands to run for Mr. Reynolds, Jesse answered. As they moved on, Penny watched the well to do women in their fancy laces and satan. Most were alone but some had young children with them. She stared in envy as one young mother and daughter walked hand in hand. The small child looked up at her mother and said, "I hope I look just like you when I grow up, Mother." Penny thought of the unfairness of life, and wondered what her own child would think of her if she had to be raised as a slave.

The streets were becoming more and more crowded. Suddenly Jesse pulled the wagon to a halt and told Penny and Celia that he would be back for them. "Well, it looks like we have plenty of time for more window shopping," Penny said. They walked slowly through the streets. As they walked along, Penny admired the fine merchandise hanging inside the stores. She wished that she could be buying for her child.

The autumn sunlight filtered down to the paved streets of New Orleans. Penny was beginning to tire easily as the weeks passed and the baby became heavier and heavier. She and Celia were passing by a shop filled with jewelry and all sorts of decorative items. A jade pendent caught her eye. At first she thought it to be somewhat like the one Brent had given her for her birthday. A sudden pang of resentment and desire all in one swept over the young girl. She walked closer to the window and stared in at the necklace. She seemed mesmerized by the similarity between this necklace and the one that had been so violently ripped from her neck the night she was captured. She thought of the good times she and Brent had shared and was unable to believe that he had been the one who had destroyed her life.

She noticed a woman with long blond hair moving slowly about. Penny found herself unable to move away from the sight. The woman's graceful movements reminded her of her own mother, Julia. Penny continued to watch. The lady moved slowly through the store not seeming to have any particular aim in mind. When she moved closer and closer to the window, Penny was even more drawn to the delicate figure within. Her face became ashen when the figure came into full view. She whirled around, stumbling as she tried to move quickly away from the store. Celia had been watching all the time. Penny walked swiftly down the street toward the wagon where Jesse now waited. Celia hurried behind Penny catching her by the arm. "What be the matta wit you, Child?" Penny stared at her for a moment but she was unable to voice the fact that she had recognized her mother. She again turned and headed toward the wagon with Celia following behind. They all rode back to Jason Reynolds mansion in silence.

Penny went straight to her room. She was numb with shock. She had been unable to tell Celia who she had seen. She now felt like crying but couldn't seem to do that either. With all the time she had spent trying to learn to hate Julia for leaving her, she was amazed at the strong feelings she had. She wanted to run back to her mother and throw her arms around her. She wanted desperately to go to her mother and ask her why she never came back for her. She wanted to understand but she fought against the idea. As all these unwanted feelings flooded through her, her thoughts were interrupted by the steady jumping movement inside her belly. As always the small miracle within her own being melted all her resentful and painful feelings and changed them to a longing to hold the one human being she felt safe in loving.

Chapter
15

Julia stood in the doorway of the merchantile looking down the street. "Penny, Penny come back." The words were uttered before Julia had time to think. Now she stood in stunned silence as the girl moved down the crowded street, climbed into the wagon and rolled out of sight. Julia had glimpsed the green eyes staring through the window just before Penny had seen her and run away. She was suddenly overwhelmed by the inclination that Penny was still alive. As she walked the short distance to her home she kept trying to wipe the picture of the young girl out of her mind but an irrevocable need to believe Penny was alive haunted her senses.

Since she and George had left Missouri and returned to New Orleans, Julia had divorced Gunther and married George. Now, as she sat at her bedroom window and watched her husband come up the walkway to the front door, she wondered how and if she should tell him that she had seen her supposedly deceased daughter in downtown New Orleans. Julia was halfway down the stairs when George reached the staircase. "Hello Darling." She put her arms around him and kissed his cheek affectionately. Julia immediately began her story.

"Julia, wanting Penny back won't change what happened. She's gone. How many times have you said you can't believe it happened? You can't keep doing this to yourself. You saw a girl who looked like Penny."

"Don't you think I would know my own daughter?"

"How long has it been since you saw her?"

"Three long years." She hesitated before speaking again. "But there hasn't been a day passed that I haven't summoned a vision of my tawny skinned, brown haired little girl." Tears rolled down her pale cheeks. "If only I hadn't left her, she would be with me now."

"You have no way of knowing that."

"She was my only child. She is my only child. I've made one mistake. I won't make another by not finding her. I'll find her if it takes the rest of my life."

George could see that his words were in vain. He could also see that his wife really believed she saw Penny. He knew that it was essential to their future that Julia either find her daughter, if she was alive, or know for sure that the terrible tragedy had really occurred. "You have the right to know, Julia. I would be doing you an injustice if I didn't help you find out. We'll hire the best private detective in New Orleans."

"Thank you, George. You have been so good to me."

For weeks, Julia and George waited for some positive news from the detective, but the answer was always the same. There was no Penny Brown to be found in New Orleans. Julia gave up. She decided to rent a buggy and search for Penny on her own. Every day she looked the crowded streets over. She often went to the store where she had first seen Penny, hoping to get another glimpse of her, but to no avail. Finally, she knew what she had to do. There was only one other person in the world who would want to believe that Penny was alive as much as she did. She had to let Brent Holbrook know about it. She began to write the letter she was going to send. She wrote all the details of the appearance of Penny, down to fact that she was very much pregnant. She sealed the letter and silently prayed that Brent would believe her. Julia continued to search for Penny, but as time passed she grew weaker and weaker.

Chapter
16

The snow pelted silently against the window panes. The fire flickered in the fireplace and the orange and blue flames cast shadows across the letter as Brent reread every word slowly and carefully. For months he had tried to overcome the agonizing pain caused by the sudden loss of Penny, but solace wouldn't overcome grief, oblivion couldn't overpower remembrance and allienation wouldn't stop love. Penny's memory was indelibly etched in his mind.

The force of the pain and the remembrance of her touch were as strong now, as they had been months ago. Brent thought he knew why. A natural instinct had told him Penny still lived even though he had continued to search for any sign or declaration of her existence and had found none. And now, as had gone through his mind hundreds of times before, he felt that all the eivdence left at the falls that stormy night, had been purposefully left, to ensure his belief that Penny had fallen to her death. And now, as then, he couldn't imagine anyone who held that kind of animosity for him or for Penny. Brent's thoughts deepened and he could see Penny heavy with child, her eyes bright, her hair glowing in the sunlight. He prayed that the baby belonged to him and that Penny's abductor had not harmed her in any way. He wiped intolerable thoughts from his mind and concentrated on the fact that whatever condition he found Penny in, it would be up to him to help her through.

He arose from the brown leather chair and walked to the window. The snow continued to fall as the wind whipped through the bare branches of the large cotton wood. Even if the storm broke immediately, he knew it would be days, or even weeks, before travel would be possible. And then, it would be next to suicide to attempt to journey through the mountain passes. He wanted beyond anything else to be with Penny when the baby was born. He knew that if it was his child, time for its birth was drawing near.

Brent felt the chill in the air and turned to see the flames dying in the fireplace. He hurriedly stirred the coals and put another log on the fire. He heard a knock and then watched as Mary moved slowly into the room.

"Is there anything I can get for you before I go to bed, Mr. Holbrook?"

Brent looked at the bewildered expression in the young woman's eyes. "I don't need anything, Mary. Are you alright?" He moved closer and searched her face for fading bruises.

"Yes, I'm fine."

Brent knew she was lying. She wasn't alright. She had told him a few days before that she had taken a fall and hit her face on the rail at the bottom of the staircase. He had his doubts, though, since he had over-heard her and Frank having a heated argument just minutes before she was suppose to have fallen. Brent was beginning to see a side of his brother that had never seen before. It created doubts in Brent's mind about his innocence pertaining to his stay in prison. But so much of the evidence had been circumstantial. He tried not to think such thoughts about his only brother. After all, anyone could lose his temper and both Mary and Frank agreed that she had fallen.

"Mary, there is no need for you to stay on here if your life is miserable. If you and Frank are having differences you can't settle, wouldn't it be better for you to get a job somewhere else?"

"Mr. Holbrook, I don't have the kind of money it would take to move away from Alder, and I don't have family anywhere. I wouldn't know where to go."

"Surely there is someone in town who could use some help."

"No. If I quit here, I would have to move far away." Mary's words were cut short by the appearance of Frank's massive frame in the doorway. Brent saw the nervousness building in Mary's actions as she automatically moved back.

"You aren't trying to get rid of our good help are you, Brent?" Frank walked over to Mary and put his arm around her shoulders. "Two bachelors like us need a good woman like Mary around. And besides, I am beginning to like her a lot. She might be your sister in law some day."

Mary looked surprised and pulled away from Frank's tight grip. "If you'll excuse me, I think I'll go to bed. It's late." She walked disheartedly from the room and up the stairs.

"Are you serious, Frank? Do you really intend to marry her?"

"You never can tell about me, Brother. But I do think a good woman would add to the quality of my life."

"Frank, prison changed you. I use to feel free to talk to you. You use to talk to me."

"Four years is a long time, especially when you're innocent,"

Frank commented with bitterness in his voice. "Prison life is worse than anyone can imagine. Men are forced to live like animals. You have to learn how to survive and sometimes that requires a drastic change."

Brent couldn't help feeling sorry for Frank because he did believe, way down deep inside that Frank had been wronged as a young man and this change for the worse was beyond his control. He just didn't reallize the depth of the change. The two brothers sat in silence feeling the chill of the cold winter storm and of the changing times.

As the storm continued so did Brent's restless night. He listened to the howling of the wind as his fitful thoughts of Penny raged on. When he awoke the next morning, he was relieved to see that the storm had broke. The sun shone through the burgundy colored drapes with a blinding intensity, but Brent was not fooled. He knew the temperature was at a dangerous low. He was also well aware that the trails between Alder and the Mississippi could not yet be traveled. He could only plan his trip and in the meantime make sure everything at the ranch was in order for his lengthy absence. He threw back the covers with one quick movement. His unsettled mind couldn't be relaxed. Brent dressed and started down the hallway. As he passed Mary's room, he heard a low whimpering sound. He stopped and listened as the sound continued. He called Mary's name. There was no answer. He called again. Still there was no answer. He twisted the knob but found it locked. Beginning to worry, he knocked on the door loudly. He listened as the crying stopped. He again called to Mary. This time she answered.

"Open the door, Mary. Let's talk."

"I'm okay, Mr. Holbrook. Really I am."

Brent didn't give up. This time his words were a command. "Mary, open the door. We're going to have a talk." He waited impatiently for Mary to open the door. He wasn't surprised when he saw Mary's freshly bruised face, but he was surprised as to the severity of the marks.

Right away Mary began her excuses. "I fell this morning. I'm so clumsy. I don't know what's getting in to me."

Brent stopped her quickly. "Mary, don't lie to me. I don't believe a word of what you're saying."

Mary broke down and began to cry again. Covering her face with her hands, she turned and went into her room. She sat down in the small chair next to the window. Brent followed slowly, wondering what to do about the problem. "Mary, you have to tell me what's going on so I'll be able to help you. Has Frank been doing this to you?" He waited for an answer.

The young woman's hair danced around her face as she shook her head in denial. Then, as if her strength had all faded away, she stopped and searched his face with a wondering gaze. She didn't know whether or not it was safe to trust Brent, but she knew at the rate things were going with Frank, she wasn't safe anywhere. She decided to tell Brent enough to satisfy his curiosity and hoped he would help her get away. "Yes, Frank has been beating me."

"Why does he beat you? Is it during an argument?"

"No, we don't have anything to argue about. He just gets that way sometime. It's like he suddenly hates me. I can see it in his eyes. He'll be perfectly calm and then this look comes over him and he starts telling me how bad I am. The more I try to explain to him how things really are, the madder he gets. If I try to walk away, he comes after me. I've been afraid to try to get away. He has told me over and over again if I tried to leave he would find me and kill me. I believe him." Brent could see her dilEma. He knew he had to help her get away from Frank before he left for New Orleans.

During the next weeks, Brent worked out a plan to free Mary. He would simply make it look as though Mary had come up missing. She would stay with friends until the weather permitted travel.

Chapter
17

"Easy Boy." Pacer danced left and then right as Brent urged him on. Pacer's ears moved quickly back and forth to hear what Brent was saying. Brent had all the confidence that the surefooted, steady beast would get him through the treacherous snow covered mountains.

The air was still, the sun bright and the snow blinding, so blinding that Brent could hardly see. But, Pacer's instincts were keen. Brent had first seen the stallion in the mountains and it was a relief to him now, to know Pacer was on home ground. The familiar sights and sounds held no threat to the horse. The crunch of the icy snow under foot, the falling icycles and squeaking of the leather saddle were the only signs of any existence in the white world.

Brent recalled the first time he had seen the stallion. He and his men had been out rounding up cattle for the branding that had to be done every year. While seeking out strays, Brent had ridden through a wide rocky creek that bordered a tall tree covered hill. Suddenly he heard rocks tumbling down the hill. When he looked up, there on a wide ledge above him stood the most magnificent horse he had ever seen. He was enormous in size. The sleek coat of his hair shone in the sun. Muscles rippled as he paced back and forth as if dancing on the stage above. Brent could feel the stallion's gaze directed toward him, communicating with him as if trying to relay an urgent message. There had been no time for thinking, for out of the blue came a fierce grizzley. He was upon Brent in seconds, growling, moving his huge head back and forth ready to attack. Brent's mount was spooked, rearing and bolting. His horse slipped and fell as he moved backwards to the edge of the creek. The horse and its rider scrambled trying to move out of range of the monster coming at them. Brent was closer to the grizzley than his mount had been. As they both came to their feet, one movement of the bear's paw sent Brent back to the ground. His head hit a boulder and he was whirled into darkness.

Later, Ben and the ranch hands told Brent about the sight they had witnessed when they rode up. "We rode around the bend just in time to see that old grizzly roll you. And then, before we could get a shot in, here came another fierce lookin animal. Same color as that bear. His ears back, standing on his hind legs, pawing at that bear with a determination to kill that I ain't ever seen. He was big, but he was quick and strong. He was pawin one second and the other he was kickin. Guess that grizzly got tired of fightin. He gavae it up in a while. And then, just as fast as that stallion appeared, he disappeared."

Brent remembered the horse on the ledge and the feeling of kinship he had felt. Now he knew why. He remembered too, the way Penny had watched over and cared for him, when he was taken back to the ranch. When he had awakened, she was sitting at his bedside, eyes swollen from lack of sleep, her tangled hair falling around her shoulders. But most of all he remembered the look of fear in her tear filled eyes and the way she leaned over with trembling lips to kiss his forehead. He had felt guilt as feelings washed over him for such a young girl. He knew early on that he was falling in love with Penny. Now, as he rode on through the silence, he realized more than ever that she was the most important thing that was now or had ever been in his life.

The bright sunshine and blue, clear sky played trickery with one's imagination. Brent pulled his parka tighter around his red, cold face. He knew how to stay warm even in these below freezing temperatures. He had spent most of his childhood and adult life combating the elements. His father had taught him and his brother well. Jeremy had been in the cavalry and had learned much about survival from the Indians.

As the days slipped one into the other Brent's hope of a future with Penny grew stronger and stronger. His imaginings were like the movements of a pendulum swinging back and forth from a picture of Penny as the beautiful and strong young woman he had last seen to a picture of a beaten and helpless woman-child. Brent traveled from daylight until dark with a tenacity that would either break him or get him to New Orleans in time to be with Penny when the baby came. The moon was full and bright, casting light enough for at least another hour's travel. Brent dreaded the cold lonely night, but more so, he dreaded the loss of time.

Pacer stepped carefully along the snowy path, constantly watching, listening for any danger signal. Far away, Brent could hear hungry woves howling with a ferocity that would send shivers up a grown man's spine. Another day was drawing quickly to an end. Pacer's ears suddenly flicked forward. His neck arched in anticipation. He began to fidget back and forth. Brent was alerted to the stallion's warning signs and immediately put himself on guard. His voice was low and raspy, but demanding, as he calmed Pacer. Soon he could hear snow crunching under approaching hooves. He heard no familiar squeaking of saddles and began to assume it could be Indians. He and his horse were still, waiting for what could or could not be a dangerous situation. Moments passed and through the low hanging limbs of the trees, Brent could see the riders. He was shocked at the sight. A small band of Indians moved along the trail. He was close enough to see their faces clearly. One dark pair of eyes after another looked ahead. And then, he noticed the girl, eyes like blue stars shining on a dark night, hair golden blond. She looked so young. Brent hadn't heard of any problems with the Indians lately.

The leader of the band stopped his paint. Without hesitation, he walked over to stare Brent in the face. It was as if the Indian had already known he and his people had a visitor. He motioned for a younger boy. The boy and the white girl he carried with him obeyed the command of the older Indian. There was an exchange of words in an unfamiliar language and then the boy spoke to Brent in almost perfect English.

"My grandfather wants to know what a white man is doing here in such dangerous land on such a dangerous night."

"I'm traveling to the Mississippi River." Brent glanced at the white girl riding behind the young boy. "What is a white child doing in such a dangerous land on such a dangerous night?"

There was once again, words exchanged between the boy and his grandfather. Again he spoke in English. "She is with my people because hers did not want her. She was left with me when the trees were still green and the birds were singing."

Brent didn't know whether or not to believe this unlikely story. The girl then spoke in a confident and steady voice. "This is true. I was left by white people for dead, although they were not my real people."

"Where are your real people?"

"The only one I had was my mother and she was killed by the white people who left me. This is my family now." Little more was said before Brent and the Indians parted and rode on in their own separate directions.

Chapter

18

The cool night breeze blew through the soft thin material of Penny's pink cotton night gown as she stood on the balcony looking at the lights of New Orleans. She wondered how she could feel so lonely while being surrounded by so many people. She thought about Brent's house and how the weather back home must be at this time of year. She folded her arms across her rounded belly to help shield herself from the cool air. The baby kicked as if to rebel against the pressure of Penny's arms. No matter how she tried to control the feelings she had for Brent during these times, there was no way. There was a part of her that would always love and cherish the man who had taken care of the little girl in the street. Warm tears fell on the floor of the balcony. The low, sad singing of the slaves wafted through the air stirring a wanting in Penny's soul.

She jumped as she felt the chill of soft hands on her flesh. She turned and looked into the cold eyes of Jason. He was a mixture of tenderness, desire and cool intimidation. She wondered how he could want her and seemingly hate her at the same time. He slid the back of his hand down her throat. Penny turned to walk away, but he grabbed her arm. Holding on he said in a low voice, "If the circumstance was different." His voice trailed off. He looked at her intensely.

Penny returned the stare with a repulsive glare of her own. "You'll never have me like you want me. I will die first."

He let her go, his lips turning upward in a mocking smile. "There are ways of getting what one wants." He backed off and looked at Penny's belly. She shivered with fear knowing what he was insinuating. He would have the baby to use against her in anyway he chose. This was the first time the thought had occurred to Penny. It was a thought that would tear all hope away from her.

Later that night Penny cried bitter tears at the realization of someone else other than Brent touching her. Not that she would ever allow him to touch her again, but she knew in her mind that her heart would always belong to him. When she had womanly feelings, the need inside her was an involuntary wanting for Brent.

The aroma of fresh baked biscuits and ham filled the air as Penny was aroused from her unsettled night. Celia smiled down at her noticing her worried eyes. "What you worryin bout this monin, Chile?"

Penny's eyebrows drew together into a frown. "I'm worried about the baby. Jason came into my room last night."

"What he gone and done to you, Girl?"

"Nothing. It's what he has in mind that scares me. I never understood before. But, now I do. I was naïve enough to think he couldn't do anything that I didn't want him to. But, he can. I understand about being owned now." Her eyes were fearful as she relayed to Celia what had been said the previous night.

Celia, knowing Jason's scurrilous nature as she did, believed every word Penny said. "Now don't you worry, Missy. Evathang will be alright. That baby of yours will be here befo you know it and evathang will be fine. We'z ain't gone let Mr. Jason o anybody hom that baby." The astute black woman knew not to let Penny see the worry in her own being.

"I know he can do what he wants. I couldn't let him harm the baby. But on the other hand, I would rather die than have Jason Reynolds touch me."

"Nonsense. What would happen to that little girl of yuz then?"

Penny looked at Celia with a total lack of hope, but Celia was wise enough to know that when the time came, Penny would survive what was to come.

Deep in thought, Celia slowly walked back down stairs to the kitchen. Her mind kept wondering back to the sadness in Penny's eyes. "You know, Jesse, we can't let Mista Jason use that baby to force Penny into doin pleasin fo him. I been thinkin. Penny told me she see her mama some weeks back. She so upset she run away. Didn't even talk to her mama. She be thinking her ma ran out on her. That girl done had so much bad in her life she confused and hurt. The worse of it is she scared to death of bein hurt again. Now you an me we kno what slavery all about. We seen how it can really be. I ain't told that little girl up stairs but I done been hearin who Mr. Jason gonna be sellin that baby to and ain't no good a tall."

Jesse knew his wife had plans but dreaded the day when he might be the one to have to help her carry them out. Right now he wanted the peace of mind of not knowing, but that was only wishful thinking. The day came early the following morning. Jesse had tried to talk his wife into staying at home and minding her own business, but that was also wishful thinking.

Now he followed Celia down the brick walkway through the early morning light, in hot protest all the way. Celia could see the two storied, peach colored stucco home ahead. As she and Jesse walked passed the delicate ironwork that surrounded the yard, she could smell the scent of honeysuckle and magnolias. The scent was faint, but definitely coming into season. She stopped and wheeled around. "Jesse, time is passin. What you think we oughta do, just let Mista Reynolds sell that little baby away from its mama?"

Jesse knew by the look in his wife's eyes that he'd been had. He respected the portion of wisdom she had been blessed with and knew from experience that she was probably right. He knew that she had no doubts about carrying out her plans. "Alright Celia, let's go git this done."

They entered the gate and walked the short distance to the door of one of the wealthiest families in New Orleans. The family was one of black decendants from the West Indies. Unlike Jesse and Celia this family had been born free. Jesse and Celia were well favored by the family ever since Jesse had saved one of the younger boys from a beating. It had been years before the family had gained their wealth and had become noted citizens in New Orleans. Their boy had been mistaken for a slave and was about to be beaten. Jesse stepped in, and as it turned out, took the beating instead. He still yet carried the scars.

Celia rasped at the heavy mahogany door. Casandra, her long time friend hugged her as she stepped into the hallway. "What brings you here today, my true and faithful friends?"

"I have a favor to ask of you."

Cassandra's brows were raised in surprise, for Celia and Jesse had been offered favors and gifts before and usually gracefully declined. She was pleased to be able to give to these two kind and generous people now. Cassandra listened intently while Celia told the story about Penny, Brent and Julia Brown. "Yes, and you wish me to send people to learn of the whereabouts and character of this Julia Brown?"

Celia nodded her head in reply.

"Consider it done, my friend."

✤

Chapter

19

The night was black. Mary had an eery feeling like she had never known before. She rationalized, telling herself she was anxious because of the misery Frank had put her through. She had been restless all evening.

The McLemores had gone into town to visit ailing relatives. These persistent feelings of anxiety had begun just a short while after they had left Mary at their home alone. They had requested that she go with them but she had declined not wanting to constantly impose on this family that had so willing taken her in. She was looking forward to the time when she could travel and safely leave Alder. Then, she would be rid of Frank Holbrook once and for all.

Mary rubbed her cold hands over her arms as she paced back and forth in front of the fireplace. She decided to light the other lanterns that set in the large room. She walked to the oval table next to the window. As she reached for the lantern, she was startled by a shadow moving across the floor. She took one step closer to the window where she could see the branches of a tree swaying in the wind. She breathed a long sigh of relief and finished the task she had begun.. The collection of books on the cherry wood shelf caught her eye. She examined the titles before selecting one. She started to read as she walked toward the fireplace. Not watching where she was going Mary walked too close to the edge of the hearth, stumped her toe and almost fell.

She could see the blood oozing out from under her toenail. She sat on the floor, squeezing her throbbing, aching toe and chiding herself for being so clumsy. When the throbbing subsided, Mary again picked up the book and started reading. After a few minutes, she was totally absorbed by the story. Time passed quickly and before she knew it she was blurry eyed and ready to sleep. She returned the book to its shelf, walked to the fireplace and stirred the coals. She made her way around the room turning down all of the lanterns but one. It, she carried with her and again climbed the stairs to her room. The house was silent, so silent that it left a slight ringing in Mary's ears. The anxiety was beginning again. Mary could hear her own heart beat as she pushed the heavy wooden door open. She set the lantern on a nearby table. Its light cast shadows across the room. As she turned toward the bed, Mary screamed in horror.

"No need to fear your lover, Mary." She knew his voice well. Mary turned to run, but Frank moved quickly grabbing her around the waist with one arm. It was enough. She could feel the wind being cut from her lungs as she struggled. She could hear Frank laughing as if he were a child playing a game. Laughing, as if he was having great fun by inflicting pain on another human being.

"You know I have missed you, Mary." He let her go, but stepped between her and the closed door. "Why did you leave? I've looked everywhere for you and finally found you."

Mary looked at Frank. He was like a hurt child. She saw the hurt in his eyes. His face was contorted as a hurt child's would be. She was still yet in a state of shock, but knew he meant his words. She was coming to realize Frank was not just a mean and vengeful man, he was a sick, mean and vengeful man. Her mind raced as panic and terror set in.

"I miss my brother too." Frank said sadly.

Mary tried to overcome her fear long enough to talk to Frank. She hoped to get in control and seize an opportunity to run, run for her life. "Brent will be back soon. You know, New Orleans isn't that far away."

"New Orleans? What on earth is he doing there?" Frank's demeanor did another quick turn around. He was no longer the hurt little boy. He was again the manacing animal he had been before. Mary knew she had been tricked. He had been searching for answers to Brent's whereabouts. Now he knew.

"You told him about Penny's jade necklace, didn't you Mary?"

Mary thought quickly. "Yes but when I tried to show it to him it wasn't there. You hid it again, didn't you Frank? So you see, he couldn't have believed me anyway."

"Don't play me for a fool, Mary. I'm sure your poor pitiful act got on my brother's sentimental side. You placed doubts in his mind. Now all I can do is get to Miss Brown before he does."

Mary was perplexed by the turn of the conversation. She had no idea why Frank was so upset about Brent being in New Orleans.

"He laughed at her confusion. Miss Brown is not dead as every one thinks. Unless she didn't survive her trip to New Orleans, that is. Slaves go for a good price in that part of the country."

"Slaves? Penny Brown is not a slave."

"She is now. A half breed slave. Who's to say with the right sellers, the right buyers and the right papers that anyone couldn't be sold as a slave?"

Mary was bewildred at what she was hearing. "But how would Brent know about that" Maybe he just took a trip to New Orleans.

Frank said angrily, "Don't toy with me, Woman. No one in his right mind would travel that far in weather like this unless he had more of a reason than a pleasant journey. Love would be my brother's reason."

"Maybe he won't find her. Then nobody would ever know what you've done." Mary knew she had to get away from Frank. She moved toward him, knowing that her chance of flight was slim.

"You know you might be right. You and I could just go back to the ranch and wait to see if Brent finds her. If he doesn't, we could just live happily ever after. Couldn't we, Sleeping Beauty? After all, you have proven to me that I can trust you beyond the shadow of a doubt." He moved around Mary and toward the bed. She knew this was her only chance. She pulled open the door and ran. Her hope was short lived. As she put one hand on the banister to make her way down stairs, her other arm was caught. She turned just in time to see the mad glint in Frank's eye and his fist coming toward her for the final time. She was flung backwards down the staircase to her death.

Chapter
20

Above the clamor and clatter of the pots and pans, Penny heard the familiar scratching at the back door. Celia shook her head and grinned as she watched the girl's eyes light up. Penny tip toed toward the bowl of meat scraps. She quickly scooped some up in her hand and headed for the door. Hungry as the dog always appeared to be, she was ever so gentle as she took small bites of food from Penny's hand. After the food was gone, Penny stepped back as Shadow pushed her huge head forward and nosed the door open.

Her long, graceful body yielded a commanding walk. She toured the kitchen area checking out everyone and everything before returning to what she now considered her space in the far corner of the room. She lay down on the rug. Penny had placed it there for her the first night she had invited Shadow in.

It had been several weeks before, on a cool, rainy night. The rain had fallen steadily all day. Penny and Celia were in the house alone. They were sitting by the fire in the kitchen after all the chores were done. The night was black and quiet. They both jumped when they heard the rasping noise. Their eyes met as they contemplated whether or not to open the door. With a skillet and rolling pin as their weapons, they moved close enough to look out the small window. There on the back door step had been Shadow, as Penny almost immediately called her. She was gigantic, coal black and appeared to be a shadow lying across the porch. She also looked as if it had been quite some time since she'd had any nourishment. Penny had no fear of the animal that looked more like a wolf than a dog. She had hurriedly brought her in and fed her.

95

"If Mr. Jason walk in an see that dog in this kitchen, they ain't no telling what he goin do."

"Celia, you worry too much. Shadow is bigger than Mr. Reynolds. Well, maybe not bigger, but I'll bet she can bite harder." Penny laughed as she walked over and stroked Shadow's head.

It was early evening. Jason Reynolds was having friends over for dinner. Both Celia and Penny had been instructed as to how their behavior should be when the guests arrived. Lately, Jason had assumed his role as the host and entertainer he had been in years gone by. To Celia and Jesse's surprise, he had been spending more time staying over with friends.

The two women had busied themselves all afternoon preparing the feast that lay ahead. On a more serious note, Penny decided that maybe Celia was right. "I'll try to persuade Shadow to stay upstairs until the party has come and gone. With one slight tilt of her head and a whisper, "Let's go, Shadow," the two headed up the back stairs and down the hall to Penny's room. "Now, you wait here, Girl. I'll be back in just a little while." When Penny left the room, Shadow walked slowly to the closing door. She plopped down, lying with her head on her front paws. She obediently waited.

Penny returned to the kitchen to help Celia. The old woman smiled as Penny walked through the doorway. She had taken on a motherly responsibility toward the girl. She felt sadness that such a young girl was made to know life so soon She looked, first at Penny's rounded belly and then at the way her hair fell in disarray around her flushed face. Penny was so unaware of her appearance. Not that it mattered, for she was beautiful and so full of innocence even in her present condition.

Penny smiled back, her eyes full of a mixture of happiness and peace. Celia had an uncanny way of relieving Penny's worry and replacing it with hope. The two worked on until the guests arrived. Celia reminded Penny to prepare herself for the serving of the guests. She did as she was asked and smoothed her hair back into the falling barrette. Then with a sigh she picked up the first tray and headed for the dining room.

She was surprised at the number of guests but was not intimidated by the whispers or the stares. She had, in fact developed quite an intrepid way of handling people. She was beginning to understand Brent's long ago words, "Hold your head up and look them in the eye." It had taken on so much meaning in the last few months. Penny smiled and held an air of self-discipline that was obviously intriguing.

She mentally, took note of the people she was serving: what they wore, how they laughed, their accent. She noticed how some were as observant of her, scrutinizing her as she was them. Those she took the time to give a warm smile knowingly striking an internal response, some of respect, some of jealousy and some of discomfort. She especially took notice of the woman sitting next to Jason. She was not at all what Penny had expected. Her look was much softer, her eyes kinder and with a glance that held more wisdom than Penny would have thought.

Penny was beginning to understand how Jason could have been undergoing some of the changes in the past few weeks. Maybe some of the kindness in this woman was wearing off on Mr. Reynolds. As she walked around the far end of the table, she detected a small bit of sincerity in the smile he cast her way. She automatically returned his smile and then just as suddenly became aware of the wrong impression that smile might have caused. She shot a glance of disdain in his direction and to her surprise received a second smile.

Although Penny was physically weary by the end of the evening, she had still been mentally alert, alert enough to hear the comments from Jason's southern gentleman friend's about the role the new black slave was to play in his household. It had brought her back to reality and her feeling of vulnerability. When the last of the guests had departed, and the work was done, Penny made her way up stairs with pain from her head to the bottom of her feet like she had never known before.

"Hi, Shadow." Penny reached down and patted the huge black head. Shadow, still lying just inside the bedroom door, tilted her nose up and looked Penny directly in the eye as if to return her greeting. "It's warm in here, Shadow." Penny walked slowly to the doors that separated her from the balcony. Pulling them open she breathed in a deep breath of cool, fresh air. "I've never seen so much rain in my life," Penny mumbled as she felt the mist beginning. She was also surprised that spring weather seemed to be coming so early in the year.

Still aching from head to toe, Penny began to undress for bed. She felt uncommonly weary and this greatly slowed the ordinary process of changing clothes. She felt as though she was moving in slow motion. Shadow followed her master's mood. Sauntering slowly to the balcony from which Penny had just come she plopped down enjoying the cool spring air.

After several minutes of readying herself, Penny all but fell into the large, feather bed. For the first few minutes she lay, amazed that she was still conscious of the world around her. In times passed, she had fallen asleep as quickly as her head hit the pillow. But, not on this night. Penny lay on her back feeling an unusual sensation in her lower abdoman. She put her hands on her belly as it hardened and then relaxed. Feeling a slight twinge of pain that she attributed to the long hard day's work, she rolled to her side.

The rain, still falling softly on the balcony, had a lulling effect. Penny closed her eyes and fell into a restless sleep. The wind began to blow, awakening her from her badly needed nap. Opening her eyes, she was momentarily startled by the dark figure sitting on the edge of her bed. She breathed in sharply turning onto her back once again. Out of the corner of her eye she could see Shadow crouched in the darkness ready to spring forward at a moment's notice. Not wanting Shadow's presence to be kown by Jason, Penny moved slowly and spoke in a calm and quiet voice. "What are you doing here?"

To Penny's surprise, Jason replied. "I just wanted to talk to you. Money is not a welcome replacement for love or a good conversation with a beautiful woman." His voice was soft, almost kind. "You know I am a very rich man." He waited as if thinking of his next words carefully. "My money has not made me happy as I long ago thought it would." There was a mixture of romorse and a new found knowledge in his statement. For the first time since Penny had met Jason Reynolds, she got a glimpse of the man he could have been.

Penny asked in a low voice,"Why are you not talking to your lady friend? She appears so kind. She is really quite pretty. She seemed to be so intelligent. The kind of woman who would carry an interesting conversation." Penny flinched at the tightening in her belly. However, Jason didn't seem to notice.

Jason laughed and then replied , "The lady is not my lady friend. She is my sister. She married a northern gentleman a few years back and has lived up north ever since. She never did believe in our southern ways."

" Do you mean she doesn't believe in slavery?"

"Exactly."

"I thought all southerners believed in slavery."

Jason wasn't surprised at Penny's naivete. Never the less, it compelled him to reach out and touch her cheek. Penny's response was to move back quickly and take in a sharp breath. Before Jason knew what was happening, Shadow was at the edge of Penny's bed crouched and ready to spring. The deep low growl and appearance of the huge animal's sharp teeth caught Jason off guard. When Penny realized he was about to move, she called to Shadow. "Enough Girl, it's alright." Shadow immediately relaxed and sat down.

Jason again surprised Penny by laughing, "So your friend is more than a companion."

"You know about Shadow?" Penny asked

"Believe it or not, there is not much that goes on around here that does not catch my attention. Do you think I haven't known for quite sometime that my kitchen door is a feeding place for any poor child or homeless white trash in New Orleans?" With that comment, Jason turned and walked toward the door. "I won't be pleasing you with my company for a couple of days. My sister and her husband have asked for the pleasure of my company."

Penny felt a surge of relief as she watched Jason walk slowly to the door. Without turning around he said in quiet but easily understood words, "I almost wish you weren't a slave."

Penny could have, but didn't allow herself to feel pity for him. Instead she turned her attention to Shadow who had grown to be a faithful and trusting friend in a very short time. "Good girl, Shadow."

Shadow eased up and lay her head on Penny's arm. Penny stroked her soft fur. Both the dog and girl communicated without words. "All this time Shadow, I thought you needed me. Come to find out, I'm the needy one." They lingered in peaceful silence, both becoming calm and comfortable, until the wind again picked up and made Penny shiver in the early morning air. "Okay Girl, let's close these doors." Penny threw the covers back and rolled from the comfort of her bed. Her belly felt heavy and tight. More so than it had early in the evening. She stood for a moment, the slight mist of rain blowing against her face reviving a sensation often felt in childhood. She closed her tearfilled eyes and pictured a small child looking up at a young and beautiful blonde haired woman. The woman smiled and tenderly wiped tiny raindrops from the round little face.

Penny could feel the moisture on her face, her eyelashes, her lips. She could feel the mist on her arms and warm wetness on her legs. Without warning, she was cringing from the pain in her back and belly. She opened her eyes and pulled up the bottom of her gown. She could see the darkened stain on her legs. The moisture was too dark to be from the light, spring rain. Although young and inexperienced, Penny knew what was happening. It was time for the baby to be born. Terror washed over her, making her tremble. Again, she closed her eyes and stood alone in the dark. Shivering like a frightened child, Penny opened her eyes only when Shadow's cold, wet nose touched her hand. The soft, high pitched whine let Penny know that Shadow sensed something unfamiliar happening, or maybe not so unfamiliar.

Penny looked deep into the golden eyes staring up at her. "Maybe you know what is about to take place, huh Shadow?" Maybe somewhere out there you have a young one of your own who is watching over someone as you watch over me." When the pain eased, Penny stepped back into her room and closed the doors leading to the outside balcony. Without any further delay she turned and headed toward the stairway that would take her down to Celia and Jesse's bedroom. The bedroom they thought was their own private home. Penny felt a touch of admiration for the old couple. They made themselves a happy home under what circumstances they had.

Carrying a small light and moving slowly and carefully, she made her way downstairs until her bare feet felt the soft rug below. The cramping in her belly was again taking precedence over the warm and uncomfortable sticky feeling between her thighs. With the pain baring down in her lower back, Penny felt the overwhelming need to sit down. In moments she found herself sprawled on the hard, dark floor in severe pain. The trembling began again giving Penny a helpless feeling. Not knowing how she would complete her walk to Celia's room, she began to call out, the pain cutting her breath short. In what seemed like hours, but was really only minutes, the pain subsided. Penny felt something wet against her cheek. Again it was her protector and friend, Shadow. She reached out to her, but the animal had gone just as suddenly as she had appeared.

Chapter

21

Celia pushed Jesse's arm from across her middle and squirmed out of the too soft bed. She quietly scurried across the room to the large wooden door, stopped and listened intently for the sharp scratching sound that had just awakened her. There, as she had suspected, stood Shadow. "Now what brings you here in the middle of the night?" The words had no sooner left her mouth than Celia realized the only thing that would have brought the dog to her would have been Penny. "Jesse, wake up." It was a command that brought Jesse straight up in the bed, stunned but never the less obeying instinctively. He threw the covers from himself and the bed as he jumped up and scrambled into his clothes.

Shadow turned and loped down the hallway, slowing down only to take a quick look back. It was as if, she wanted to make sure the two were following. She came to a sudden halt when she reached Penny. Putting her nose close to the girl's face Shadow walked away, seemingly satisfied that all was still well.

Celia knew by the blood stains and soft moans what this night was to bring. She took Penny by the hand looking into her jade green eyes that were already filled with agonizing pain and childlike fear. "Help me git her back to bed, Jesse and then you bes go git the Doc." Together they helped Penny back up the stairs and into her own bed where Celia felt she would be most at ease.

With Jesse on his way to get the doctor and Penny as settled as possible, Celia prepared what she already knew would be needed. In no time at all she was ready, and not so patiently waiting for Jesse and the doctor. Another moan, louder than the last, brought the old woman back to

Penny's bedside. She wiped the young girl's flushed face with a cool wet cloth and then took her trembling hand in hers. "Everything gonna be jes fine, Baby. The pain be gone befo you know it." For the first time, Celia was feeling a bit of guilt for what she felt she had to do. Seeing this much pain made her realize the devastating effect her decision would have on Penny.

The decision was quick and to the point. "Penny, they is somethin I want to tell you befo you have this baby." The last pain had eased up enough so that Penny could concentrate, somewhat, on Celia's words. "I be knowin I should a told ya befo now, but I thought you and da baby would be safa if you didn't know."

"Know what, Celia?"

"I heard Mista Reynolds talkin bout what he gona do wit da baby afta it come. He be sellin it to some awful mean slave ownas."

Penny's eyes widened with fear. "He, he wouldn't do such a thing! Would he, Celia?"

"I ain't havin no doubt, Baby or I wouldn a told ya anythin about it." She continued with an all knowing look that erased any doubt in Penny's mind. The young mother looked into the shattered eyes of her friend and knew she was trying to protect the baby.

"Listen. I know of a good family right hea in New Orleans that would be willin to take that little baby and raise it like they own."

"Why would Jason let someone have the baby if he intends to sell it? I don't understand."

"Mista Reynolds wouldn haf ta know."

"How could we hide such a thing from him?"

Celia patted the girl's arm. "Well, ya see if the old Doc be willin to tell Mista Reynolds the baby din't make it, they wouldn be no problem."

"Why would the doctor do such a thing?"

"The doc, he be a man that would like to put an end to slavery his self. He helped a many a people in his time."

"I see." Penny's eyes saddened but she knew she had to do what was best for her child, even if it meant being away from her. Her next thoughts were of her own mother and the same feelings of hurt that she must have felt that night long ago when she left Penny standing alone. Suddenly Penny saw things differently. Before she could open her mouth to speak another pain overtook her. What had previously been low moans, now became muffled screams.

Without hesitation, Shadow moved quickly to Penny"s bed and again put her nose close to the girl's face. As before, she returned to her place in the far corner of the room.

To Celia's astonishment Penny's will had been intensified by their conversation. Although she had a long, hard labor, Penny held an air of inner calm. What Celia did not understand was that Penny had already made a promise to herself, that no matter what, she would get her little girl back. Now, after hours of struggling, Penny's small infant girl was placed in her arms.

Penny looked up at Celia. "How long do I have with her?"

Celia looked across the bed at the old doctor with a questioning expression. The old doctor answered brusquely, "That's a decision the two of you will have to make. I'm going home to get some rest." Then in a gentler voice he said, "Take care of our patient, Celia. If there is any problem, send someone after me."

Penny looked at the old man and then at the baby snuggled in her arms. "Thankyou Sir for giving my child a chance to live." With only a nod of his head, he turned and left.

For the next several hours, mother and child were together constantly. Penny hoped she could form some sort of bond with her daughter before another one of life's cruelties took her away. Although, so very tired, she watched the small being in her arms as it greedily suckled at her breast. "I've never felt anything so soft and warm, Celia," Penny said as she kissed the baby's rosy cheek.

Celia looked at Penny with great admiration. She knew the young mother was trying to consume as much happiness as possible while she could hold her child in her arms. "I'z send Jesse ta find out when we might be spectin Mista Reynolds. We don wanna wait too long."

Penny watched Celia leave the room before she looked into the blue eyes now watching her. "You have your Daddy's eyes," Penny said in a voice filled with wonder. Penny was also amazed at the similarities she saw between the baby and herself. She ran her finger down the small soft arm. To her surprise, she found a small heart shaped birthmark on the inside of her left wrist. It was identical to the one on her own arm.

Chapter

22

Brent stole one last look before turning to knock on Julia's door. He had felt as though he was being watched ever since he arrived in New Orleans.

"Brent, come in." Julia said as she took Brent's arm and escorted him into the study where George awaited them. Both she and George watched anxiously as Brent walked across the room and looked out the window. Julia shot a quick glance in her husband's direction, her eyes telling him what they both already suspected. There was still no news of Penny.

Brent finally turned with a down cast look. "I've searched everywhere. I've gone to the sheriff and told him the whole story. I have told as much as we know, anyway. I've looked in every corner of this city. Every day I ask anyone and everyone I see. If we only knew how Penny got here, who brought her here and why." He slammed his clenched fist into the palm of his hand. "I'll never stop looking." He looked at Julia. "I promise the both of you I will find her if it takes the rest of my life."

Julia was visibly relieved but also weak and shaken by the heavy burden. She walked to the desk in the corner of the room. Handing a sealed envelope to Brent, she said, "This was left for you today."

Brent took the envelope. Scratched on the front side were three letters, Ema. "Who brought this?"

"A slave boy. I did see a dark skinned woman waiting in the buggy. I had never seen her before today."

Brent tore open the envelope. Inside was a short note. Penny Brown was sold at an auction as was I. They called her Shanda. His heart raced. He slowly and almost silently mouthed the words. "It's unbelievable."

The couple across from him took the note. "Will this help us find her?"

"At least we know now, why she was brought here." If this is true and not a cruel joke. Never the less, this information is all we have and we will have to use it. If our girl is here we'll find her."

"Thank you, Brent for loving Penny so."

"And now, said George, Let's all go into dinner. It looks as if there is work to do."

They all ate and for once since Brent had arrived in New Orleans, they really enjoyed their meal together. They all had hope that the next day would bring the information they needed to find Penny. They reminisced about Penny's childhood, both before and after Julia left Alder. They all learned things about Penny's past that made them feel closer to her than they had before. They all had an urgency to find her, but Julia most of all. She and only she knew how her own physical stamina was quickly dwindling away with each passing day.

A sharp knock at the front door brought them from their own private thoughts. "I'll get it." Brent slid his chair back and moved toward the door, always hoping the next face that would appear would be that of his beloved Penny. It was dusky dark and all that could be seen was that of a dark figure moving through the far gate. Just before he turned to close the door, Brent heard another noise, unfamiliar at first but then all too familiar.

Brent couldn't believe what lay in front of him , a large basket. A basket holding a small infant wrapped in a pink and white shawl. He took another look in the direction of the fleeing figure but who ever had left the baby was gone. Brent carefully picked up the basket and carried it back into the dining room. He uttered not a word, but stood in silence holding the basket and staring at Julia and then George, as if he couldn't comprehend what was truly happening.

After the initial shock wore off, Julia stepped in and took over. Setting the basket on the table, she took the infant in her arms and carried it into the living room. There, she layed it on the sofa and gently unwrapped it, looking it over for any injuries it might have had.

"It was just abandoned, Brent said. I saw a figure hurry away in the shadows."

"Was it a man or woman?"

"I couldn't tell. They were too far away and it was too near dark."

Julia continued to look the baby over. As she ran her fingers down its small arm, she and Brent gasped at what they both saw. They both knew the birth mark very well. Penny had the same heart shaped spot on the inside of her left wrist. They looked in disbelief at one another.

"I don't believe it," Brent said to Julia.

"Don't believe what?" asked George. "Will you tell me what is going on?"

She held the baby close to her husband showing him the mark.

"Yes, it is a little unusual but I wouldn't say that it's extremely unbelievable."

Brent and Julia looked at each other, amused. "Darling, Penny has a birthmark identical to this one. The same arm in the exact same spot." Julia smiled at her husband.

"I See. This does seem more than a coincidence."

Suddenly and without warning an unexpected feeling washed over Brent. Not a shallow feeling but one that started in his chest and worked its way down to the inner pit of his gut. A feeling somewhere between happiness and sadness, excitement and fear love and hate. Happiness to think he might find his beloved Penny: sadness for the time they had already lost: excitement in thinking he might be able to spend the rest of his life with her and this beautiful child: fear that today's events could be just false hope: love for the girl he had loved so long that it reached to the inner most part of his soul and a hate for whoever might have caused her any hurt. The turmoil was displayed in every manly feature of his face and in his strong physical stature as he ever so slowly and gently took the small baby girl out of Julia's arms and into his own.

Brent looked at Julia and then at George. Both the man and woman reflected his own feelings. The three stood in silence, their eyes wet with unshed tears. Brent held to the hope that all of today's events would lead to othe discovery of Penny's whereabouts. He refused to accept any possibility that someone could have abandoned the child because something had happened to Penny.

At last, George spoke up. "I wonder if maybe, just in case the baby does not belong to Penny, should we contact the authorities?"

"I understand your reasoning. The same thought crossed my mind but I believe the odds are; this child does belong to Penny. And to keep this to ourselves will just lessen our problems." Brent looked at Julia, "What do you think, Julia?"

She remained silent for a time and then spoke. "I believe you're right. If the baby is truly Penny's, we don't want any interference from outsiders.

Evidently, from what you say, the sheriff hasn't been any help in finding Penny. Why would we think they could find the mother of this child?"

Brent looked at the couple. "Then it's agreed?"

George smiled at his wife, "Yes, agreed."

Julia hesitated another moment and then suggested, "She doesn't look to be over a few hours old. We should have a doctor look her over: just as a precaution."

Both men agreed. "Since you've been out all day, Brent, I'll go get the doc."

"Make sure you have Doc Henson to come out, George. We will be able to trust him," Julia said thoughtfully.

George turned toward the stairway, ascending the stairs two at a time, he entered the bedroom and quickly slipped into his coat and hat. As he came back down, Julia was waiting for him, a light in her eyes that he had never seen before. He thought as he kissed his wife goodbye and walked out the door, "We'll find her, Darling."

Brent sat in the living room cuddling the small form lying in his arms. He was thankful for these tranquil moments in such disquieting times. Reconciled to the hope that this was indeed his own daughter, Brent was determined to provide a safe and secure enviorment for her.

Julia stood in the doorway, watching and listening to the man so tenderly caring for her granddaughter. It was comforting to her to know that no matter what happened, this small infant would be well taken care of by Brent. With these thoughts tucked deeply in her mind, she again took over the situation, knowing they had to get things together for feeding and clothing the baby.

Chapter

23

Brent's night was short, but a more restful one than he'd had in months. He awoke the following morning before dawn. The moon still shone in the dark sky as he walked to the barn and saddled up Pacer. Julia and George owned a small ranch just on the outskirts of New Orleans. He looked back as he rode down the lane. Seeing the light , he surmised that the baby kept early hours too.

Brent first visited some of the larger plantations. He was astonished at the elaborate life style of these southern aristocrats. The size of the mansions was overwhelming. The vast fields with the slaves so busy at work, and the over-seers watching over them was a sight he could hardly comprehend and didn't really want to. He kept thinking about Penny and all that could have happened to her during these last few months. As he made his way from one plantation to another, unimaginable thoughts kept trying to cloud his mind. The life style of some of these people haunted him. The day grew shorter and shorter. A worrisome, nagging fear continued to be like a pesky insect that had to be constantly shewed away, but Brent would do so as long as it took. His love for Penny was steadfast and immeasurable.

The sun was warm but to the east, Brent could see the clouds building again. He couldn't recall ever seeing so much rain. Again he rode Pacer up a narrow road, through fine gates and toward a sprawling plantation home. His heart leaped at the first sight of a lovely dark haired woman. She was leaning against one of the huge pillars on the front porch. She was tall, slender and appeared graceful as she walked down the steps to gain a better view of the visitor. But, as Brent drew nearer, the same feelings of discouragement enfulfed him as had again and again since his journey had begun.

A smile lit up the young woman's face. "So you came back."

Brent was somewhat stunned, but before he could speak, he was confronted with yet another person.

"Hello Sir." A big, burly man suddenly appeared. Pushing open the door and stepping onto the porch, he looked at Brent through squinted eyes. "What brings you here today?"

Brent spoke up. "I'm looking for a slave girl."

The man shrugged his broad shoulders before replying. " Don't have any slaves for sale, right now."

"You misunderstand me." I am looking for a slave girl, called Shanda."

"What's the wench done? Is she a run away?"

"No, she's done nothing wrong. She was sold by mistake, several months ago."

The man laughed and so did his daughter. "Pardon my saying so, Sir, but if she was as good as you say, you'll have a hard time getting her back. Once papers have been signed, a slave is the other man's property."

I'm afraid you don't understand. This girl has somehow been mistaken for a slave, but is truly white. She was kidnapped from Missouri and brought to New Orleans. Someone has sold her under the pretense that she is a slave. One other thing, she was suppose to have been called Shanda, but that is not her real name.

The man paused. He took in a sharp breath. "I'll be darn. There was a slave auction several months ago and a high falutin wench stood up like she was a queen and told how she was being sold as a white slave. Of Course, no one believed her."

"Who bought her?"

He bit his lower lip and wrinkled his forhead. "I can't say as I recollect who that was. But, I'm sure if you keep asking you'll find her. She stirred up quite a fuss that day."

"Thank you for the information, Sir." Brent turned and rode out, feeling as though he had come one step closer to finding Penny. He rode back down the lane and started his search again. "Another small piece of information, another fragment of hope," he said to himself as his eyes roved over the fields where the people were bent low and singing in unison as they worked.

Julia and George waited impatiently for old Doc Henson to come. George had left a message the night before when he found out Doc had been called out on an emergency.

"You know, she seems so healthy, but I will feel much more relaxed when we have her checked over by Doctor Henson."

George looked at his wife admiringly. I can see what kind of a mother you must have been to Penny, Julia."

"Thankyou, Darling." Julia's eyes shone with a new found hope. She arose from the huge rocker and walked slowly and quietly to the crib her husband had already bought for their grandaughter. "I can see what kind of father and grandfather you will be."

After reassuring herself that the baby was still doing well, Julia turned to George. They sat together in silence listening to the distant thunder. As the day progressed, the air had cooled a bit.

Julia looked into the fire that was crackling in the fireplace. Her thoughts were directed toward the past and all that had happened. "How many times have I prayed for Penny to be alright until I could return to her?"

"Yes, and thus far it looks as though your prayers have been answered. Keep your faith, Julia. Keep your faith." He patted his wife's frail hand affectionately.

"What would I do without you George? You have been my anchor every time I've needed you and I love you for it."

A knock on the door brought them to their feet. Old Doc Henson didn't wait to step inside. Julia took his hat and coat. "I came as soon as I received George's message. I was afraid you were ill again, Julia. But, I have to admit you are looking better than I last saw you."

Julia bit her bottom lip before flashing a sincere smile at the gentleman. She turned to George. "Would you like to tell him or shall I?"

The doctor smiled back, glad to see Julia in such good spirits. "Well, it's a bit too early in the year for Christmas, but I believe I am about to be surprised." At that the couple laughed out loud.

Julia and George led the way through the hallway and into the living room where the newborn lay, eyes wide open and staring as if she was listening to every new sound she heard. Doc Henson looked at the dark haired infant. He gazed over his wire rimmed spectacles. "Now Julia, I know it hasn't been that long since I saw you last. Where did this little bundle come from?"

Julia hesitated for a moment, took a deep breath and after a wave of her hand the old man sat down. She began her long story.

After listening to the incredible tale, Doc Henson arose with only a nod of his head and stared into the crib. He looked at the baby for a good long while. With a smile and a mischievous, but also satisfied gleam in his eyes, he said, "So what they told me was true. Not that I doubted it. There are probably many more people than we know who are held in bondage." He stopped and looked at Julia. "I know where your daughter might be." Before Doc Henson could get another word out, they were interrupted by yet another knock at the door.

"I'll see who it is." George immediately left the room. Opening the door he saw a welcome sight. "You couldn't have come back at a better time, Brent." Neither of the men delayed, but went quickly back to where Julia and the doctor waited. With just a quick glance at the two men, Julia said, "Brent this is Doctor Henson. He knows where Penny might be." Her words were urgent. "Please continue, Doctor."

Doctor Henson had no sooner given directions to Jason Reynolds home until Julia turned and whispered, "Bring her home quickly and safely, Brent." She wasn't sure he heard, for he was half way across the room before anyone else had a chance to move.

Chapter

24

Brent rode into town once more, Pacer's hooves clinking and clanking over the cobble stone streets. The clouds that had hovered over head earlier had passed on and taking their place was a full moon and bright shining stars. The yellow orange ball hung low in the sky and the shadows fell deep as the rider searched through the crowded city. He had been, not only, to rich areas of the city but to back street huts and what ever lay in between. Still yet, he had not scratched the surface of the large area. The clattering of Pacer's hooves came to a sudden halt. Standing with ears forward, he began prancing and swinging his head in an up and down motion. He nickered softly. Looking upwards, Brent followed his gaze. There, on a balcony, stood a figure that again made Brent's heart race. He watched as she stood in the shadows. When she moved, it was slowly. There was something about her unhurried movements that made her seem fragile. How similar her stature was to Penny's. So many young women Brent had seen on this very day who could have been Penny. He rode on down the street past the powdery brick homes with their pastel shades of color. He could see slaves through the open shutters, tending to the work at hand as carefully and efficiently as if they were the owners themselves. A way of life so uncommon to the one he had always known.

He couldn't fathom Penny, the wild and free girl he had known so well, being held in bondage. He ached from the need and wanting of her. He could almost feel her presence. The city lights faded in the background as rider and horse moved farther away from town and on toward the small ranch where Julia and George waited.

Pacer moved smoothly with a fast gait. Brent reached down and patted the horse's neck. "Well Boy, another day is coming to an end and we still haven't found our girl." Ears flicked back. Brent knew his mount couldn't understand his words, but he was sure Pacer could read his moods. The gait slowed, ears flicked forward again. Pacer nickered quietly. Brent listened as he reined his horse in. In the darkness an approaching rider came closer. The large figure on a black horse passed quickly. He was too far away for Brent to make out who he was, but something about the way he sat in the saddle looked familiar. Brent shrugged it off and rode on.

Through the large front window, he could see three people inside the house. He opened the door and saw Julia, George and and an older gentleman. All three stood without uttering a word and stared at Brent. Within seconds, Julia moved around Brent and looked outside. She turned, "Where is she, Brent?"

Brent saw the over whelming look of disappointment on Julia's face. "I'm sorry, Julia, I had no luck again today." He added, " I did get some leads, but it still may take some time."

"But, Doc Henson told you where she is." Julia sounded almost hysterical.

Brent looked in the older man's direction. "Doc Henson?" Brent stretched out his hand.

"Yes," Doc Henson nodded his head as he shook Brent's hand.

The two men eyed each other almost suspiciously for a moment before the younger of the two spoke up. "Could someone please tell me what is going on?"

It was George who spoke next. "You weren't here while ago, were you, Brent?"

"Of course not." Brent no more than got the words out of his mouth until he began to understand what was happening. He remembered the girl at the plantation. Her words were beginning to make too much sense. She had said, "So you came back."

Julia took in a sharp breath, "It was Frank."

Next, it was Doc Henson's turn to ask, "What is going on?"

"I have a twin brother. "He must have gone after Penny. Tell me how to get there." After learning of Penny's where abouts, Brent said to Julia, "We'll bring her back. I promise you this." A dread momentarily stunned Brent into stillness before he turned to rush away.

Brent rode Pacer hard and fast. He could only imagine what would happen to Penny now, if Frank got to her before he did. All the haunting thoughts that had come to his mind about Frank were back. This time they couldn't be easily dismissed. Brent had never wanted to consider the idea that his only brother might truly be demented, but now he had no choice. He had to deal with it. Pacer seemed to know the emergency at hand. He ran without provocation. Brent only had to rein him in the right direction. His heart pounded hard in his chest. He knew it would be unbearable to lose his beloved Penny again. It was heartbreaking for him to know what the young girl must have gone through in the last few months but he was so thankful she was alive.

Chapter

25

Penny peered at the street below. Although she was still weak from her recent ordeal of giving birth to her first child, she couldn't seem to rest. The night before had been long and sad. The distress of having given her own child away had left her with a feeling of desolation. She knew in her own mind that she would somehow get her daughter back, but couldn't shake the despair building on the inside.

It had been over twenty four hours since she had felt the soft, warm child in her arms. Tears streamed down her face as she wondered about that night so long ago. She whispered to herself. "Did Mama hurt as I am hurting now?" She thought about the day she had seen her mother in New Orleans. She didn't realize until now, that her mother hadn't carried the graceful and delicate appearance that she had remembered about her. It had been replaced with a pale and fragile look. Penny found herself not only hurting for the loss of her child but also for the loss of her mother.

The cool air chilled her to the bone. Rubbing her hands over her arms, she shivered. The tiny chill bumps remained. Weakness came again and she shuffled toward her bed. The pillow felt comforting beneath her head and neck. Sleep came quickly and so did her dreams. They were vivid dreams that brought back the most haunting happenings in her life time. Her eyes fluttered open but she squeezed them shut again. She tried to block out the image. Her dreams were too clear. Eyes opening again, she couldn't shut the image out. She pushed herself up in the bed. Opening her eyes wide, she tried to awaken herself and shake the picture before her.

In the large chair near the foot of her bed, she could see him. The moonlight shone on his black hair. Shadows cast over his face, but she knew it was him. She remembered the dreams well.

The longer she stared at the figure slumped in the chair, the clearer it became. Fright began to wash over her and a lump began forming in the pit of her stomach. She swallowed, another tightening forming in her throat. Her heart raced and her breathing was shallow now.

"Hello, Miss Brown."

Penny began to tremble. She wanted to pull the covers over her head but could only sit rigid in her bed. She knew the voice.

So quickly, before she had time to move, only a pitiful whine was coming from Penny's throat, for a rough hand was crushing her tender lips against her teeth. She could taste the blood as she tried to move out from under the grasp. She stilled herself and looking up into the face above her she could see a glint of excitement in the eyes looking down at her. She knew there was no where to flee, no place to hide. She calmed herself and waited. The excitement quickly vanished from the eyes before her and anger took its place. She had a flash back to the night by the falls. She had fought until the demented man had easily put her into a state of unconciousness. This time Penny wanted to know where she was being taken. He scooped her up as if she were no heavier than the pillow that had lain beneath her head.

The stairs creaked from the pressure of feet descending them. Penny could hear low moans coming from the room below. She began to kick and scream at her opponent. "What have you done with them?" Frank kicked the door open as he effortlessly carried his thrashing burden into the cool night air.

The saddle horn gouged Penny's hip when she was thrown upwards onto the beasts back. A sudden weight shifted the saddle and Penny, as Frank slipped his foot into the stirrup and swung a leg over the horse. The ride caused the new mother great misery as she bounced up and down in the saddle. The eerie sounds of the night echoed in her head. The howling, croaking, crackling noises of the swamps made her heart pound hard in her chest.

Penny had no idea how far they had traveled when Frank pulled her from the saddle and her bare feet touched the wet ground. A low growling sound caught their attention and they both glared at the nearby woods. Her abductor seemed to dismiss the sound as just another of the many noises of the swamp, but Penny would have recognized the familiar sound anywhere. She now had an unexpected feeling of hope mixed with a near overwhelming fear. She knew she was no longer alone on this dangerous journey. As the night lingered on, Penny caught sight, more than once, of her friend moving in and out of the shadows.

Despite the discomfort of the whole ordeal, sleep finally overtook Penny. Her weakened condition allowed her to drift into a semi-unconscious state for a short while. Her awakening came all too soon reminding the exhausted young woman of her dire curcumstance. Frank tossed her a small chunk of jerky as he threw the saddle on the still tired horse. Penny realized that neither she nor her adversary had spoken a word since the ride had begun. She summoned all the courage she could muster and spoke for the first time since the kidnapping earlier in the night. "Where are you taking me this time? Haven't you done enough to destroy my life? Why have you hated me so?" The words came from her throat in a shrill scream. She suddenly felt delirious, unafraid, almost as though she was floating away from herself. She felt the warm tears running down her face, her eyes blurred and she was unable to see her enemy clearly. She choked on her words. "You have taken everything from me. You pretended you cared, all the time you helped me, took care of me. How could you do this to me?"

Penny was in a state of shock, no longer in control of the words echoing in her ears. She was suddenly dizzy, her legs feeling like rubber beneath her body. She thought she must be dying or dreaming when out of nowhere came the black blur flying through the darkness. She caught sight of white teeth in the orange glow of the camp fire. The sound of tearing flesh brought Penny back to a sharpened awareness. The huge man's body was writhing beneath Shadow's ferocious attack. He was big and strong but no match for the animal. Penny knew this was her only chance to get away. She moved toward the horse, grabbed the saddle horn and threw her leg over the horse, barely touching the stirrup. She felt as if she was flying through the darkness. She didn't know how far she had gone before she realized Shadow was in hot pursuit of her. She pulled up on the reins bringing the horse to a sudden stop. Penny slid from the saddle throwing her arms around Shadow. Both the girl and dog were gulping for air. She was again conscious of the weakness over powering her.

"How much damage did you do back there, Shadow?" Penny wondered if she had gone far enough to be safe. She had no idea where she was or which way to go next. The swamps were not far away. She could still hear the swamp creature sounds. A thick fog covered the earth like steam coming from a boiling kettle. Everywhere she turned, thick vines stopped her progression. The night sounds came again making Penny shiver, her hair tickling the back of her neck. She leaned against the tree behind her pulling Shadow close and holding tightly to the horse's reins. Penny slept.

Chapter
26

Pacer's hooves beat against the stone street as he ran full speed to the entrance of Jason Reynolds home. Brent felt sick to his stomach when he thought that only a few hours earlier he had watched Penny on this same balcony and not realized it was her. Now he was convinced the fragile girl he had seen earlier in the evening was Penny. The heavy wooden door stood wide open. Brent didn't slow down as he entered the dimly lit room. He moved quickly but carefully as he searched the home. No one was to be found. His hopes began to dwindle before he heard the muffled groans coming from the closet just off the kitchen. He opened the door and found the two old people tied and gagged. He had them untied in moments, but only to find himself in a precarious predicament. He was soon at the wrong end of a shotgun.

"Where did you take our girl, you sorry no account?"

Brent knew it would do no good to try to explain, but he tried. He felt by the look on Jesse and Celia's faces that he was talking his way right into a killin. He was very relieved when he saw Doc Henson come through the doorway. He was even more relieved after the old doctor told them his story and they laid the shotgun down.

"Do you have any idea where he took her?" Brent looked old beyond his age as he stared hopefully and intensely at the couple.

"He was laughin and talkin bout how he was takin her through the swamps and feedin her to the alligators. He's a crazy man. No good."

"We'll never find them." Brent looked helpless as the words burst from his taut lips. The old doctor rubbed his chin, slowly took a deep breath and spoke, "Maybe there's someone who can help. I've heard Old Samuel and that hound of his are the best pair of trackers in this part of the country. The story goes, they can go into the worst gator territory known to man and come out alive."

"I be goin wich ya. I can take youz to his place." Jesse spoke up.

The three men left the worried Celia standing in the big empty house alone to wait for the return of the girl she had learned to love as a daughter.

The dog met them with a low growl, teeth bared, crouched and ready to spring at the intruders. He was suddenly called to a hault by the gigantic man standing in the doorway of the old cabin. The dog stopped, but was still yet growling a warning to the men to stay put.

"Who there?" The coarse voice could be heard loudly over the growling dog.

"We was needin help." Jesse called back.

"That youz, Jesse?"

"Yea, it be me."

"Down Dog." With the words the threat was gone. The dog that had looked so vicious a moment before was lying like a gentle puppy on the ground.

The three men walked closer to the rickety porch where Old Samuel stood. With trembling lips, Jesse told Old Samuel about Penny. Brent stared intently into the eyes of Jason Reynold's slave, realizing he wasn't the only one who was suffering. Without hesitation the tracker began his job. Within minutes the men were on their way to find the missing girl.

They followed Old Samuel down the winding dirt path, away from the cabin, and back toward Jason Reynolds. The tracker knew it would be the best place to start. They road in silence until they reached their destination.

"I be needin somethin, maybe somethin the girl wore so my dog can sniff her out." Celia moved hurriedly to Penny's room. She grabbed the dress Penny had worked in. She suddenly changed her mind, thinking of all the food scents that might interfere. She dropped the garment and stripped the sheet from Penny's bed.

"Hea, take this. Find hu. Find hu fas. She in danga."

Dog smelled the sheet, and with a howl, lunged forward in the direction of the swamps. Again, Brent was listening to the clanking of hooves moving down the streets of New Orleans. But this time, his heart beat with hopeful anticipation.

The group moved swiftly and steadily, each man determined that the hunt would be successful, no matter what it took. Brent tried to keep his mind off what might be happening to Penny. The farther he rode, the better he controlled his emotions. He blocked out any worrisome thoughts and grew more and more confident that he would soon have Penny back. The riders rode without delay with only one thought in mind.

The search was tedious and all eyes were watchful as the animal ahead moved in and out of the dense thickets. At times, the trackers were so far ahead, Brent was fearful of losing them He and the others pushed faster as time wore on. They hoped the light of the moon would prove to be steadfast, for the search would have to be delayed until dawn if the clouds, now hovering in the distance, blew their way.

The resounding night noises were in perfect harmony and were a distraction for Brent, but he was well aware of the danger lurking within. An abrupt and eerie howl came from the darkness ahead, and then for a moment, all was silent. When Brent, Jesse and Doc

Henson located Old Samuel, they didn't have to be told that a significant struggle had taken place there. Only the life long tracker was able to offer an explanation.

"It look like a big animal got a big man hea. No doubt, he been beat up Purdy bad. He on foot but the girl she be on the horse and lit out a hea like a bat out a hail storm." Without delay all mounted again and followed the eager dog until the fog and thick vines consumed them.

Chapter

27

Penny was exhausted, but relieved by the first sign of the morning sun peeping through the leaves above her. Drawing all her remaining strength together, she pulled herself from the moist ground and searched the saddle bags for more nourishment. Her mental and physical discomfort were relieved somewhat when she found more of the tough jerky within the wet, smelly leather. She chewed the meat hungrily, biting her tongue and bringing bright red blood to the corners of her mouth. She took one bite after another tasting the fresh blood as she swallowed. After only seconds of hesitation she mounted the horse and headed out. Penny rode short distances resting her weary body, pacing herself, attempting to devise a plan as she traveled her uncertain path. Not knowing where she would end up, she headed toward the sunlight.

The long tiresome day wore on. Penny was mindful of the changing environment. She had left the swamp lands behind and had now entered a celestial domain. The horses hooves kicked up small clouds of dust as he carried the girl up the shaded, winding dirt road. She breathed in the fragrance of the pink and white flowers dotting the green grass. All the while, she was careful to dodge the enormous tree branches sheltering her pathway. She was leery when she spotted a small cabin in the distance. Dismounting she wearily but cautiously eased her way to the shelter. Penny peered through the window. The cabin looked uninhabited. Relieved, she tied the horse's reins to the porch post, slid the rifle out of the leather straps and stepped inside. Penny moved, on shaky legs, toward the small unkempt cot in the corner of the room. Although small and dusty, no bed had ever felt so good as Penny lay her tired, aching body down to rest. She knew her time had run out. She bled heavily again and her strength was dwindling away. She closed her eyes and darkness over took her.

It was hours before Penny was, only slightly, aroused by Shadow's low, warning growl. Her green eyes fluttered open and then shut again. She heard the creak of the door, but her eyes only wanted to open. Next the most ferocious sound she had ever heard took hold of her. She was sitting upright on the small cot, eyes wide open, staring into the eyes of her worst enemy. The massive figure stood fixed in place in the open doorway.

Penny reached for the rifle beside her. Without hesitation, the gun was in hand, cocked, with Penny's finger on the trigger. Splinters flew from the wall beside the man. "One more step and you'll be gone." He had no doubt.

Shadow still yet kept guard as the girl held the man at bay with the deadly weapon. Penny swung her legs off the cot and moved to stand. She wilted like a flower in the hot summer sun. Her legs gave way, and she fell lifeless to the floor.

"Penny," Brent felt sick when he saw the blood. Unexpectedly, the threat vanished for both man and beast as Brent moved forward. He ever so gently scooped Penny's limp, still body up in his arms and laid her on the cot. Her skin was cold and clammy to his touch. He ran his hand over her forehead, smoothing her thick, tangled hair from her face.

Brent felt a hand on his shoulder. It was Doc Henson. He also saw that Jesse had reached the doorway of the cabin. "Will the chile be alright, Doc?" Jesse asked.

"Only time will tell," said the doctor as he took charge.

Brent, Jesse and Old Samuel waited outside.

"We los da man a while back. He took off down riva. We hud gun shots and headed dis way. Figued he might a doubled back." It sho be strange how he still be movin afta takin such a whippin from dat dog."

Brent's mind was tormented about all that had happened. When Penny had looked at him with such terror in her eyes, he knew his suspicions had to be right. His only brother was a cruel and sick man.

When Doc Henson came out, he looked at Brent, "She is very physically weak, but worse than that is the mental anguish she has suffered. She needs sleep now more than anything. I told her what I knew about the situation. I told her enough so that she won't be trying to shoot you, Brent."

The day was wearing to an end and all agreed it would be best for everyone to bed down and get some sleep before heading back home. All slept except Brent. Too many thoughts muddled his mind. Morning was a long time coming for him, but when it did, he was very anxious to see Penny. He wondered if she would be able look at him. He again remembered the terror in her eyes and wondered if she had blamed him all these months.

"Penny needs rest before she is able to travel," Doc Henson said as he walked out of the cabin.

Both Brent and Jesse waited to see Penny. Brent spoke. "Jesse, Doc will the two of you go in with me? I think it would be best if Penny is not alone with me just yet. She might be able to talk to me better if she's not alone." His own words tore at his heart. After all, this was the girl he had loved and protected for so long. His gut knotted up at the thought that Penny was afraid of him.

At first sight of Jesse, tears welled up in Penny's eyes. "Jesse, I'm so glad you are here." Jesse said nothing as he put his arms around her.

Brent watched from a distance, fearing what Penny must think of him. But when their eyes met, he knew nothing could ever change the love they had. She held out her arms and heart wrenching sobs broke the silence as Brent embraced the girl he had cared for so long.

Jesse and Doc Henson slipped through the cabin door. They saddled their horses and prepared to go home. Before riding out Jesse said to Brent, "We know Penny be in good hands."

After the others had gone, Brent left Penny long enough to get his saddle bags and the few supplies Celia had packed for him. To his surprise, he found not only food enough for them both, but clothes for Penny. He began the task of cleaning the old cabin and preparing food. Penny set up long enough to eat the food Brent had brought her. With his help, she ate as if she was starved. She lay watching in amazement as he moved around the room. She was overwhelmed with love. She could hardly believe what was taking place. They both knew they had much to talk about, but for now, it was enough for them to be together. A time for healing was needed. They had both had too much at one time to fathom it all. Brent kept watch over Penny as she slept off and on through out the day. Sleep came easy and peaceful now. For the first time in months Penny felt her life was back. There was so much she needed to say, but for now, she just needed to enjoy the peace of mind. She felt safe again.

Brent, on the other hand, knew of the danger that could be lying in wait. He didn't know how much Doc Henson had told Penny, and he didn't want to cause her any more distress. He wanted her to gain her strength back. In the evening after another nourishing meal, Brent walked to the nearby creek for a bucket of water. He warmed it in the fireplace. When Penny aroused he offered her warm water and a cloth for bathing. He hung a blanket beside the cot to give her privacy. When Penny finished washing, Brent replaced the soiled cot coverings with a fresh blanket that had been sent by Celia. He gave Penny one of his shirts. She put it on feeling she had just been given the finest of silks. Brent began making a pallet on the floor next to the cot, but Penny stopped him. Moving to the far edge she laid her hand on the cot beside her. "Sleep here beside me. I've missed you so." He eased into the small bed and kissed his beloved on the cheek before she drifted into yet another peaceful sleep. Brent looked at the barred door and then at the protective animal lying next to it before he too fell asleep.

Chapter
28

With the morning sun came the sound of a meadowlark outside the window. Penny's eyes opened wide. "I smell food." The aroma of breakfast filled the air. She saw Brent by the fireplace. She barely got the words out of her mouth before he was giving her a plate of food. She sat up and began to eat. Brent returned with a plate of his own and sat beside her. They ate in silence, both feeling the serenity of the moment. When their plates were empty, Penny swung her bare feet off the bed. She was standing, not so steadily, when Brent put one arm around her waist and took her hand in his.

"I need sunlight. Will you walk with me to the porch?"

They walked slowly into the warm spring sunlight, listening to the chirping of the birds and smelling the sweet scent of freshly bloomed flowers. Penny wanted to say something. She needed to talk about everything that had happened, but when her lips parted no words came. She stood in silence again, breathing in the warm air. For now, there was peace for her in the way Brent held her. She could feel the strength in his arms as he held her beside him. She leaned into him, her head resting on his chest.

"I love you, Brent." is all she could say.

Brent was just as much at a loss for words as Penny. He didn't know where or how to start. Not knowing how much she knew, he was still yet afraid to say anything that might cause her more mental anguish. They clung to each other, drawing strength from their undying love. Both knew there would be a time for talking, later. Together, they walked to the old porch swing. They sat rocking back and forth soaking up the sun.

As the days passed, Penny grew stronger. The ghost white pallor of her face was being replaced with the natural tawny color. The gleam was appearing in her jade green eyes and with the nourishing meals served by Brent, her fragile look was beginning to disappear. They knew it was time for them to leave the small cabin and head back toward the city. The horses were saddled, the saddle bags packed and the two were ready to make their way back to new Orleans. Before stepping from the porch, Penny sat down in the swing for the last time.

She stared at Brent with the wide eyed innocence of her past. "There is much to talk about before we leave."

Brent moved to sit beside her, taking her small soft hand into his larger calloused one.

Never taking her eyes from Brent's, Penny began. "We have a child, Brent. A girl. A baby girl." Tears swam in her eyes even as she smiled. Her smile was lost by the quivering of her lips. "I tried to protect her the best way I knew how." Tears spilled down her cheeks.

Brent put a finger to her lips. "Penny don't. She's alright. She's beautiful, just like you."

Penny opened her mouth to speak, but was so confused she didn't know what to say.

"She's with your mother. We have been caring for her."

"So, that was Celia's plan. She saved my daughter. She has saved me."

"Julia came to Missouri to get you and start that new life she had worked so hard for."

Penny took in a deep, shaky breath. "But I was gone, wasn't I?" She sat staring off into the distance, remembering the night she was first taken.

Brent told Penny about all that had happened.

Then, it was Penny's turn. She left nothing out as she let the nightmare flood from her lips. It was like poison spewing from her mind and body. She felt drained when she finished, but knew it was part of her healing. She told him about the kidnapping, the slave auction, Jason Reynolds and about the beautiful little blonde haired, blue eyed girl, Lisa. She told him of their attempt to escape and that Mildred had never let her see Lisa again.

"I didn't even get to tell her goodbye."

Brent remembered the white girl who rode with the Indian boy. He knew now, their story was true. He pushed it to the back of his mind, knowing this was not the time to tell Penny. He slowly moved from the swing to the porch post. With one arm on the post and his head bent low, his whole body shook with pent up sobs. Without delay Penny had her arms around Brent, knowing that it was he who was in need of comfort now. She realized the depth of his love. The nightmare had not only been lived by her but by all who was involved.

The couple knew it was time for them to go. They had so much to be thankful for. They had their lives back. Suddenly the sky was bluer and the grass greener than Penny ever remembered. They rode down the narrow trail away from the cabin. Trailing close behind was Shadow. Penny smiled at the sight of her.

Brent looked first at Penny and then at Shadow. The young woman never ceased to amaze him. She was captivating, beautiful beyond belief and seemed always oblivious to the fact. His passion and love were stirred as he watched her intently. The air was warm and filled with the sweet scent of spring flowers. Nearby thickets held the sounds of animals and birds calling to their young. The squeak of leather resounded rhythmically with each step their mounts took.

Penny's health had improved with each passing day and Brent intended to keep it that way. He kept a close watch on her, stopping regularly to rest. He made sure Penny took time for proper nourishment too. Even though they were both anxious to get back to the city, Brent was firm in making their trip an easy one.

Brent pulled his horse to a stop as they came to a Live oak. He dismounted and immediately turned to Penny. Putting both arms around her, he carefully lifted her from her horse. Ducking under the low hanging branches, he spread his blanket on the ground. He took Penny by the hand and they walked together to the pallett. He pulled her to the ground.

"I'm really not tired yet, Brent." Penny grinned, as she quietly said the words.

"Good, now I know my plan is working. I want you to keep your strength up." He ran a finger along her cheek tracing a path to her chin. Tilting her head so that he looked directly into her eyes, Brent ever so lightly toucher her lips with his before getting to his feet and moving toward his saddle for a canteen of water.

Penny took the cool liquid offered her and then lay back on the makeshift bed. Brent rested beside her, taking her hand in his. They watched the white, fluffy clouds float through the turquoise sky.

Chapter

29

"I want everything to be just right when Penny gets home, George. It has been so long. Do you think she hates me? Will she ever understand? How could a child understand when her mother deserts her? What if she can't forgive me? Will she ever love me again?"

"Julia, stop torturing yourself. Things will work themselves out. You did what you thought was best. How could she condemn you for that?"

Julia took in a deep breath. "I hope you are right. I couldn't stand it if things are not good between us." With that, Julia again busied herself with the task of preparing Penny's room.

George soon took her by the arm, leading her out of the room and down the stairs. He insisted that his wife take a break. "You want to feel good when Penny gets here, don't you my darling?"

"Yes, you are right." Julia smiled.

The baby slept soundly in the cradle. Julia tiptoed into the room taking a quick peek, before sitting on the sofa in the spacious living room. Time passed slowly but Julia was glad for the time of relaxation.

The sheer, mint green curtains blew lightly in the breeze, as Penny and Brent walked arm in arm up the walkway to the huge mahogany door. "I'm scared." The young woman clung to Brent, tightly.

Brent patted Penny's hand and smiled lovingly at her. Before knocking on the door, he turned to her. "If you only knew how loved you are, there wouldn't be an ounce of fear in you." He kissed her softly.

Julia opened the door. For a moment, she stood motionless. She looked into the tear filled, jade green eyes. It was as if they had been hurled back

133

in time. All fear melted away as the mother and daughter were lost in a long awaited embrace.

Julia, gently wiped the tears from Penny's cheeks. "Come with me." She took her daughter by the hand as if she were still a young child. They entered the living area. Julia led Penny to the sofa. Penny sat down and Julia crossed the room. She lifted the small bundle out of the cradle, took her back to Penny and placed her in the young mother's arms. Overwhelmed with emotion, Penny took her own daughter and with trembling lips said in a low, pain filled voice, "For so long I tried to hate those who loved me most. Now I know why I couldn't."

As painful as it was, Brent went to the sheriff soon after he and Penny got back to the city. Frank was no where to be found. It was as if he had vanished. Brent knew they might never know wat had happened to his brother. The law and trackers had followed Frank into the swamps. That was where they lost him. They said it was next to impossible for a wild animal to survive the area. They said a man didn't have a chance. Brent knew he would be haunted by thoughts of the unknown for a long time, but he was determined not to let those thoughts ruin anymore lives.

Brent was torn between giving the family time to adjust and bringing up the subject of marriage. He didn't want anymore time to pass before he gave Penny and the baby his name. He walked toward Penny's room, feeling a bit nervous. It suddenly entered his mind that, maybe Penny wouldn't want to marry him. After all, he hadn't talked to her about marriage since they were in Missouri. What if she said no? It was one thing for her to love him and be grateful that she had been rescued. It was another for her to spend the rest of her life with him. So much had happened to her. He took a ragged breath and knocked on the door.

"Come in." The voice was soft and sweet. His heart raced. Brent stepped into the bedroom, closing the door behind him. When he didn't move away from the door, Penny giggled. What's wrong, Brent?" She thought he looked much like a little lost boy, quite a contrast to the self-assured man she knew him to be. Penny kissed Maggie on the cheek and laid her in the cradle. She walked the short distance to Brent. Taking him by the hand, she pulled him toward the bed. "Sit by me. Tell me what is on your mind."

Brent was even more giddy now, because Penny was having just the opposite effect on him. She portrayed a self-assured young woman instead of the young girl he had first proposed to. He was mesmerized by her beauty. Now, a more mature, womanly beauty. He felt as though he was being held captive.

Penny had no idea, the effect she was having on Brent. The silence grew longer. It was Penny who so abruptly, became aware of intense feelings. It was a breath taking awareness of the womanly feelings she had toward this man. She was no longer the little girl who needed someone to care for her, but the woman who needed to love the strong and gentle man sitting so closely to her. She leaned into him, put her arms around his neck and kissed him with a passion neither of them had ever felt. The kiss was long and tender but filled with a desire that threatened to consume them both. Brent moaned with pent up passion and returned her lingering kiss. When their lips parted, they were both dizzy and breathless.

The silence came, once more, but this time it had nothing to do with doubt. Brent was sure of the love and trust between them. "Will you marry me, my love?" Penny kissed Brent again. "Yes, I love you. You are my life." They spent the afternoon discussing their plans. They both agreed that under the circumstances they would need a quiet wedding with only family. They also agreed that Celia and Jesse were now included in that family.

Penny had made sure Jason Reynolds would set Celia and Jesse free in return for her silence. He had agreed, willingly, much to Penny's surprise.

Chapter

30

When Julia and George returned home, Penny and Brent were waiting on them. Julia took one look at the two young people and knew they had something unique. It was a once in a lifetime sort of love.

"Mama, we have a wedding to plan."

Julia moved toward her daughter, taking her by the arm, "Let's get started." The two walked away leaving the men alone.

Julia and Penny spent the next few days planning the wedding. The time brought mother and daughter even closer than they had been before. Celia was included in the plans, and since the baby was only a few weeks old, helped with much of the shopping. They walked through the streets of New Orleans. Penny could hardly comprehend the change in her life. She remembered a time not long ago when true happiness seemed forever out of reach. Penny was filled with joy. She looked down at the small baby girl wrapped in the snow white blanket Celia had made for her. She touched Maggie's pink cheek, then ran her hand gently over her downy soft, black hair. Julia watched Penny, so proud of the young woman her daughter had become.

The wedding was as planned. The preacher came to Julia and George's home. Celia and Jesse were there and, of course, Maggie.

Brent couldn't take his eyes off Penny as she descended the stairs and walked to stand beside him. He had never seen her looking more beautiful. She wore a lavender dress that clung loosely to her, still slim, figure. Her dark brown hair hung almost to her waist. The white pearls accented her tawny skin. Her full lips turned up slightly in a smile for Brent. He returned the affectionate smile with a wink. The light in Penny's green eyes told all. In only a few minutes the two had exchanged vows and were husband and wife. Brent kissed Penny tenderly, and the two turned to face their happy family.

With the baby being so young, the couple didn't have any intentions of leaving her while they went on a homeymoon. They had both agreed their family had been separated for too long.

Julia and Celia had planned a feast for the evening. George, not wanting Julia to over do it, had wanted to hire help, but Celia and Jesse had insisted on taking over the task. The rest of the family had, in turn, insisted they join in at dinner time. Now, in celebration they all sat around the large, cherry wood dining table. They all knew they were truly, a blessed family.

The night was warm and filled with springtime sounds and smells. Brent and Penny had decided to go out for a walk. Hand in hand the newlyweds strolled down the trail that led from the house to the creek. The big yellow moon hung low in the star lit sky.

Brent turned to his wife. "I thought I would die without you." His words were barely audible.

Penny moved closer to him, wrapping her arms around his waist and laying her head on his chest. "I felt the same, but now I could not feel more alive. What we thought we couldn't live through will make us stronger."

The couple strolled through the garden, and finally made their way back to the family room. Julia and George were sitting on the sofa together, looking as if they were at peace with the world. Penny gave Julia and George a hug, took the baby in her arms and the bride and groom walked up stairs to their bedroom.

Brent twisted the knob and moved back, allowing Penny to go in. He watched as she slowly scanned the room. He heard her take in a deep breath. "You were all in on this, weren't you?"

Her husband chuckled. Penny walked deeper into the room, smelling the roses. She looked down at Maggie. "I can just imagine how your daddy will spoil you, little one." She turned to Brent with a smile. Laying the baby in the cradle, she continued walking around the room taking in the aroma of each boquet as she went.

Penny felt as though she was, again, the girl in Alder Missouri. She looked at the oversized bed in the middle of the room. Her eyes fell upon the most delicate gown she had ever seen. It was snow white and made of pure silk. The little girl in her was replaced again by the young woman. "It is beautiful. It's something that a princess might wear."

"I chose it. It was made just for you." He closed the distance between Penny and himself. Putting his large hands on her arms, he gently turned her around. Moving the thickness of her hair from her neck, he unbuttoned Penny's dress. She turned to him. He pushed the material from her shoulders and let the lavender dress fall to the floor. Penny never took her eyes from his. She watched the changes in his expression as he proceeded to undress her. He took the white gown from the bed and dropped it over Penny's head. She pulled her arms through the smooth material and Brent pulled it into place. He stepped back, taking in the full length of her. "Now, Sweetheart, it looks like something a princess might wear." They both laughed. They crossed the room and looking down into the cradle saw that Maggie was fast asleep. Penny took care to hang her wedding dress in the armoir while Brent got ready for bed. She walked to the dresser, took the pearls from her neck and placed them in the jewelry box. Catching Brent's reflection in the mirror, she knew he was moving toward her. She felt his strong arms enfolding her. She felt his warm breath when he put his face against hers. She turned just far enough that their lips met in a sensual kiss. Brent bent and slipped an arm under knees, easily lifting her from the floor. He carried her to the bed and slipped in beside her.

He held his beloved wife in his arms, tenderly, caressing her with kisses and hugs. Although it was with great restraint on both Brent and Penny's part, they knew, instinctively, that this was not the time to be intimate in a sexual way. The baby was only a few weeks old and there would be time for the literal marriage bed later. For now, they were happy beyond belief to be together again. Penny loved Brent more than ever, for she knew the strong man beside her would spend a lifetime caring for her and their children.

Brent awoke in the early hours of the morning to a dim light and his young wife feeding their child. He watched, intrigued by the soft, pink, little lips suckling at Penny's full breast. He saw a tender young woman willing to give her all to him and his child. He reached up and kissed his wife on the lips. "I love you, Mrs. Holbrook."

Chapter
31

The next few weeks passed in a hurry, bringing tumultuous feelings. Everyone knew at some point, Brent would have to return to the ranch and handle business. The time was drawing nearer with each passing day. Until now, no one had made mention of it. Brent had been distracted lately due to the colossal decisions that would have to be made soon. He didn't know how to approach the situation. He knew it would be devastating for Penny and her mother to be separated again, so soon, after everything that had happened.

Brent had given the circumstance much consideration before he finally decided it might be best if he talked to George first. They could talk to Penny and Julia together. Brent had noticed George leave the house and figured he had headed for the horse barn. Brent had found the older man to have quite a unique liking for the outdoors, especially to be a city man. Just as he had suspected, George was in the barn mucking stalls and putting down fresh hay. The younger man grabbed a pitch fork and began helping. As the men worked, they talked.

"What's been bothering you, Brent?" George asked.

"I don't know how to begin talking to Penny and her mother about us going back to the ranch." I've been keeping in touch with Ben, my forman, but there is going to be a time, soon, that I will have to go back. I don't know how the girls are going to handle it. They have renewed their bond quite well." Both men laughed.

"Yes, and I am quite thankful for that. Julia was so worried that Penny would never forgive her."

"And, I can assure you, Penny had fears of her own." Brent shrugged his shoulders. "What am I going to do, George? How can I possibly take Penny away from Julia again?"

"Believe it or not, Brent, I have been pondering this thing myself for quite some time now. We can't separate them, not now, not so soon."

"I can't leave my wife and daughter. What am I going to do?"

George walked over and put his hand on Brent's shoulder. "You, son are going to take your wife and daughter home. I have been thinking about retiring. I have a good savings and can provide for Julia and myself quite well. I have been thinking I'd like to settle down near a small town, spend more time with Julia, maybe have a small herd of cattle."

Brent was relieved to here what George had to say. It was too good to be true. He had thought about how good it would be if they could all go back to Missouri, but never thought it could possibly happen. "Do you think Julia would be willing to move from this beautiful home and go back to Alder?"

"Yes, we have discussed it. We just wanted to make sure you felt okay about it."

"Brent reached for a hardy hand shake. "Sir, I can't wait to tell my wife."

A heavy load had been taken from his shoulders. The two worked steadily all morning feeling all was well with their world. Before long, Penny came walking briskly into the barn. "Are you two hungry? We have made a special lunch just for hard working men." She giggled as she said the words.

"What is that special lunch, my Dear?" Brent asked.

Penny yelled back over her shoulder as she headed toward the house to set the table. "It would be fried chichen, mashed potatoes, corn on the cob, chocolate cake." Her voice trailed off as she moved out of sight.

Brent and George looked at each other and grinned. They lost no time getting cleaned up and ready to sit down at the small table on the back porch. Penny and Julia bustled around happily, serving the men they so desperately loved.

After everyone was seated and the blessing had been said, Penny looked around her. She thought, "To be loved so deeply and to so deeply love, what could be better?" Julia was looking stronger and healthier with each passing day. Brent and George were happily enjoying their meal and Shadow lay next to the cradle watching over Maggie with a motherly instinct of her own. Penny knew she was truly blessed.

Chapter

32

Jason Reynolds peered across the room at the lovely creature who seemed to be attracting the attention of every man in the ball room. His abrupt recognition of her was both embarrassing and shocking. His sister looked at him in disbelief. She had also recognized Penny.

"I guess she was telling the truth after all" Jason said.

"She is gorgeous, isn't she, Jason?"

"Quite." He responded.

Brent caught a glimps of Jason. He tightened his hold on Penny as they waltzed around the room. He wouldn't let anything or anybody stain this time with his wife. He wanted their brief time alone to be flawless for Penny. This time that had been so long in coming. "I am a lucky man. The most dazzling lady in the world is mine."

Penny looked up at her husband. Her eyes took in the black hair falling across his forehead. Her gaze fell to the broad shoulders. She felt the strength in his arms as they held her close. She was breathless as she looked into his blue eyes. "You are my hero. More than once you have saved my life, heedless of your own safety. No, my love, I am the one who is most fortunate."

Brent pulled her even closer, listening to the rustle of her lemon yellow dress as he guided her around the dance floor. He had made a gift of the dress and the strand of emeralds she was wearing. He was fascinated by the stare of her velvety green eyes. Oblivious to the crowd around them, the couple was lost in their passion for each other.

When the music stopped, Brent whispered in Penny's ear. "Are you hungry yet?"

"Starved."

They went arm in arm up the stairs to the hotel room where Brent again surprised Penny with an evening meal. They enjoyed the quiet time and ate leisurely while they talked. It was then, Brent brought the topic of Missouri into their conversation. A look of sadness washed over her face but was quickly squelched when Brent told her of Julia and George's plans.

Penny jumped up, ran around the table and flung her arms around Brent's neck. He pulled her down into his lap. "What about Celia and Jesse?" Her words shouldn't have been a surprise to Brent. After all he knew his wife and her need to care for everyone in her life.

"That, Sweetie, is something you are going to have to talk to them about."

They finished their meal in a perfect state of bliss. Brent was glad now, that he had decided to tell Penny about the plan. After they had finished eating, both agreed they would like to take a walk. They strolled down the city streets, listening to the soothing music wafting through the air. By the time they got back to the hotel they were eager to be alone. The soft bed felt good to Brent as he lay watching Penny.

Penny stood in the doorway leading to the balcony. The moonlight filtered into the room, casting just enough light for Brent to see her full silhouette. He watched her delicate body with each fluid movement she made. She was unaware of the enticing display she was presenting to her husband. He could see the fullness of her breasts, her small waist line and the roundness of her hips. Her long legs looked silky smooth as she moved toward the bed. Her long thick hair fell in disarray around her face. Her green eyes shone with loving anticipation of what this night would bring. Brent could smell the sweetness of her scent and see the fullness of her lips as she slid into bed beside him. He could hardly contain pent up desire when he moved to kiss her moist lips.

Penny's whole being opened up to her husband. They were both consumed by the urgency of their desire. They wanted to make up for the time that had been stolen from them. Penny's lips and legs parted as Brent searched every line, crevice and hollow. He was strong but ever so gentle as he loved her slowly and deliberately. Penny could feel the taut muscles in his arms and chest. She could also feel the soft quiver of his self inflicted restraint. This night belonged to them, and they now belonged to one another. They loved and slept and awoke to love each other again. They drank in the moment as if this would be the last, for they knew life was full of the unknown.

They awoke the following morning, late, but that was okay by them. They were stilll yet not ready to give up the new found freedom they had found in each other. They lay in each others arms and planned for a bright future together. The two of them not only had passion and desire for one another, but they also had much in common as they were quickly learning.

Chapter

33

The passengers heard the horn blow and watched the crowd slowly fade from sight. They were leaving New Orleans to travel to Missouri. With babe in arms and surrounded by family, Penny was off to her brand new life. The muddy Mississippi rolled as the boat moved through the waters. Every now and then land was close enough for rabbits, squirrels, and even white tailed deer to appear in the early morning light. An occasional cardinal, purple finch or woodpecker would fly into sight.

There was no sadness now for Penny, except for the sporadic thoughts of Frank. "I won't let him take any more of our lives than he already has," she whispered. Once again, she erased the memories from her mind.

The trip back to Alder was peaceful and all were enjoying their time together. They all knew much was to do when they arrived back home. Each day held excitement and anticipation for all, as they made their journey.

Gunther had passed away soon after Julia and George left Alder leaving the old home place for mother and daughteer to deal with. They had both agreed to keep the farm, since it connected to the far side of the Holbrook's ranch. Julia and George had decided to build a new home there, but in a different spot. They knew even though the old home place held good memories, it also carried bad along with the good.

"I think I have an idea," Julia had chimed. "What about Celia and Jesse? They will need a place to stay. Do you thik we might talk them into letting us build a new cabin for them to live in?"

Penny's eyes lit up as she hugged her mother. "We could tear the old cabin down and put them a new one in the same place. I will talk to them."

"We can't be takin no handouts. Ya'll done too much fo us now." Seeing the sadness in Penny's eyes and after the pleading, Celia and Jesse had agreed, but only if they could work for the Holbrooks. All was settled, a new cabin would be built.

"Mother, everything will be perfect," Penny had said. Her eyes shone with tears, so much different than the ones that had rolled down her cheeks years before.

Now, Penny stood on the boat overlooking the waters of the Mississippi. The sun was sinking slowly into the western sky lighting up the horizon with orange light. The air held a slight mist that cooled her skin. Feeling the, now familiar, warmth of Brent's arms slide around her waist, she rested her head on his chest and leaned back into his embrace. His lips came down to touch her cheek. The words he whispered sent a warm flush through Penny and she lifted her lips to meet his.

"I was afraid you were gone forever. I am not dreaming, am I?"

"No, my love, you are not. I felt the same. My life was over without you. I only existed. Each day, even when I was working on the ranch herding cattle, breaking horses, no matter what I was doing, I was not whole without you." Their kiss was lingering, demanding ,arousing such a searing passion it left them both breathless and weak. They clung to each other in the dusky dark shadows.

After short, treasured moments together, Penny and Brent walked wistfully back to their cabin where Julia and Celia waited with Maggie. The two women had suggested Penny take some time for herself. Soon after, Brent had left his conversation with George and Jesse and joined her. He could hardly stay more than a few feet away from his wife.

Penny went straight to Celia and took Maggie in her arms. "Thanks so much. I enjoyed my walk on deck. The night is so beautiful. I don't know when I have seen such a colorful sunset."

She walked to her mother, kissing her on the cheek. "We are going home, Mother."

The farther up the Mississippi toward Missouri the steamboat took them, the more excited Penny became. She stood holding Maggie looking so much a child herself. Brent watched her intensely admiring her innocent nature even after everthing that had happened. Everyday it seemed she was becoming the light hearted young girl he had known. Penny hugged

Maggie to her chest rubbing a finger over her soft pink cheek. Julia and Celia said their goodbyes and went to find their own husbands.

The next few days travel were much the same. By the time land was reached again, everyone was eager to walk down the planks and off the boat.

"It is good to feel the land beneath my feet," George said as he looked at Julia.

All agreed, but Brent thought to himself, "Now it feels good, but what are they going to think by the time we make the trip the rest of the way home ? Up until now, it has been just a vacation." He dreaded it for them. Especially, the women who were not familiar with the type of travel it would take to get back to Alder in a wagon. He looked at Penny and was reminded of the journey she had taken more than a year before. It brought a sudden surge of anger for him to think about her kidnapping. It also brought relief to know that Penny was strong and could probably make it fine.

Brent suddenly realized he had been staring for long moments at Penny. He saw the questioning look in her twinkling eyes. He smiled affectionately at his wife and gave her a flirtatious wink. She smiled back her heart light and filled with hope. Maggie squirmed in her arms taking Penny's attention. She bounced her daughter up and down as she walked her back and forth, waiting for the men to direct them to the next step in their trek home.

Brent turned to George and Jesse. "What do you think about getting the ladies into a room over at the hotel for tonight?"

The others agreed since it was getting well into the afternoon. There was still yet much to do in order to get supplies ready for the trip. Wagons would have to be bought, not to mention getting the livestock off the boat and ready for the long awaited excursion.

When the women were settled in at the hotel, the men went to handle the business at hand. The livestock and personal belongings were taken off the boat. Wagons were bought and the livestock was taken to the livery stable. "Can you keep her here until morning?" Brent asked.

The old man looked down at the dog standing close by. "I suppose I could bed her down too." He eyed Brent. "She is friendly, no problem with her and the livestock? She looks like she might have some wolf in her bloodline."

"She'll be fine. You won't have any problems like that out of her. Shadow you stay here, girl," Brent said firmly, before heading back toward the hotel with the other men.

Evening came quickly and everyone gathered in the hotel lobby for supper. Plans for the trip back to Alder were discussed over the evening meal, then all went their separate ways, once again, for the night.

Penny sat on the edge of the bed feeding Maggie while Brent watched in amazement. He crawled up onto the oversized bed behind Penny, kissing her on the neck and then the cheek. She turned her head just enough to press her moist lips to his before turning back to focus on her beautiful baby girl.

Maggie slept without awakening and so did her mom and dad. All too soon, came the morning sunlight peeping through the sheer curtains and warming the room. Brent felt the soft feathery feel of something on his face. His eyes opened to Penny's wide eyed stare. He pulled her down on to his bare chest holding her gently for long moments before she suggested they get up and get ready to go home.

Again, all met for a nourishing meal before leaving civilization and heading off through the wilderness that lay in wait. With much work, baggage and supplies were packed and loaded on the wagons. Horses were saddled up and the family was on its way toward Alder. Although, Shadow was left to come and go as she pleased, she was never far away from Penny and Maggie. She fit into the family with ease and it was evident that the dog had a basic need for the wild. It was obvious to all, that Shadow was in no need of their care. Instead, it seemed to be her intent to look out for them.

↓

Chapter

34

Hours turned to days and the toll of traveling through the rough country was beginning to leave its tiring effects on all. No one complained though, for they all looked forward to each new day they spent together. Another day was slowly passing and with everyone being tired and needing some extra rest, they had decided to camp early. They had found the perfect place. A flower covered meadow with a nearby creek. Everyone was at their leisure and enjoying the warm, sunny day.

Jesse, sitting quietly and at peace, was the first to notice the visitor. He nodded his head toward the opposite side of the creek and spoke. "Mr. Brent, I think we be havin compney."

There, at the water's edge, rested a magnificent figure of a man on a paint horse. He appeared to be alone, but the men suspected appearances were probably deceiving. His eyes locked with Brent's. It was at that moment, both men remembered the cold, snowy, winter night when they spoke of the girl child traveling with his tribe.

Without hesitation, Brent swung a leg over Pacer's back and started toward the creek. He moved forward with no fear, only pausing to glance back over his shoulder and say to Penny, "This is the tribe."

Penny knew, and gasped in shock. Brent had told her about his meeting with the tribe of Indians. He had chosen a time when he felt she was able to handle the thoughts of Lisa being left behind so many months before. In a way, she had been glad to hear that Lisa was no longer being held captive by the band of thieves that stole and then sold human beings. Neither Brent nor Penny had held any hope of ever seeing the tribe or Lisa again. Now, standing with her own child in her arms, Penny watched eagerly for any sign of her long lost friend.

When Brent reached the far side of the creek, he was surprised when the old Indian began to speak to him in English. "I see you made your journey well."

"Yes, and you also. I am taking my people home."

"My grandson told me the story of the girl who saved his life. She is traveling with you."

Brent was somewhat taken aback to hear that anyone had been following them closely enough to know details about who was traveling with him and it was a little unsettling.

"I would like to meet her."

"And the girl, Lisa who travels with you, where is she?"

With a movement so slight from the old man, came Jerome and Lisa, out of the forest beyond and into the clearing.

Tears welled up in Penny's eyes as she put Maggie in Julia's arms and started to run across the shallow creek toward the beautiful girl in the buckskin dress. Sliding from the prancing palomino, Lisa ran to meet Penny. They met in midstream flinging their arms around one another, both girls in tears. Penny took Lisa by the hand leading her to dry land.

"I have someone I want you to see."

When they reached the bank, Penny took Maggie in her arms and turned toward Lisa. "She is mine, Lisa. She nodded her head toward Brent who was still on the other side of the creek. He is my husband. We are going home to Alder. He came and found me, Lisa. She turned toward Julia. "This is my mother." Lisa looked, in amazement, taking in all that had happened during the last months. Julia stepped forward and hugged Lisa.

The sound of splashing water drew attention toward Brent as he came toward them on Pacer. "Jerome's grandfather would like to meet you, Penny. He is grateful for the life of his grandson."

With no more said, she returned Maggie, once again to Julia, took Lisa by the hand and waded the creek to meet the majestic looking man. He dismounted and without taking his piercing black eyes off Penny, came to stand in front of her.

"It is as my grandson said, Girl with the green eyes. My family will forever be indebted to you for saving Jerome."

The old man stepped to the side and Penny was confronted with yet another astounding sight. Penny noticed first, the long black hair and then the blue gray eyes. He was very tall and lean but muscular. If he hadn't been so spectacular looking, Penny would have been frightened.

"This is my son, Jerome's father, Blue Wolf. He has a gift for you."

The man spoke for the first time. "As my father said, my family and I are forever indebted to you for what you did for Jerome. I would like for you to take this gift. She is from my finest herd. I broke her myself."

Penny was overwhelmed with happiness and again astonished that these noble people were giving gifts to her. She took the reins in her hands. "She is beautiful, thank you."

"Try her out, Penny," Lisa said, enthusiastically.

Penny looked questioningly at Brent and then at Jerome's father. Since she heard no objections, Penny grabbed a handful of mane, jumped and swung a leg over the paint filly's back. She was gone before the men could comprehend what was happening. To say the least, they were surprised, with the exception of Brent. He was well aware of Penny's riding abilities. Penny and the filly were moving in fluid like motion as they loped across the clearing. There was no restraint from either of them when they came to a downed log. The filly flew over it with ease. As they made a wide turn to gallop back toward the group, now watching in silence, Penny leaned to pick a flower. With one quick move she was down and then back up. When she reached her destination, she was off the filly and putting the yellow wild flower in Lisa's hair, both girls giggling and remembering their last journey together. The men watched in utter amazement and admiration.

"We would like to invite you and your people to our camp tonight," Jerome's grandfather, Lone Wolf said.

"My family and I would be honored to come to your camp, Lone Wolf."

The band of Indians turned and disappeared into the forest.

Penny watched Lisa ride with them, her palomino, walking beside Jerome's.

The young married couple had a lot of explaining to do. Neither of them had told the complete story about Lisa, to anyone else. The rest of the family was relieved when they heard of the gratitude the Indians held for Penny.

Later in the afternoon, when they were alone, Penny turned to Brent and asked, "What are we going to do about Lisa, Brent?"

He knew the question was going to be asked. He had just wondered when. He could see the concern in her eyes and hear it in her voice. "What do you think we should do?"

"You know what I want. I want Lisa to come with us. That is where she belongs, isn't it, Brent?"

"I don't really know, Sweetie." He pulled her down on his knee as if she were a child. "You know, we can't just take her, don't you?"

"Yes, but isn't there something we could do?"

"She doesn't seem to be afraid. I believe if we talk to Lone Wolf and Blue Wolf, they would release her. We should still yet take her wants into consideration."

"Yes, you are right. We should talk to Lisa. I think she would not be afraid to say what she really wants."

The remainder of the day was uneventful in comparison to its beginning. The rest seemed to be having the anticipated effect on the travelers. Chatter and laughter rang in the air. Every now and then a giggle from Maggie could be heard as the women passed her from one to the other, spoiling her and loving every moment of it.

Julia said, "You know, I never thought I could feel so good again. Happiness can do wonders for a person. She looked at her daughter and smiled. And, you know what, ladies, we don't have to cook supper tonight since we are eating with Lone Wolf and his people." They all laughed lightheartedly. Soon the men joined them.

"We can't miss out on all the fun." George said as he sat down and looked at Julia fondly.

Chapter

35

Time passed quickly, but long before the big orange ball in the western sky rolled behind the distant mountains, an Indian brave was sitting among the travelers ready to take them to the Indian village. All saddled up and riding one behind the other along the narrow trail, they followed the figure in the lead. He sat straight on his pony and rode with ease, darting in and out of the branches. Finally, they came to a clearing that held the Indian village. Dogs barked at the intruders passing through, while children clothed in buckskin watched with interest.

The pale skinned people were more than surprised at what they saw. The people they now visited did not appear to be living as savages, the way others had described their habitation. Much to the contrary, they had a very functional community. Gardens of fruits and vegetables were plentiful. The homes were neat and clean. Tools had been made of stone, pots were made of clay and woven baskets were used for a variety of activities. Evidently, these were intelligent and hard working people. They were a beautiful people, tall and proud. The women and girls wore deerskin dresses and moccasins decorated with brightly colored beads and leather. Their hair was black and shone in the light. Their black eyes sparkled with a hint of mystery and intelligence.

Penny could not help being a little jealous when she noticed more than one of the young maidens watching and smiling at Brent as he rode by on his prancing stallion. She watched him intently, feeling the warm flush wash through her veins. She loved him with a depth that she felt no other woman could ever understand. Maybe she considered herself the most fortunate woman in the world. The man she had found, or the man who had found her had become everything to her. She took in the color of his jet black hair, the deep blue of his eyes the masculinity of his build. She could almost feel the strong hard muscles as she watched his mount stay under perfect control.

Her husband cast her a sideways glance smiling a smile that not only curved his desirable lips but put a mischievous glint in his blue black eyes. He sent her his usual wink, easing any anxiety she could have been feeling about his love for her. Penny had no idea, the feelings she aroused in Brent as she shot back an easy smile. He too, had tumultuous emotions about the lustful stares she was getting from the handsome braves.

Without warning the brave who led them into the camp stopped his horse. People seemed to come out of no where to gather around their guests. It wasn't until then, Penny took note of the fact that Jesse and Celia were getting more attention than were the whites. The brave signaled for them to dismount. Brent swung his leg across Pacer's back and was on the ground with his hands around Penny's waist before she knew it. She slid off her horse into his arms before landing solidly on her feet. She held Maggie, protectively in her arms, while taking in the manner in which the Indian women carried their young. It seemed to her, at the moment, a good idea, since they had their hands free to take care of other necessities.

When Lone Wolf and Blue Wolf appeared, the crowd moved back quickly letting the two men approach their guests. They did so without interference. Beside them stood Jerome, but Lisa was no where in sight.

"Welcome, to our home, my friends."

"It is our pleasure to be here, Lone Wolf." Brent replied.

"Come with me."

The chief took the travelers to a somewhat secluded area where he stopped and began to speak. "I asked you to come here, to our home. As I have said before my family will forever be indebted to you for the kindness you have shown to my grandson. Yet, I have seen what you and the girl, Lisa, have meant to each other." He looked at Penny with a knowing and empathetic look. "You will want to take her with you, but I will ask you before anything is said, to take the girl's needs into your heart first. My family loves her as one of our own. She is safe as long as we are safe. My son and Yellow Moon, his wife, have taken her as their daughter. As you know, color of the skin, has nothing to do with love for some of us." He said the words as his eyes swept from Penny to Jesse and Celia.

Penny was beginning to understand that Lone Wolf was a very wise man. "I love Lisa as a sister. I want nothing for her but her happiness and safety."

"And this is what I want. Before you talk to her, spend time with us and see what you will. Now let us enjoy our time this day."

As they all walked back toward the camp Lisa could be seen coming from one of the teepees. She ran toward Penny and the others. "Penny, come with me. I want you to meet Yellow Moon."

Penny followed Lisa into the teepee. There she saw a very unexpected sight. A young woman was hurriedly preparing sleeping areas in the huge teepee. When she saw Lisa, she stopped what she was doing and, very graciously, came to meet Penny.

"Penny, this is Yellow Moon. She and Blue Wolf have made me a part of their family."

Yellow Moon moved to embrace Penny in a quick hug. "I am so happy to meet you. Lisa speaks of you often. She has missed you very much."

Penny was momentarily, speechless. She opened her mouth to speak but no words came.

"You are surprised."

Penny let out a breath, "Yes, I am," is all she could say. She gazed at the woman admiringly. A long braid trailed down Yellow Moon's back, but it wasn't the color she had expected. Instead of the coal black hair, like the other women in the camp, Yellow Moon's was the color of honey. She had a look distinctly her own, with almond shaped eyes the same color as her honey colored hair. Her skin was smoothe and tan.

Yellow Moon's eyes danced with delight as she told Penny the story of how Lone Wolf and his people had found her. She had wondered from a wagon train that had carried her and an aunt and uncle westward.

"They had at least called themselves my aunt and uncle. My parents had died back east when I was very young. I can barely picture them in my mind, but I remember the love. I had no other relatives and when the Sanders offered to take me that was all it took. We lived in the east for a while. They often said they had a little live in maid. One day they decided to head west. We made it together as far as Missouri, and as I said, I wondered away from the wagon train. I was lost in the woods, scared and half starved when Lone Wolf found me. They took me in and raised me as one of their own. I was raised with Blue Wolf, but I have loved him from the start. When he realized we would never be like brother and sister, we married. Jerome is my son. I will always be grateful to you, Penny, for giving him back to me.

Penny took the story in, realizing how much the same, Yellow Moon's life and Lisa's life had begun. As their time together wore on, Penny watched Yellow Moon and Lisa. She knew they had a true mother - daughter relationship.

Although Penny, Brent and the others had not intended to stay the night, at Lone Wolf's request they did so. It was late into the night and just before the festivities had ended, cries from the far end of camp could be heard. The fear was evident. Penny could make out the word, wolf. She felt a sudden surge of terror as she realized what could be happening. She quickly put Maggie into Celia's arms and ran as fast as she could to where the commotion was. Brent was right behind her, but couldn't stop her in time. She ran between the warrior and the huge black animal that was crouched and ready to spring.

"No!" Penny's command was loud and sharp, as she stood in the way of the spear. She stood facing the warrior until he put his weapon down. Then, she was immediately on her knees with her arms wrapped protectively around Shadow's neck. The Indian stepped back and looked at the unusual green eyed woman and the wolf. Penny heard the gasps of horror. She stood up slowly and wondered in amazement what could possible be so frightening about a dog, even though Shadow probably was part wolf.

By this time, Julia and George, Celia and Jesse and what seemed to be everyone else in camp, had made their way down the row of teepees. Penny walked over and took Maggie from Celia. She held the baby near Shadow so their protector could see all was safe. Again, the Indians gasped. Lone Wolf looked first, at his son Blue Wolf, and then at Jerome. They assured the others that the camp was safe, and the white woman who walked among them was in control of the animal. No longer, did Lone Wolf's people look at Penny in horror. Those feelings were replaced with awe. They held Penny with high regard after that night.

Later within the confines of the large teepee, all the visitors chatted and teased Penny about being a spirit woman. The peaceful night's sleep was astonishing to Penny, Brent and the others.

"I had no idea animal hides could make such a comfortable bed."

"Nor I."

"We might have a lot to lun bout travlin and sleepin in the wildaness," Celia laughed.

"Jesse might have to go huntin and make us all a good bed fo the res of ou trip to Alda." She looked at Jesse with a sparkle in her eyes.

"I sho might do that. Yes um, I jes sho might."

They all walked out of the teepee to learn breakfast was awaiting them. After a time of visiting with their new found friends, Penny knew it was time for her to seek out a private place to talk to Lisa. She took her by the hand, and they walked to a nearby creek. Sitting on a fallen log, Penny began.

"Lisa, are you happy and well here?"

"I am, Penny. I still miss my mother, but Yellow Moon is so good to me. Everyone here is. I have missed you too, Penny. You are my sister."

"You can come with us if you want. I would like it if you did, but I want most of all for you to be happy."

"I don't know how a person could want to be in two places at one time." Lisa looked at Penny so seriously and with such dilEma it put a knot in Penny's stomach.

"Perhaps it is because we have been created with such an ability to love more than one person."

Lisa sat down beside Penny and put her head on her knee - much like she had on the trail to new Orleans so many months before. Again, she cried until Penny's dress was wet with tears. They both knew, this place - with these people - for at least now - was home to Lisa.

By the time Lisa and Penny were back at the camp they had it settled in their minds. They would forever be sisters and this would not be the last time they would see each other. Before they left camp, Penny made sure everyone agreed that they would meet again before the end of life's journey.

Penny hugged Maggie closely, as they headed back to their own camp. The same Indian brave that had led them the day before was now leading them back to the wagons so the trip to Alder could continue.

Julia watched Penny as she rode beside Brent. She thought to herself, "Where did the little girl go?"

At the same time her heart was lifted with pride at the woman her daughter had become. "So much heartache in her young life - but so much love to give."

The day was still fresh and before too long, the wagons were packed and everyone ready to go, leaving behind the quiet of the forest for the animals.

Chapter
36

The party was now well into Missouri. The travelers were casting their attention on the natural wonders of the country side. All were overwhelmed with feelings of familiarity as they came closer to Alder - all except Celia and Jesse. Each day was new and different for the two as they journeyed on.

Penny and Julia had been anxious about their two loyal friends making the trip, but soon, learned of their strength. They found too, that Celia and Jesse had acquired, what seemed to be an unending supply of skills.

"We didn't always work fo Mista Reynolds, ya see. Sometime it seem we been round this big ole world."

"We ain't neva been to Missouri befo, though," Celia said with a big grin.

Julia and George looked at them and smiled. They both knew it would take a lifetime to repay Celia and Jesse for taking care of Penny and Maggie. "We are so glad you came with us." Julia said, earnestly.

Much of the trip had been warm and sunny, not too hot, not too cold, just right for traveling. Now, black clouds were beginning to form in the southwestern sky. It reminded Penny of the time she and Lisa had to make their way into the cave to avoid being blown away. She was nervous about the darkness that was now hovering over them. Penny left Maggie in the wagon with Julia, untied her paint from the back of the wagon and rode to seek out Brent. He had gone ahead to find shelter. She was eased when she found him, not too far away.

When Penny reached Brent, he saw the terror in her eyes, even though she didn't make her fears known. She only said in a calm voice, "I believe we need to find a place soon. I have seen this kind of cloud before."

"Just up ahead, there is a cavern with high bluffs around it. It should keep all safe until this storm passes."

Penny breathed a sigh of relief as they rode back to help move the wagons to safety. They reached their destination just before the brunt of the storm hit. The rain was pelting down hard, and the harsh wind was beginning to uproot small saplings when the group disappeared into the cavern.

Before the storm lifted, it was almost night again. They decided to stay put until the morning. A fire was built and the women cooked a supper that was both nourishing and tasty. Bedrolls were laid out, and once again, the family was down for a peaceful night. Penny snuggled close to Brent. She lay with her back pressed against his chest. She held Maggie in her arms watching her sleep, peacefully. The firelight cast shadows on the baby's sweet, soft face. Penny kissed her cheek, thinking how safe she always felt with Brent. She drifted off to sleep.

With the dawn, came another serene day. The warm, morning sun peeped through the trees to the east. There was not a cloud in the blue sky. The splash of water, running off the cliffs, hit the pool below with a welcoming sound. Penny was the first to be up and out. Julia came out of the cave shaking her head much like she had when Penny was a child. There in the water, she could see her daughter swimming in the pool. Maggie was near, on a pallet, kicking in the warm morning sunshine, while Shadow lay protectively, just off to the side.

"Mother, we are back in Missouri!"

Making her way to the pool, Julia smiled. Brent, George, Jesse and Celia could already see how life was going to be back in Alder, with the three generations before them. Before long, Penny had talked them all into joining in. By the time dry clothes were put on, the morning meal was eaten and the wagons were rolling, the sun was far above the eastern horizon.

The following days were made of, fields of Indian Paintbrush and Marsh Ferns, clear mountain streams and waterfalls. The travelers had never seen the like of wildflower covered meadows and cool, blue springs. The closer to home they came, the more lush the grassy valleys were. White tailed deer leaped gracefully in and out of sight. Bluebirds flew overhead. Night owls screeched. Wolves howled. The thunder roared and the spring rains came pouring down. Rainbows arched in breath taking colors across the sky, and then, they were home.

Tired, but filled with joy, they made their way up the lane toward the ranch house. Penny rode with Maggie in her arms. She was on her paint filly riding along side Brent, who was on Pacer. Both horses and riders moved with ease and rhythm. Julia, George, Celia and Jesse followed behind in the wagons.

During the weeks that had passed, Brent had not allowed himself the weakness of thinking about the loss of his brother, but now it hit him. The hurt, the anger, the disbelief, the fear were threatening to over power the sweetness of his family's home coming. A sudden rush of strength soared through him.

"I will not let anything or anyone interfere with my wife and daughter's happiness. This is a promise I will protect with my life."

Chapter
37

The remainder of the summer months were very hectic but full of excitement. Julia and George found the perfect spot for their new home. They both decided on a log cabin with a huge front porch. "I want rocking chairs to rock my grandchildren," Julia had said. With that in mind, the men built a porch the length of the cabin. Julia admired the roof over her enormous porch. "George, we can watch the sunset from here."

He was happy to please his wife. "I am holding you to that, my Dear." George leaned down and gave his wife a quick kiss on the cheek.

Celia and Jesse were just as pleased with their new cabin, although theirs was not as big. They had both agreed that it would be nice not to have to spend all of their time cleaning and repairing.

"Freedom be real nice." They both wanted to enjoy their years together.

"We might just do some thangs we always talkin bout but didn't neva git to do."

Penny looked at them in her curious way, "What will you do?"

"Well I sho do think fishin would be good hea."

"An, Mz. Penny, I thought if you don't mind I might do a little rockin myself." Celia had reached for Maggie and the child had leaned toward her without reluctance.

"It be on my mind too. Maybe I could teach some chilen, bout some horses."

"It was Brent who spoke next. "You know horses, Jesse?"

"Why, yes Mr. Brent. I sho do. I worked animals a long time on one of the plantations. They sho did have some mighty fine horses."

Brent knew Jesse well enough, by now, to know he wasn't bragging, just stating a fact. He hadn't carried the conversation any farther, but had tucked the information away, knowing that at some point in the future he would be finding out just how much Jesse did know about horses.

The Holbrooks had also done some settling in since they had gotten home. Even though Penny had been in the house many times before, it had felt so unusual to her to be living there as the wife of Brent Holbrook instead of the little girl he had protected from the world. It was an unfamiliar feeling but one that Penny loved.

They had made some changes in the house to accommodate Maggie. Penny was finding it very difficult to let Maggie out of her sight, so they made the adjoining room, to the master bedroom, into a nursery.

Now, Penny lay thinking about the time she and Celia had been in the city of New Orleans and how she had wondered about the future and what it held for her and her child.

"I prayed, Brent, so many nights I prayed. Now, I know my prayers were answered. It is a miracle that we are all back home. I love you, Brent." Penny felt Brent's lips on hers, softly and gently guiding her into another night of passionate love making.

The hot summer months had ended, releasing the most brilliant colors to an autumn, like no other Penny could ever recall.

"Celia, Maggie is down for a nap. I think I'll go for a ride."

"She be jis fine, Mz. Penny."

Penny walked toward the barn breathing in the cool fall air. Her eyes drifted from one magnificent color to the other. The sun shone brightly in the sky, giving her a light hearted feeling as she walked down the trail. She stopped at the water well drawing the bucket up to fill her canteen. As she made her way into the barn, Penny could hear the paint nickering. She stopped, giving her an apple and rubbing her nose before going to her palomino's stall. Both horses were exceptional, and both meant a great deal to Penny. Although the paint held much sentimental value for Penny, there was a special place in her heart for the light colored filly Brent had given her. It had been the first horse she could ever really call her own, and it had been given by the man who had loved her then and now. She smiled as she opened the stall gate slipped a halter over Dolly's head and led her to the corral just outside the barn.

"Afternoon, Mrs. Holbrook," came a friendly greeting from Ben.

"Hello Ben," replied Penny. I thought I might take a ride before Brent comes in from the north pasture."

"Yes Mrs. Holbrook. I'll get your saddle."

Ben returned with saddle in hand. "Ben, you know you don't have to call me Mrs. Holbrook."

"Yes, ma'am."

Penny grinned and shook her head. "Thanks, Ben."

Ben placed the saddle on Dolly's back and Penny took over. When she had the saddle just like she wanted it, she grabbed the saddle horn and swung a leg over Dolly's back.

"I won't be gone long."

Dolly held a smooth stride as the two rode, leisurely away from the ranch and into the meadow. When they reached the clearing, Penny turned Dolly loose letting her lope through the field. The golden palomino jumped downed logs, creeks and all other obstacles with ease and grace. The terrain began to change. Penny was riding closer to the old home place. She could see the pines jutting up through the golden yellow mass ahead of her.

Penny slowed Dolly to a walk as they followed the trail up to the creek. She hadn't meant to go to the waterfall, but felt somewhat compelled to keep riding in that direction. It was the first time she had ventured there since she had been back home. She dismounted and tied Dolly's reins to the limb of a small tree.

She remembered the log she had sat on the night of the kidnapping. She could almost hear the thunder roar, almost hear the water as it tumbled down the rocks and into the deep ravine below. She could almost see the face of the man who had stalked her with his treacherous plight. She could almost see the glimmer in his eyes as she had that night when the lightening flashed and lit up the sky. The memories were real and vivid but the visions were a blur. Before Penny realized what was happening, she felt hot tears flowing down her face. She wiped them away with the back of her hand. On shaky legs and with trembling hands, Penny continued walking until she came to the exact place. She saw the boulder she had hidden behind. How dangerously close to the ledge she had been that night. How easy it would have been to slip and fall to her death. Now, she saw the faces of Brent, Maggie and her mother. The visions were clear and the fear was suddenly gone.

"Penny, what are you doing here?"

Penny turned to see the concern in the blue eyes gazing at her. "I didn't intend to come here, so I was wondering the same thing just a little while ago. Now I know - I needed to face the past." She stared straight ahead - a haunted stare. "He came like a panther in the night, hunting me down. He came so quietly, I didn't hear the danger until I was trapped.

A crease formed between Brent's tear filled eyes. "Penny, I'm so sorry."

Penny went to her husband. Standing on tiptoes she wrapped her slender arms around his neck. Brushing her moist lips against his, she said, "Don't be. It's over now. I am the most blessed woman in the world to have you and our child." The two rode home with a feeling of peace surrounding them. They looked forward to their life together.

Jesse was in the barn grooming the horses when Penny and Brent led their horses through the doorway. Penny loved the feeling she got when she walked into the big, red barn. She loved the smell of horses, hay and the leather from the saddles. She didn't know why such things would give her such a feeling of security, but it never failed. She and Brent looked on as Jesse worked with one of the new colts Brent had recently bought. She knew he had plans he hadn't yet told her about. She also knew that he would tell her, when he thought the time was right. She was eager to hear what he had in store for the ranch, but waited patiently.

"I am going to the house to check on Maggie and Celia. Celia and Jesse have put in a days work and I'm sure they have things they want to do." She smiled at Jesse, eyeing his fishing pole in the corner of the barn.

Penny took a brisk walk home, still yet enjoying the fall colors. She opened the front door and called Celia's name. Celia came from the kitchen with Maggie in her arms. Maggie reached for Penny. "Hi, Sweetie. Did you have a good nap? I bet you did and then lots of fun with Celia." Penny giggled while looking at the guilt on Celia's face. "My little girl will be the most spoiled child in Alder, and that's okay by me."

Celia smiled then and went on about her business. Penny called out to her as she headed back toward the kitchen, "Celia, you and Jesse have put in enough work today. I'll finish up here. Mother and George are coming for supper. I'll finish up."

"Yes, Mz. Penny. I'll see ya in the monin."

"Penny worked the rest of the afternoon preparing the evening meal and before she knew it the sun was low in the sky. Julia and George were knocking at the front door. Penny met them smiling, and reached for her mother giving her a hug and kiss on the cheek. She then gave George a quick hug before turning and inviting them into the kitchen. By this time, Brent was down the stairs, cleaned up and ready to eat.

"I'm hungry as one of those bears we saw in the north pasture this morning, aren't you George?"

"Sure am!" George boomed out.

"Then, let's eat." Penny had the table set and enough food to feed an army. Brent was first to bow his head as he thanked God for the food and family. When the meal was finished, Julia helped Penny with the dishes while the men retired to the living room. The air had cooled off after sundown and Brent had started a fire in the fireplace. They were all entertained by Maggie before she fell asleep in Julia's lap.

"I'll put her to bed, if you don't mind, Penny."

"I would be happy for you to, Mother."

Penny knew it would be a while before Julia came back down stairs. She always spent time just watching Maggie sleep and remembering Penny when she was a baby. Sometimes Penny was afraid her mother still yet felt guilty for leaving her behind and going to New Orleans, but she did not want that. Penny did everything in her power to save her mother from any bad feelings at all. She hoped that in time for Brent and her mother, the guilt and pain would go away. Penny was deliriously happy, for she knew no two people could love her more. The blame could not be placed on them. Brent didn't know what his brother had planned and her mother had to leave in order to stay alive and make things better for Penny. Penny shook the thoughts from her mind. She felt that if she let her true happiness shine through, everyone else would have to see this family's world as a very blessed place.

Chapter

38

Autumn passed too fast for Penny. She didn't want to let go of the beauty or the pleasant weather, but it did pass and then came a winter like she had never seen before. She often wondered, during the snow covered days, about Lisa and her ability to survive the cold. But, her mind was eased when she thought of the people who were looking after Lisa and their promises to take care of her. Penny had seen for herself the protective ways of the tribe and the loyalty they shared for each other. They were a strong people and Lisa was probably learning to be just as strong.

Penny again looked out at the snow covered trees. Icicles hung from the eave of the house and barn. The sun was shining brightly in spite of the deep snow on the ground. Penny decided to check the weather out. As she suspected, the sun was warming the white fluff outside and small drops of water were falling. She decided to bundle Maggie and herself up and go to the barn. She often took Maggie to the barn and let her see the horses. The toddler was old enough now to take notice when Penny held her small hand and ran it across Dolly's nose. She seemed to have no fear of the huge animals. She giggled and jumped in Penny's arms as they neared the horses' stalls.

"You will be quite a rider when you grow up. I can tell right now." Penny said as she entered Dolly's stall.

Shadow nudged the back of Penny's leg and whined. "And you want your share of the attention, don't you my friend?" Penny bent down to rub a hand down the dog's neck. Maggie was, like wise, just as attentive to Shadow. She was at perfect ease with Shadow's presence. The animal's ability to move in and out of their lives never ceased to amaze Penny. "How do you keep up with us so, Shadow?"

Penny untied the bundle she had carried with her and Maggie. She gave an apple to Dolly and then walked to Star's stall and did the same. Star, her paint filly, took the fruit, gently from the palm of Penny's hand. She admired the fine horse. Penny looked at Maggie and then pointed to the horse. "This is Star." She turned and pointed to Shadow. "This is Shadow. Someday you will say the words, my sweet child." Penny carried Maggie back to Dolly's stall. "And this is Dolly." She again took Maggie's hand into her own. Rubbing it over Dolly's neck she said, "This is Dolly - Dolly." Penny was more than pleased when the words came out of the pink little lips. "Da de."

"That is it. Dolly!" Penny kissed Maggie's chubby cheek and headed for the barn door. She was stunned when Shadow jumped in front of her, blocking her pathway. She heard a pathetic whine as Shadow tore at her boots almost tripping her. She continued to walk. "Shadow, stop that you got your share of the attention. We have to go in now." Penny pulled the barn door open, Shadow following behind her almost stepping on her heels with every step she took. The air was still yet warming, but the snow was deep and difficult to move one's feet in.

Without warning, Penny heard Shadow again, but this time it was not a whine. She turned around just in time to see the white fangs. Shadow let out a sinister growl as she sprang at the hungry cougar. The two ferocious animals clashed in mid air. They were a blur of teeth, fur and blood. Penny let out a blood curdling scream, "Shadow!" Her mind raced. "How foolish I have been to come out alone, with no gun." She ran as fast as she could in the snow and with Maggie in her arms. She put the baby safely into the crib, grabbed her rifle on the way out and ran again to where the animals were. They rolled and tumbled away from one aonther before they again got their footing and sprang once more. Penny was a good shot but now realized, not good enough. Each time she tried to take aim and shoot, the animals would roll and tumble, putting Shadow in harms way. Finally, with one more roll, she shot, putting a bullet in the heart of the cougar. The yellow hump of bloody fur lay on the ground beside Shadow. Shadow was still, too still. Penny ran. "Oh, Shadow." She saw that something would have to be done. Moving quickly, Penny made her way to the barn. With saddle blanket and rope she was able to pull Shadow home. Without a second thought, she took Shadow into the house and started to work on her deadly wounds.

She cleaned and sowed wounds until her back ached with the strain. Shadow was finally bandaged and lying on a soft pallet on the floor, near the fireplace. "I have done all I can do my friend." Penny's head dropped; her face in her blood covered hands. She sobbed, "Shadow, I should not have doubted you. I should have known something was wrong."

Shadow watched Penny. Her eyes were the only part of her that had the strength to move. The almond eyes moved back and forth, as if still yet trying to comfort her master.

Penny smoothed the fur on Shadows head, talking to her softly and realizing that now was a time to comfort her. "You must feel so helpless. Your only job seems to be taking care of everyone else. But rest easy Girl. It's my time to take care of you. Penny sat, stroking and setting a serene and peaceful place for her. Shadow's smoky, brown eyes closed in a peaceful sleep. Her breathing was easier now. Her muscles were no longer twitching and jumping. Her gigantic form was lying quiet and still.

Penny was soon lost in thought. She had known how to shoot and ride for a long time now, but today had made her even more aware of life's ever lurking dangers. She knew what she would do. She knew she would sharpen her skills so that in case of any emergency she could move automatically and precisely. She made this promise to herself.

Chapter
39

Brent, Ben and the rest of the cattle hands had been chasing strays all day. Some of the cows and calves had been wondering out, farther than was safe, with the hard winter that was upon Missouri. It seemed more than a usual number of cows was having trouble calving this winter. The sunset was catching up with the men and they all started back toward the ranch house. The farther the sun sank in the western sky, the colder the air was. By the time the men got to the stables, they were ready to unsaddle, chow down and hit the sack.

Brent waved and continued on to the barn. He first noticed the barn door standing open. He called for Penny, thinking she might be doing her usual visiting with Dolly and Star. No one answered. He took a quick look around and then continued the task of unsaddling his horse and brushing him down. He hurriedly put Pacer in the stall, pulled his coat up around his neck and moved in long strides in the direction of home and a hot supper. He abruptly stopped when his eyes fell upon the dark stains soaking up the snow. Brent knew right then it was blood. He knew by the amount, someone was in trouble. His heart pounded hard in his chest as he ran full speed. He almost tripped when he came to the cougar. He couldn't stop fast enough and had to take a flying leap over the dead animal. He saw what it was and didn't turn around. He followed the trail of blood into the house. By the time he got the door open and ran from room to room calling out Penny's name, he was blurry eyed and dizzy from the fear that had over powered him. He saw Penny on the floor, her face, hands and clothes covered in blood. He moved quickly to her, still yet believing she was wounded. Penny knew what was happening and immediately started trying to calm his fears.

"I'm alright. I'm not hurt. It's not me. It's Shadow." She saw the fear slowly leaving his eyes and the relief flooding in. She felt his hands trembling on her arms and saw the pallor of his face. She knew if he didn't sit down, he was going to fall. She moved to pull a chair closer to him. She pulled his arms and he began to slowly back up until he was sitting on the edge of the chair.

His voice still trembling, "What happened, Penny?"

She told him the story in detail.

"Is Maggie, alright?"

"Yes, to check on her is the only time I have moved from Shadow's side. Our daughter is playing happily in her crib, thanks to our ever loyal friend." She said it with tears again pouring down her blood stained face. Penny told him about the defenseless mess she had gotten herself into by not taking a gun with her.

"It's not your fault. You had no way of knowing that a cougar would be this close to our barn. It's just that this has been such a hard winter, everything is hungry. We will be more cautious from now on. All of us. I'll tell the men to be on the look out, and I'll ride over and tell your mother and George tomorrow. Celia and Jesse will need to know too. He put his arms around her and let her head rest on his chest.

"I have made a promise to myself. I won't let another season pass without learning to be the best shot and rider this side of the Mississippi."

Brent offered to watch over Shadow while Penny got cleaned up and then she did the same for him. They took turns tending Maggie and working on a good hot meal. Finally, the baby was asleep and supper had been eaten.

The night was long, but Penny kept constant vigil on her guardian. She had read much about the healing of illnesses and wounds. Her father, Gunther, had also told stories about how the Indians used certain herbs and plants for healing. She never knew where he had heard them, but now she knew they were true. She decided after Jerome's wound and now Shadow's, she would make sure to learn all she could about tending to the sick and injured. After all, she did have a family to take care of. She wanted to be able to help them as much as possible.

Soon after Penny had fallen asleep, it was sunrise, and she was up again. She saw that Shadow was still breathing and sleeping peacefully.

She quietly went upstairs to find Brent holding Maggie. Maggie's eyes were closed while Brent watched her.

"Her lashes are as black and long as her mother's."

Penny looked at him tenderly before he got up from the chair and put the child back in her crib. Penny headed to the kitchen, knowing Brent would need to get an early start. She had a hot meal ready in no time.

With his last bite of food down, Brent said, "I'll go clean up outside. We don't want the carcass to attract other animals and bring them close. Ben and the boys will be out and about soon and we don't want a house full of men trying to save you. I'll tell your mother and George and then go to Celia and Jesse's before they have a chance to get out into dangerous territory." He added, "That could be right in their front yard. The boys and I will be on the look out. Ben and I will go to the north pasture where we saw those bears last week. I don't want them to make their way down here."

"Be careful, my darling and come home safe."

Brent kissed Penny goodbye and walked out the door.

Still yet nervous from yesterday's near fatality, Penny watched Brent until he was well on his way to the barn. She knew he was probably safe because he always carried a rifle with him. Still yet, she couldn't shake the anxious feeling that possessed her.

Chapter
40

All went well for the rest of the winter. Shadow healed and the men had been able to thwart other attempts of the hungry animals to come too close to the houses. By the time spring was on its way, everyone was ready for the sunshine. None, not even Ben, could remember a winter so harsh with so much heavy snow. Although Penny loved it and thought it beautiful, she was happy with the change of season.

The days were warm and the green on the trees had just begun to show. Celia was busy preparing lunch and Julia and Penny were doing some spring cleaning.

"I want to start my garden, soon," Penny said, looking at Julia and then Celia. "I want to make sure we have plenty of fresh vegetables. I also want to put up all the herbs we could possibly need for those little surprises in life. With all that has happened in the last two years, and especially, since I have a child, I want to be prepared for illnesses and the like."

Maggie was making her way around the kitchen trying out every pan she could make a sound with. "I can hardly believe she's walking." Penny watched her daughter's black curls bounce as she walked from one end of the room to the other. Her blue eyes met Penny's and she came running with outstretched arms. Penny picked her up twirling around in a circle, while Maggie giggled. "Mama." Penny looked at Julia in surprise. "And Talking," she said.

Early spring came and went. New life had begun on the ranch as the new season was born. Baby calves ran along side the cows that grazed on luscious green grass in the pastures. The gardens were planted and already producing the vegetables that Penny now gathered for lunch. She had her basket full, carrying the uncooked meal in one hand and leading Maggie with the other. Brent came walking up from the barn with what Penny deemed as mischief in his blue eyes. She loved the look. She always felt as though she might have a pleasant surprise coming when he looked at her that way. Since she had both hands full, Brent put his arms around her and kissed her lips. He turned her loose, took Maggie in one arm and the remainder of Penny's load in the other hand. She laughed and returned the favor. Putting both arms around his neck she pulled his head down and kissed his lips softly.

"What are you doing home so early?" She asked.

I have some things I want to discuss with you. I have been waiting for the right time and I believe this is it. But, let's wait until after lunch. I might need all the energy I can muster up if you don't think my idea is as good as I do. That way I'll have more stamina to convince you."

The afternoon was pleasant for the small family and they took advantage of it. The times had been few, when Brent had not been working with the cattle and Penny had not been busy with all of, what might be considered, the woman's work. Although the Holbrooks had people who worked for them, both Penny and Brent took part in running the house and ranch.

When Maggie tired out and fell asleep for her nap, Brent led the way to the porch. Sitting in the swing, he moved his head toward the horses and their colts running in the meadow. "Do you like what you see out there?"

"Well, yes, you know I love horses. They are beautiful animals."

"Do you think we have enough of those beautiful animals?" Brent watched Penny as he asked the question.

"No, I don't. I have often wondered why there wasn't a whole herd of horses running these fields. With all you know about horses, why have you never started a horse ranch, as you did the cattle ranch?"

Brent was more than happy with Penny's response. "We really do belong together, Penny. We think alike." He was excited now. "I have a plan. Not a complete plan. I have found that nothing in my life will ever be complete without you. I want us to do this together. I want to build a life with you and our children. We'll have the best known horses in the country."

"Well, what is the plan?" Penny asked with anticipation.

"Do you remember the day Blue Wolf gave you the paint filly?"

"How could I ever forget that day? I was shocked, afraid and over joyed to have been presented with that gift."

"You will never know how proud I was of you that day. My wife had been taken as a friend by some of the most noble and proud people in the country. But, it wasn't that. It was the way you rode that day. You were so humble but yet so very skilled at what you were doing."

"Brent, darling do you not remember? You are the one who taught me to ride."

"I gave you some advice and you took it and turned it into skill that is unequal to any other I have seen. Now you can see that even though I am telling you what my plan is, you were the one who put this vision in my head. When I watched you ride that day, you were like royalty."

"How did we get off horses and on to royalty, as I sit here in my gardening clothes?" Look at me again and tell me that I look like royalty."

Brent laughed at the way Penny always kept her feet on the ground no matter what compliment she was given. "Okay, back to the plan. This couldn't happen over night but within a few years we could have a herd of horses like no other. I was thinking about those Tennessee Walkers over in Tennessee. That gentle natured, smooth riding horse, the way it carries the plantation owners, it's a calm breed, easy to train. A horse like that could easily handle mountainous terrain. And, then there is the Morgan. The Morgan is a sound and strong horse. I don't have to tell you about the Indian ponies, since you have one yourself. You know at one time, they were crossed with English Thouroughbred horses. That gave us the quarter horse, which is faster than most on running at high speeds for short distances."

"Yes, what does this have to do with your plan?" Penny was excited, now.

"I figured, if we crossed those breeds with the Arabian, with his endurance, we would have one heck of a horse. I would suspect we would have a horse with an easy gait, dependable, durable and gentle natured enough for even the youngest riders."

Penny's eyes lit up at the thought of having the magnificent creatures on the ranch. She moved closer to Brent, taking his hand. "I think you have more than a plan. It's a dream that could be right at our fingertips."

"You know, at first I would have to be gone at times to buy the choice animals. Would that bother you?"

"Of course, I would miss you, but if that is what you must do, I would just have to suffer until you return. We could enjoy a long goodbye and homecoming." She looked at him with a teasing smile.

"I should have told you about this sooner." He scooped her up in his arms and carried her up the stairs to their bedroom. They were both laughing and giggling like children, all the way. "Let's start practicing that long goodbye," Brent said as his lips met Penny's in a long and passionate kiss.

"You are a dangerous man."

"What do you mean by that, my lovely wife?"

"You make me dizzy." Penny laughed, and then kissed Brent again. Taking a deep breath and pulling her lips from his, she said, "You know you are right. With Maggie being so young and all, I wouldn't feel comfortable leaving her for long lengths of time, but when she gets a little older, I could go on some of the shorter trips. Who knows, maybe she could go too when she gets older. After all, I intend to teach all our children to ride as well as their father does."

"How many children do you plan to have, Mrs. Holbrook?"

Penny's light laughter chimed through the air. "That does depend a lot on you. Perhaps that is another plan we should discuss."

"I don't know. Some things are better left to nature, don't you think?"

Penny sat up, abruptly. With a more serious tone to her voice she looked at Brent. "Do you remember the promise I made to myself last winter when Shadow was attacked?"

"Yes, I do."

"I would like to get started on that, especially since you will be gone more often in the future."

"You are a good shot and handle a gun very well as it is, but I do believe you are right. You should hone your skills in order to be as safe as you can possibly be. If you would like, we could do some practicing this evening."

"Yes, I would. I would like that very much."

Brent gave Penny a quick kiss on the cheek. "I better get back to work. The boys are going to wonder where I went. Why don't we meet down by the creek in the southwest pasture at about 7?"

"I'll be there." She watched as he moved across the room and through the doorway.

Chapter
41

Penny was looking forward to the evening. She knew that developing her skills with a gun and horse was something she needed to do. It was something she also wanted to do, for she enjoyed both so much. She looked in on Maggie, who was sleeping peacefully. She watched her for long moments before going down stairs.

"Hello, girl," she said, when she noticed Shadow lying by the swing on the back porch. "You look as though you never had a run in with that cougar last winter. You gave me quite a scare. Lucky for Maggie and me you were there." Penny turned when she heard the wagon pull up in the lane beside the house. Walking to the west corner, she could see Celia and Jessie bringing in the supplies she had sent after that morning.

"We'z back, Mz. Penny. Got all you sent afta."

Penny didn't hesitate when Celia and Jessie started unloading the goods. She walked quickly to the wagon, picked up an arm load and headed for the back door. Soon the kitchen was restocked. Jessie took the wagon to the barn to unload the farm supplies.

"Celia, would you mind watching after Maggie this evening? I need to meet Brent for some target practice down by the creek in the southwest pasture. Unless, you and Jesse have plans."

"I'd be happy to stay. If you like I could cook up the suppa too."

"Thanks Celia, that would give me some extra time to spend with Maggie before I leave. Speaking of, I believe I hear her now." Penny ran up stairs to find Maggie standing at the side of her crib. After tending to her, Penny took the toddler down stairs and out doors for some sunshine. As usual, they were followed by Shadow. Penny thought, as she walked along leading Maggie, "I know now, why Shadow was the best name for you."

"Mama," Maggie called out to Penny as she pointed toward a butterfly in flight.

"Yes, butterfly," Penny returned.

"Do you want to swing?" Penny took Maggie in her arms and sat in the swing that hung from a tall oak tree. The little girl giggled so hard her laughter almost turned to tears. Penny leaned her cheek against the small head and pressed her lips into the black curls in front of her. Leaving the swing behind, she carried Maggie on down the shaded trail to the creek. Both mother and daughter sat on the bank, bare feet dangling in the cool water.

Penny breathed in the sweet scent of summer in Missouri. She was surprised at some of the vivid memories that flashed through her mind. Memories of life before the drunkenness of her father, Gunther Brown. Events that must have somehow pushed themselves to the farthest places of her memory were now challenging her emotions. Time slipped by as she remembered the earlier days of her childhood. She contemplated the times before the liquor took over her father's mental stability. The feelings were fresh and good, reaching into her being and turning some of her bitterness into pity. Bitterness that was, until now, unknown to even her.

When Penny had first heard of the death of her father, she didn't allow any room for her own time of healing. Now she realized, that time had been greatly needed. All the good things about her father had been repressed. Penny felt an odd sense of peace. She finally felt as though she had a father, even if things had gone bad in his life. She now remembered the love that had surrounded the family, before weakness had strangled the life from Gunther. Penny thought about her mother and how she must have been so strong to live through all the abuse. She had known love and lost it. Penny was hit, full force, with the pain her mother had endured when she had to leave her only child behind. "All the time you worked so hard to come back and get me."

Penny reached for Maggie with a renewed thankfulness for her blessed life. She walked back up the trail with babe in arms. The barn was in sight, and as always, Penny was lured in by the nickering of the horses. The door stood open, letting only enough light in for Penny to see the dark figure in the far corner. Randall, the newest hired hand was stacking feed in the feed bin. He had been highly recommended by another ranch owner.

"How do, Mrs. Holbrook?"

"Hello, Randall. What are you doing here at this time of day? Brent told me he would be going into town for supplies later in the week. We had planned a day out." She was disappointed but knew Brent must have a good reason. "He probably forgot to tell me. He has had a lot on his mind lately."

"Yes, Mrs. Holbrook." He looked pleased. Penny assumed it was because he had been hired for the extra work to be done to start the horse ranch. When the Holbrooks had first heard about the young man they were skeptical. They didn't know how he could have so much knowledge about the care of horses when he was so young. To their relief, though, they soon found out he was far more skilled than they had anticipated. Both his father and grandfather had been veterinarians in Tennessee. He was carrying on the family tradition.

Penny and Maggie went on with their daily ritual of feeding apples and talking to their favorite horses. In a short while they left the barn and continued walking up the path toward home. It was getting late and almost time for Penny to meet Brent for her target practice.

Celia took over, leading Maggie to the kitchen while Penny ran up the stairs and changed into her riding pants. She pulled on her buckskins and slipped a brown shirt over her head. Walking to the dresser she picked up her brush, gave her long hair a few quick strokes and pulled it back, tying it at the nape of her neck. She made her way back down stairs to the study. Opening the gun cabinet, she took out a rifle and her pistol She started to step away, but having second thoughts about the amount of ammunition Brent might have with him, she reached back into the cabinet and loaded up with ammo. "If I'm going to do this I might as well do it right," She thought to herself.

Penny walked out the door and down the trail to the barn. When she walked into the barn, she heard Star nickering. She saw Dolly's head pop up out of her stall. I would like to take you both on this ride, but I can only ride one horse at a time." She rubbed Dolly's neck as she stopped and gave her an apple. She continued on to Star's stall. In no time she had the paint saddled, loaded down with weapons and on the trail to meet Brent.

The evening was giving way to cooler air and both Penny and her mount were feeling lively and energetic. When they reached their destination Brent was waiting patiently. Smiling, he reached for her. Pulling her off the horse, he held her in his arms for long moments before turning her loose. Penny felt a warm flush run through her body as the familiar feelings came.

"We better get started, Mr. Holbrook." Penny flushed even more with Brent's knowing wink.

He admired the way she slid her rifle out of the scabbard with one quick, smooth movement. He heard the click of her gun as she pulled the lever and the shell moved from the magazine and slid into the chamber. She walked the distance back to Brent, eyed the target and pulled the trigger. In an instant she had pulled the lever, ejected the empty shell and was ready for the next target. Each time she pulled the trigger the target was demolished.

"I don't know if you need any practice, my Dear. Remind me never to make you mad." Brent sounded half serious as he said the words. He heard Penny's soft giggle as she turned and walked to her horse. Replacing the rifle with her pistol, she came back to stand the same distance from the target area, To her husband's surprise, she slid the revolver from the holster, that was now, strapped around her waist. He watched as she spun the cylinder and shoved the gun back into the leather. He stepped back, and just before he opened his mouth to suggest she move closer to the targets, she had drawn and emptied the gun. He stared in disbelief, as calm handedly, the feminine creature standing before him, took each empty shell out of the still smoking revolver.

"When, uh, where, did you learn that?" Brent asked in astonishment.

She said with a look of far reaching anger, "I practiced some when I was a slave. Sometimes I went with Jesse and Celia to do chores on other plantations. They were both trusted, because they had always returned to their owner. But, Jesse knew, at some time, it might be a choice for me to defend myself or die. He knew someone who took the time to teach me while no one else was watching." Penny shrugged her shoulders. "I was afraid I might be a little rusty."

Brent laughed hardily. "I wouldn't call that rusty." He looked at her with that questioning gaze still lingering in his blue eyes. He grabbed her. With both arms around her small waist he swung her around. "Let's go home. I'm starved." The two rode home light hearted and in love. By the time they reached the creek, where Penny and Maggie had played earlier, it was dark. "How about a little dip in the water before we go in?" Brent leaned from Pacer and whispered in Penny's ear.

She could feel his warm breath on her face. She turned her lips to his barely touching them before her tongue found its way into his mouth. The touch was brief but seemed to answer his question. In only minutes, they were in the creek. Penny shivered as Brent's hand found her. The trembling stopped when his hot lips came down upon hers. The full moon shone on her dark wet eye lashes. She closed her eyes and Brent lightly touched first one and then the other with his lips. Their love making was slow and lingering, but the solitude of the moment was fleeting.

I could never get enough of you, Brent told Penny as he took one last taste of her full moist lips and carried her out of the water.

↓

Chapter
42

Celia had supper waiting and Maggie in bed asleep when they stepped inside the house. Celia looked at the two shaking her head. "This looks mighty suspicious to me." She mumbled something about Penny catching her death of cold with a wet head before she went back into the kitchen. Brent and Penny followed her, hand in hand like two children who had been caught misbehaving. When they got to the kitchen they were also met by Jesse. Brent and Penny tried to avoid eye contact, but the harder they tried, the more comical the circumstance became. Before too long, they were all laughing so hard they were in tears.

"I will take my wife and go home now," Jesse said as he put a hand on Celia's elbow and started to guide her toward the doorway.

Penny looked at Brent in a sudden state of panic. Before she could get a word out, Brent responded. "Why don't the two of you stay over tonight since it is so late. After all, it is our fault you're leaving so late."

Jesse started to decline, but when he looked at Celia, thought better of it. After all the years the two had been together, he still yet, was mindful of his wife's safety. "We sho do ppreciate the offa."

"Good, I'll set a place and you can eat supper here." Penny was relieved.

The two older people never ceased to amaze Penny. She had noticed the difference in their speech and knew the black dialect was a thing of their own will . They could both speak as well as any of the highly educated people she had met in the south or in Missouri. Her thoughts were interrupted by a knock at the door.

"Go ahead and start eating. I'll see who it is." Brent went to the door and then returned with Julia and George by his side.

"We went by to visit with Celia and Jesse earlier. We got worried and thought we had better check and see if they were here."

Penny, hurriedly took more plates and silverware from the cabinet. After they all sat down and began the evening meal, Brent spoke. "I'm glad you are all here. This will give us a chance to do some more talking about the horses." The room was filled with excitement as the family ate and discussed details of the travels that would have to take place in order to purchase just the right horses for breeding. Everyone had some input on which horses would be best. They all had their own experiences and knowledge of horses and the unique characteristics of each breed to be used. Even the women had their opinions and ideas about the new venture.

Penny was proud of her husband. He was self confident without being self indulgent. He felt comfortable discussing his future plans and knocking ideas around with George and Jesse. Penny knew a lot of men would probably feel out of control doing so, but not Brent. He was strong without being brutal, gentle without being weak, loving beyond what she could ever have imagined. She didn't realize she had been staring at him hopelessly, until his eyes met hers and his lips turned up in a smile that she knew would always be just for her.

Later, after all had been taken care of and beds had been made for the whole family, Penny slid into her own bed beside Brent. Resting her head on his muscular shoulder she fell into a deep sleep. The restless and frightening dreams that had tormented Penny when she first returned to Missouri had long ago subsided. Thanks to the love and trust she and Brent shared, a new sense of security and peace had taken over.

The sun was shining through the bedroom window when Penny woke up the next morning. She took in a deep breath smelling all the smells she had loved as a child. A mixture of honeysuckle and roses drifted through the air. She threw the covers back and rolled out of the bed, anxious to find Brent and enjoy waking Maggie. She loved the times when she could watch her little one sleeping in the early morning, before she reached down and gently picked her up. Those times were few and far between, for Maggie was usually the first sound she heard. She walked into the nursery but Maggie was not sleeping as she expected . Since Brent was no where in sight, she assumed the two of them were already up and starting the day. Penny couldn't believe she had slept in so long. She was usually the first up and ready for the excitement each dawn brought to the ranch. She dressed hurriedly in a simple riding skirt and blouse and descended the stairs two at a time. She met smiles and stares as she stepped into the kitchen.

"Good morning." She heard more than one voice ring out.

"Good morning. Sorry I slept so long. Breakfast smells delicious. I'm starved."

They all laughed as Penny pulled a chair out from under the table and joined them.

"We intentionally let you sleep in. I was telling everyone about your rusty target practice yesterday and we all knew you would be tired." Everyone laughed again.

Maggie was seated in her high chair beside Penny. The young mother leaned over and kissed her only child on the cheek. Maggie was old enough now to attempt eating on her own. Penny could taste the blueberries that were smeared on her small face.

The conversation about horses continued on as if the night had been no interruption at all. Penny was elated with the idea and could hardly wait until Brent would bring some new horses to the ranch. Even though she already knew how much she would miss him, she also knew that it was a must for him to go. "Where do you intend to go first, Brent?" She asked with enthusiasm.

"Kentucky," he answered. Randall has put me on to a Tennessee Walker. His grandfather was a vet for the owner of this horse. Randall still remembers the stories about some of the horses in the lineage. One in particular was born and bred on a South Carolina plantation. It has been told the mare had stamina and intelligence that was unmatched. From what I hear, none since has lost quality."

"And how soon will you be leaving?"

"Next month, more than likely. There is still plenty of work to do in order for us to be prepared for this thing. I do want to make sure the trip is over by winter. But, in the meantime, there are barns to be built, extra feed to put away and," he stopped in mid sentence.

"And?" Penny repeated, "Firewood to cut?" The room was filled with laughter as Brent agreed.

Soon, the morning meal was done and the men were off to their outside work, leaving the women alone to do their own chores. The morning passed quickly and when Julia and Celia were ready to go home, Penny offered to ride along with them. She felt secure, again, in her ability to handle a gun. Julia and Celia were somewhat surprised when Penny put her riding pants on and gathered her weapons once again to escort them to their own homes.

"Is there something I don't know about?" Julia asked.

"No, it's just that after the incident with Shadow and the cougar last winter, I want to take every precaution I can when it comes to protecting the people and animals I love."

Julia and Celia looked at the young woman and knew without a doubt her words were not idle.

"Lord have mercy on the man that eva messes with that child again," Celia said as Penny walked out the door and headed toward the barn to saddle Dolly.

Julia looked at Celia with a humble heart. "Celia, I can never tell you enough, how grateful I will always be to you and Jesse for giving my family back to me. All the nights I prayed for God to give me the strength to endure the tragedy of losing Penny, and now," She couldn't get another word out for the lump that had formed in her throat.

Celia walked to her side. "Thank you for sharing your family with Jesse and me. In a way, it has been a blessin fo us not to have ever had children. I don't believe I could have stood havin um sold off away from me. But, it sho be a blessin now to be a part of you family, Mz. Julia." Julia put her arm around Celia's shoulders. Much was said without either of the women saying another word.

Chapter

43

Everyone on the ranch had been busy preparing for the venture ahead of them. By now, all who worked for the Holbrooks had some idea about the future plans for the ranch. No specific details had been discussed with any of the ranch hands, except Ben. It wasn't too difficult, however, for the other men to figure out something was about to change. Orders were given about new barns and corrals, more men had been hired and another bunk house was being built. It was obvious to everyone that something was about to take place.

The early morning sun was beginning to light up the eastern sky, when Brent and Penny walked down the trail toward the barn. The barn door stood open. Without hesitation the two looked at each other with a questioning gaze.

"Wonder who the poor bored soul is who is up and busy before the owners?" Penny watched Brent's lips turn up in a half smile as he said the words.

They were both surprised to see Ben saddling Dolly. "Mornin," he said, as the couple stepped inside the barn. They both returned the greeting, with a questioning look at Ben. Finally, Penny asked, "Ben why are you saddling Dolly?"

Ben looked at Penny and then at Brent, puzzled. "Well, that new man you hired, Jeff Hunter, told me last night, you wanted to go for an early morning ride. Said, Mr. Holbrook spoke to him about it yesterday afternoon."

Brent looked at Penny and shrugged his shoulders. "I don't know how these young cow hands get so confused. Maybe nerves over a new job."

193

He shook his head as he walked away. Suddenly turning to Ben, he asked in a baffled voice, "Who brought the feed in?"

It was Penny's turn to speak. "I was here a few days ago when Randall was unloading the feed. He told me you had sent him into town to pick it up. I was surprised and a little disappointed because I thought you had forgotten about our plans to go for supplies together."

"It's not like Randall to get so confused, but I guess it can happen to anyone, can't it?"

"Well, I guess, since Ben just about has Dolly saddled, I will take advantage of his mistake and go for that early morning ride." Brent and Ben watched as Penny led Dolly out of the barn and climbed up into the saddle. She headed toward the sun.

"We are lucky to have her back, aren't we Brent?" Ben nodded his gray head as he looked affectionately toward Penny.

Brent chuckled. "We are that."

Fleeting memories of the times after Penny was kidnapped came and went as the two men gazed at each other with knowing eyes. No more time was spent on the past, for they both looked forward to the future with renewed strength and energy.

Hours turned to days, days to weeks and before they knew it traveling time was upon them. Brent knew that he and the men who were making the trip to Kentucky with him, were going to have to move out quickly in order to get back home before winter weather set in. He could see Penny sitting on the steps as he approached the house. Although they were both weary from a hard days work, their passion for one another was strong. Each time they came together, no matter how short a while they had been apart, the passion stirred in them. They knew how fragile life could be. They had learned how much they loved and needed each other. They had learned that no one else could fill that place in their hearts, even when they thought they were separated forever. Brent sat beside Penny, taking her hand in his, he leaned close to her. Her lips were moist and so were her cheeks. Brent could taste the salty flavor of tears.

"I am so glad you are going to get the horses from Kentucky, but I'll miss you so."

He put his arms around her and pulled her close. Resting her head against his chest, she found comfort in his strength. His fingertips stroked her arm gently. "I feel the same, Sweetie. I would like to be able to take you with me, but I know Maggie is still too young. George and Jesse will be here to watch over you and the ranch. Of course, some of the men will be staying to take care of the cattle, but I won't get a good night's rest until I'm the one taking care of my own family again."

Penny sat up, wiping the tears from her cheeks. "I didn't mean to be such a child. I am happy and excited about the horses. I will miss you so much though." She smiled and looked into the blue eyes staring down at her. "You know darling, when I was so young, before our lips ever touched, before the touch of your hands ever made me a woman, I knew we were meant to be together. From the time you first rescued me in the streets of Alder, I have loved you."

Brent's heart beat hard in his chest when he heard his wife's words. He could feel the desire stirring as he watched her in the moonlight. Her full lips parted beneath his and he kissed her, with a long, demanding kiss. His hands found the material on her shoulders. With a gentle push, her skin was bare to the top of her waist. His head moved downwards until his mouth found one nipple and then the other. He scooped her up into his arms and carried her through the doorway.

The night was long, but sunlight filtered through the curtains way too soon for the couple. With a mixture of dread and anticipation, they both rolled out of bed. Brent would have to make the trip to Kentucky without delay if he wanted to get the stock back to Alder safely before winter. In no time, the men were ready to leave. Brent twisted in his saddle, one last time, to see Penny standing barefoot on the porch. She held Maggie in her arms, both mother and daughter waving goodbye. Brent lifted his hand and then turned to face the eastern sky. Ben and Randall kicked their horses out taking their places on either side of Brent. The other men followed behind.

Chapter

44

Summer was drifting away and the cooler days of early fall were making the trip to Kentucky an enjoyable one, but no time was wasted. Brent was anxious to do his horse trading and head back home to Penny and Maggie. He knew his days of cattle and horse drives would never be the same as they once were. He had too much of a longing to be at the ranch with his wife and child. He was looking forward to the time when Penny and Maggie could make some of the trips with him, but for now, he would have to make the best of the situation.

The days came and went and so did the hills and forests of Missouri. Soon the rich soil of Kentucky was under foot. The grandeur of Kingston's horse ranch was even more than Brent and Ben had expected. Randall watched the two of them as they approached the colonial style home. He couldn't help the smile that lit up his face when the two looked at each other.

"Wait till you see the horse," Randall said.

"We'll let you do the honors of knocking on the door, Randall, since you know these people."

Randall took the steps leading to the porch two by two. His rap at the door was somewhat unusual. It was almost as if he was tapping out a code at the telegraph office.

Suddenly, the door was flung open and a young girl was on the porch with her arms around Randall's neck.

"Ma, Pa, it's Randall." She was yelling excitedly.

The young man was twirling the girl around as she clung to him. Only moments later an older man and woman appeared. The woman was next in line to give Randall a hug and then the man was slapping him on the back.

"Welcome home, son." Randall was wearing the biggest smile Brent had ever seen. Brent thought to himself, "He told us his grandfather had worked as a vet for Mr. Kingston, but I didn't know they looked at the young fella as part of the family."

The attention of the people was suddenly on Brent and his men. "This must be Mr. Holbrook."

Randall had told Brent how welcoming the Kingston's were, but his words couldn't describe the extent of their hospitality. He and his men were treated as good as royalty during their short stay at the Kingston Ranch. Mr. Kingston and his family would not let him rest until it was agreed that he and his men would stay at the ranch until the business concerning the horses was taken care of. Their horses were unsaddled, taken to stalls and supper was on the table in no time. The dining room was enormous. Brent had never seen anything like the chandelier hanging over the table, that is until he had gone to new Orleans. He remembered the night he and Penny had gone dancing. The rich life style of the plantation owners had been a shock to him His mind drifted to the time he and his new wife had spent together that night. Ben noticed that Brent seemed to be momentarily out of touch. He poked him in the side with his elbow. Brent smiled, gratefully, because in the next moment Mr. Kingston was asking him a question about the horse business he planned to start. Thanks to Ben he had been able to carry on an intelligent conversation with the man. After everyone finished eating, the men walked to the barn to take a look at the famous mare. The deal was made quickly when Brent saw her.

He knew she was the horse he wanted to use to start the breed. Not only did he take that mare, he bought ten more mares of equal quality. Brent had also learned from Mr. Kingston, about a herd of quarter horses in Missouri. He decided to travel the few extra miles and take a look at them before going back to Alder. After all, that would save him another trip later. The new barns and corrals that had been built at the ranch would easily accommodate the new herds. The remainder of the evening was spent taking tour of the ranch. Mr. Kingston was very helpful with information about starting a horse ranch.

"Randall spoke very highly of you in his letters. He is a fine lad. His grandfather and his father have taken care of Kingston stock. You couldn't ask for a better vet, Brent. Randall grew up with horses and he learned his business from two of the best vets I have ever known. He loved to care for horses even when he was too small to get in the saddle by himself. If there ever comes a time when you don't need him, there will be a place for him here. You know he is like family."

Brent had been watching Kingston's daughter and Randall. They seemed very fond of each other. Brent couldn't tell whether it was in a sister and brother sort of way or not, but it was obvious they were very glad to see each other. Of course, the entire family appeared to have the same feelings about the young man. Never the less, their time at the Kingston Ranch was very enjoyable.

"I really appreciate your hospitality," Brent looked at Mr. and Mrs. Kingston. I only wish my wife, Penny, could have been here. She would have very much enjoyed meeting all of you."

"If you are ever back this way you and your family are more than welcome to come stay with us." Mrs. Kingston took Brent's hand in hers as she said the words.

"Who knows, maybe when you get that horse ranch started, we might just need to make a trip up and take a look at your horses."

Mr. Kingston smiled, but his words held a ring of seriousness.

"We will be expecting you." Brent tipped his hat, turned Pacer around and rode toward Missouri.

Chapter
45

Penny stopped the rocker and looked down at Maggie lying in her arms. She ran a finger across the sleeping child's chubby, little cheek. Moving slowly from the rocking chair, Penny laid her daughter in the bed, and gently pulled the pink and white quilt over her. She tiptoed away.

Shadow took her place between the two rooms. She had slept curled up in the doorway of the adjoining rooms since Brent had been gone. Penny stroked her head and neck for long moments, and then returned to her own bedroom. She looked at the big empty bed before crawling in with a sigh of relief.

For the last few nights, Penny had been too tired to lie awake missing Brent, as she had the first few weeks he was gone. Tonight, like so many nights before, she was too tired to think about anything when she finally got to bed. The hectic days at the ranch had worn her down. So many unusual things had happened lately. Fences were knocked down. Cattle had been straying. Horses had gotten out of the corrals. It wasn't until some cattle had come up missing that they knew without a doubt they were being hit by rustlers. Penny had been riding out to help with the extra work that had to be done. She had gone to the sheriff, but no one else in the area had been having the problem. She figured who ever it was, had for some reason, thought them to be an easy target. She was anxious for Brent to be back. What a relief it would be to her.

Penny closed her eyes and very quickly fell into a deep sleep. Her peaceful night didn't last. She was awakened by the sound of gunfire. She knew the men must have heard it too, and they would be out to protect the cattle. She went in to check on Maggie. The child was sleeping peacefully. Penny quietly left the room. She again reached down to pat Shadow. "Come on, girl, outside." She walked down the stairs with her faithful companion following closely behind. When Penny opened the door, Shadow pushed her way to the front. She stopped in the doorway. Her attention was focused in the direction of the gunfire. Shadow let out a low growl. She sensed a threat. Penny rubbed the goose bumps that had immediately formed on her arms. She had learned with the cougar attack, that Shadow knew things no human could possibly fathom. Shadow moved forward to jump off the porch, hesitated, and once more, looked back at Penny, as if she wanted reassurance that her master was alright. She leaped off the porch and within a very short time was back at Penny's side. Penny opened the door and Shadow followed her in.

When they returned to the bedroom, Penny watched as Shadow went to Maggie's bed and sniffed at the sleeping child. When the dog was convinced all was well, she again curled up in the doorway between the two rooms and rested. From that night on Shadow was at Penny's side. She watched Maggie with an intensity that amazed Penny. The child could hardly make a move without the loyal dog. Shadow breathed in her scent, as if, to convince herself, the little girl was still there.

More cattle had come up missing, not a whole herd at once, but a cow here and there. It was like a dirty game they were playing. Regardless, no one had been caught or even seen. Penny rode out to help as often as she could. She felt a strong sense of responsibility as mistress of the ranch. George and Jesse had done a wonderful job taking care of everything, but Penny still felt her obligation heavily.

Of course, there had been times when her riding ability had been absolutely necessary in order to round up the cattle and horses after the fences had been torn down. Today would be another one of those days. The night had held more trouble for the Holbrook Ranch. A commotion had been heard again in the middle of the night. The hands didn't bother Penny with it until early morning. More calves had been stolen along with one of their best horses. Still, no one had been seen. The men were taking turns on night guard but the rustlers seemed to know where to hit each time. The ranch was too big for the men to cover every inch of it, constantly.

Penny planned to take Maggie to Julia. She wanted to see what had happened the night before, but for now she was enjoying her early morning time with Maggie and Shadow. She looked across the yard and saw Maggie's black curls bouncing in the sunlight. Shadow was with her every step of the way. Penny knew the sight would be a permanent mental picture. The air was just nippy enough to bring a pink glow to the toddler's little nose. Shadow was jumping back and forth trying to keep up with the little girl's every twist and turn, her sleek blue black coat shining. The fall foliage was more beautiful than Penny could remember. The crimson red, flaming orange and bright yellows made a beautiful background for the scene. Penny stood, watching while the image was burned into her mind forever. She sat down under the tree where Maggie and Shadow had been playing.

Penny pulled Maggie into her lap while Shadow took her place beside her. "Girls this is a good day to just steal away for a while and enjoy the quiet of nature." She hugged Maggie close and reached over to run a hand down the soft, silky coat of hair covering Shadow's neck. "You are matchless, girl." The dog laid her head on Penny's available knee. Her eyes moved to look at Penny and then she took a deep breath. The three sat, ran, played and escaped the turmoil that had been abundant in their lives lately.

After a while, Penny knew reality had to be faced once again. She swung Maggie into her arms and walked to the house.

Penny climbed the wooden stairway and dressed in her riding pants and a long sleeved, black, cotton shirt. She sat on the edge of the bed and shoved her feet into the tan leather boots that were more than broke in. Maggie was soon changed and dressed for the cool fall weather. "Alright girls we are ready to go to Grandma's house." She pulled her child up into her arms once more and headed for the gun case in the study. After arming herself she headed out the door, this time, Maggie and Shadow tagging along behind her. She saddled her paint mare, slid her gun into the scabbard and climbed into the saddle with Maggie riding in front of her.

Julia was waiting patiently for her daughter and grandchild. She always looked forward to a day with Maggie. She watched Penny slide out of the saddle her long hair tied back. Her velvety green eyes looked at Maggie and then at her. Julia couldn't get enough of just watching her lively daughter. She stepped down from the porch and hugged Penny and Maggie at the same time.

Penny kissed her on the cheek as she had done so many times as a child. "You look pretty, Mama." Penny meant those words with all her heart. To her, Julia was the most beautiful woman in the world. All the years of hurt had turned into an intense bond between the two. They understood one another's pain and remorse. That made them closer than most. "Penny, be careful when you go out. Maybe the sheriff will find these people soon and we will all feel safe again."

"I'll be careful, Mama. Shadow will be with me. She hasn't left my side in weeks." Penny gave her mother another quick hug, kissed Maggie on the cheek one more time, climbed on her paint and loped away.

Jesse first, saw her coming over the hill. He looked at George. "Mz. Penny is a natural born horsewoman."

"She is that."

"Good afternoon." Penny pulled her horse to a stop. "How are things today?"

"Nothing since last night. I guess the thieves had to get some sleep, sometime."

Penny took a good look at George and then Jesse. The men looked ten years older than they had when Brent left on his trip to Kentucky. She said in a low and gentle voice, "You two need to go home and get some sleep. You know, if those thieves need sleep the good guys will have to have some rest too."

They started to object, but when they took a good look at Penny's face, they knew she was not going to have it any other way. They also knew they might be needed more later.

She turned her horse toward the distant ridge. Her paint was lively and wanted to run, but Penny wanted to make sure she didn't miss any signs the rustlers might have left behind. She knew if everyone at the Holbrook Ranch ever had any peace, those people would have to be stopped. Approaching the tree line at the foot of the ridge her horse slowed and threw her ears forward. Taking control of the situation, Shadow moved ahead. Penny trusted the natural instinct of the animals and was on guard, but before she coud remove them and herself from the danger, a rider came running at full speed out of the wooded area.

He was on Penny before she could draw her gun. Still on his horse, he grabbed Penny from behind and pulled her from the paint. Only half on his horse, she found herself being carried through the thicket. She was held on, only by the vice like grip around her waist. As they slowed, all hell broke loose. Shadow flew through the air hitting the attacker and knocking him from his horse. Penny was instantly on the ground. Her head hit hard. She heard an explosion and then a desperate whine. At the moment, she couldn't tell whether it was her head or gunfire. She scrambled to her feet. Next, she heard the pounding of horses hooves hitting the earth hard and fast. She knew the men had heard the shot ring out and were on their way. The rustler turned to look in Penny's direction before he was again riding out of sight. Still yet blurry eyed from the fall, she saw Shadow lying still. When she got closer Shadow raised her head and for one final time, stared deep into her master's eyes. Penny fell to the ground beside her beloved friend and felt her last heart beat. Shadow was gone.

Several of the ranch hands had been working to replace a stretch of fence that had been torn down by the intruders. They heard the gunfire. They were in a frenzy when they found Penny. The sight of her on the ground, covered with blood, brought them to state of panic.

Cody was the first to dismount and reach her. She was limp as he pulled her to her feet. The others scouted the area, searching for the gunman. There was no one in sight. By the time they returned, Penny was able to tell what had happened.

"Did you see who it was, what he looked like?"

Penny shook her head. "No, he wore a bandana and his hat was pulled so low, I couldn't see him at all."

"Well, John, why don't you go into town and tell the sheriff what's going on? I'll take Mrs. Holbrook back to the ranch house. The rest of you men can get back to work. Oh, Sam, you better ride over and lelt her folks know about this."

The broken hearted young woman wouldn't leave until Shadow was laid across her saddle so she could be taken home. Penny's thoughts drifted back to a time, only a few hours earlier. She could picture, in her mind, the peaceful morning she and Maggie had spent with Shadow. She rode straight to the beautiful Red Maple.

"This is where we will bury, Shadow."

By the time the difficult task was finished, Julia and George were by Penny's side. Maggie reached for her mother and Penny took her in her arms holding her tightly. Celia and Jesse were soon to follow. All were teary eyed. They not only hurt for the grief of Penny, but also, for Shadow herself.

Even with frequent visits from Julia and Celia, the days were lonely for Penny. The empty doorway between her own room and Maggie's was almost too much for her to handle. Not only did she miss her loyal friend, the empty space evoked an inexplicable fear. Shadow had kept her from danger so many times. To know she was the primary protector in Brent's absence weighed heavily on her mind. All on the ranch had learned to expect some sort of disturbing activity, but it stopped as suddenly as it had started.

Chapter

46

The horses were a bit nervous as they were herded through the rolling pastures of Kentucky, but it didn't take the knowledgeable horse wranglers very long to get them under control and traveling at a satisfactory pace. By the time the herd was in Missouri, the days were shorter and significantly cooler. The hillsides were again, blazing with the fiery colors of autumn. Every mile traveled carried with it the promise of another winter approaching. Another day had come to an end and the men sat around the campfire watching the night shadows and talking about the rest of their venture.

"Cash, I want you to take the hands and head on toward Alder. There should be enough of you to keep the herd under control until we catch up with you. I'll take Ben and Randall with me to check on that herd of Quarter Horses down in Canton. If you get as far as Beaver Mountain, wait on us there." The air had turned cool enough for the coffee mug to feel good against Brent's hands. He thought of Penny and could hardly wait to see her and Maggie again. "I'll send her a telegram from Canton and let her know when to expect me home." With that thought, he flung the remaining drops of coffee from his mug into the fire. He unrolled his blanket and fell asleep.

By dawn, Brent, Ben and Randall were on their way to Canton. A short time later, Brent was in the telegraph office sending a telegram to Penny. Brent looked at the little man with the wire rimmed glasses. "I'm looking for a J.L. Benson. Do you happen to know where I might find him?" Brent asked. "I heard he has a herd of Quarter Horses for sale."

"Yes Sir, everyone in this neck of the woods knows J.L.." The laugh was muffled. "J.L. raises the best Quarter Horses in this part of the country. The ranch is just west of here, right outside of town."

"Thank you, Sir." Brent tipped his hat and headed out the door and down the steps toward Ben and Randall. "Lets go have a look at those horses, boys."

The three loped their horses down the streets of Canton and to the west. Pacer lifted his feet high as he stepped into the clear creek water. Brent could look down and see the small perch swimming between the rocks. It reminded him of when he was a boy. His dad would take him and Frank to the creek often and let them fish. He took a deep breath, shut the feeling in the pit of his stomach out of his mind and kept traveling toward the Benson's ranch. The horses could be seen in the distance, their muscles well defined, as they ran through the fields. Brent saw, at first glance, the quality of the animals.

Ben gave a whistle. "Man, this must be just what you were looking for, Brent."

"As far as I can tell, at this distance." He tilted his head toward Randall. "Our man Randall can give us an okay, as far as the health of the horses. The three cantered their horses to the ranch house. They were met, at the door, by a red head wearing a straw hat and jeans. Her blue eyes shone as she looked out from under the brim of her hat. She swung open the door and stepped out on to the porch. Randall stared at the girl. He didn't know what to think. He noticed her bare feet and her slim, almost boyish figure as she set her boots on the edge of the porch and sat down to pull them on.

"Can I help you, men?" The words came out of her mouth, as if she owned the place.

"We're here to see Mr. Benson. We heard he has some stock for sale."

"Well, there is some stock for sale, but you missed my dad by about six months. He passed away. A rattler got him when he was out rounding up the cattle for branding. I'm J.L.." Tears formed in the blue eyes, but she quickly blinked and hid all traces of sadness with a quick glance in the direction of the horses. "I'll get Sandy saddled and take you to see them." She was back in no time. She sat on her horse as if she was as comfortable as a matron in a rocking chair. The red head led the way, loping her bay across the field. She had hardly pulled her horse to a stop before she was out of the saddle and had both feet planted firmly on the ground. The men dismounted and walked over to the wooden fence that surrounded the horses. The girl's red hair fell around her shoulders as she climbed over the fence with one quick motion. Randall looked at Brent and then at Ben, shaking his head. It was easy for them to see the young man was taken with the girl.

The sun had dropped low in the sky before the men chose just the right horses, but before sundown, they were on their way back to join the rest of the men and make their final drive to Alder. They pushed hard to get back to the herd of Tennessee Walkers.

They moved the Quarter Horses as quickly as they could without stressing them or taking a chance on starting a stampede they couldn't get stopped. Brent knew they would have to rest for at least one night before they could join the other men. They traveled as long as daylight would allow them and then made camp for the night.

The three took turn about watching over the horses, but all were up at day break. A quick breakfast was wolfed down and the herd was again moving out. Bright streaks of sunlight broke through the shadows of the red and gold leaves. The air was crisp, clear and easy to breathe. Everyone was looking forward to getting back to their familiar beds.

"We should catch up to the others by mid day and be back in Alder by dusk tomorrow evening." Just then, Pacer moved his ears forward as he did when he heard something drawing near. From a nearby thicket, came a small group of men.

"That's him Sheriff. He's the one that did those terrible things to my little Betsy. The man jumped from his horse running like a crazy man toward Brent. The sheriff was off his horse and had the man in a headlock. It took him and two of the others in the group to control the man. His eyes were wild with a feverish gaze. Two more grabbed Brent from behind and tried to pull him off Pacer. They soon found out that was not an easy task. Before Ben and Randall could get off their horses and reach the men, Brent came out swinging and knocking all in his reach to the ground. The sheriff pulled his pistol and fired two shots into the air. All stopped and stood in silence.

Brent was the first to speak. "What is going on here, Sheriff?"

The crazed man started in again. "You know what you did, you worthless animal."

The sheriff spoke then. "You'll have to come with me, till we can get this straightened out." He aimed his gun at Brent's chest. "Get on your horse."

"Ben, you and Randall take the herd on and meet the boys. I'll be there as soon as I get this thing taken care of."

"Are you sure Boss? I think maybe I ought to come with you."

"No, Ben you go on with Randall. He'll need you to get those horses to the rest of the herd. I haven't done anything wrong. I'm sure I can get this lined out."

Chapter
47

The buggy bumped along on the uneven trail. "It is a relief not having to worry about waking up to some disaster each morning." Julia said.

Both, Penny and Celia agreed. "It sure is."

The women were all enjoying the ride to Alder. They had wanted to go into town for some shopping for a while, but didn't feel safe until they had stopped having trouble at the ranch.

The sheriff from Avery had sent word about some cattle rustlers pulling some of the same tricks down there. They were tearing down fences and stealing horses and cattle. Sometimes whole herds and sometimes a few at a time. It looked like they had moved on.

Penny felt like a boulder had been lifted from her shoulders, but she still yet had the empty, sick feeling in the pit of her stomach from missing Shadow so much. Thinking of her now brought tears to her eyes. She tried not to let them spill down her cheeks, but to no avail. Julia patted her arm. She knew.

The young woman looked at her mother. "You know every time the hurt comes, it is quickly replaced by a happy memory. She filled our lives with such good things for that short while she was with us. I am thankful she was sent our way."

With those thoughts, Penny took in the beauty of her surroundings. She vowed to herself that she would live each day as though it would be the last. She would love as though she would never see those close to her again. She said a silent prayer of thanks.

The day was a good one. It was so different now than what Penny or Julia had once thought it could be. Penny remembered the day she met Brent in the street. She felt a sudden urgency to see him. She could hardly wait until he was home again. When the women got to the General Store, they all picked out material for new dresses. It was a day for them to remember. It was a day of leisure. They had not had many of those days lately, and they all soaked it in.

As they finished up and walked out the door, two young women were on their way in. "Hello, Penny."

Penny recognized them right away. They looked at her, not with the smug and scornful grins she remembered, but with what appeared to be sincere smiles. Penny smiled graciously as she greeted them.

"Mrs. Holbrook, Mrs. Holbrook."

Penny turned around to see Mr. Riley, standing across the street, waving a piece of paper in the air. She smiled and ran, dodging everyone in sight. She knew it must be a telegram from Brent. Penny was the one waving the paper in the air now. Running back across the street with a smile on her flushed face and a gleam in her green eyes, she breathlessly said, "It's from Brent. He says he will be home soon. He says he has a surprise for me."

Julia couldn't get enough of Penny's happiness. She loved to watch her smile. "We will all be glad to see Brent too, my darling. I am happy for you."

The ride home was a good one. The women laughed and sang, and talked about good memories and future plans. They were just as excited about the horses as were the men. They were all quite capable when it came to handling a horse and they could hardly wait to teach Maggie.

"She will have to be a natural," Julia said.

Celia held the little girl. "She will be good at anything she does. This is the smartest chile I have eva seen." Penny took note of her speech. She knew by now that both Celia and Jesse spoke as they wanted. They could pick and choose, at any moment, just how they wanted their speech to sound. It made Penny wonder how many languages they would have spoken with the proper education. But more important than that, was the kind of friends they had been to her and her family. It was immeasurable. She still yet didn't know how she could have survived in New Orleans without Celia and Jesse. She sighed and thought to herself, "I know the good Lord must have been watching over us." She looked at Julia and then at Maggie. She watched Maggie's eyes light up at every little thing she saw along the way. "You have your father's blue eyes." With that thought came a light hearted feeling. She was eager for her husband's return to the ranch. She knew it would only be a short while now, until he was back home.

The sun was shining brightly, but the air was getting cooler with each passing day. The leaves were just beginning to fall from the trees. It was a beautiful sight. The red, yellow, orange and purple colors of the leaves twirled round and round as they floated to the ground. The laughter, the horses hooves hitting the ground, even the squeeking of the wagon wheels as they rolled toward home were like a song to Penny. She could almost see Shadow running along beside the wagon. "I will never forget you, my dear friend. I will always be thankful for my time with you." Penny took a deep breath and felt the cool air fill her lungs.

George and Jesse watched the wagon coming up the path toward the ranch. They could see by the smiles on the women's faces. The day had been a good one.

"Maybe we should send them to town more often," Jesse said with a mischievous grin.

The supplies were unloaded in no time at all. Much to the surprise of the women, the men had cooked supper. They all sat down and enjoyed the good hot meal. It was almost dark by the time everyone left for their own homes.

Penny knew she had a busy day ahead of her and decided she needed to get Maggie in bed and get a good night's sleep herself. She wanted everything to be just right when Brent returned home. Sleep came easy for both mother and daughter. Penny laid Maggie in her bed and before she could pick up the scattered clothes from the floor, she turned around and her child was sleeping peacefully. "Such a busy day." Penny smiled and walked to her own room.

The moon was shining a bright orange, casting a light on the bedroom wall. The tree limbs made a pattern moving like waves as the wind blew through the trees outside. The soft sound of the autumn breeze was soothing and like her daughter in the next room, Penny drifted into a deep and peaceful sleep.

She awoke early the following morning, and practically jumped out of the bed. She wanted to get a good start on getting things ready for Brent to come home. She slipped in and saw that Maggie was still sleeping and then started down stairs before she remembered she hadn't even dressed. She laughed at herself for being so excited about seeing her husband again. Penny's aim was to get all of the work done so that she would have time to devote, only to Brent.

Chapter
48

Brent could barely restrain himself as he rode along with the sheriff and his so called posse. He had a suspicious feeling about the whole ordeal. He couldn't quite believe his arrest could be anything but a hoax. He eyed the burly looking man riding beside him. Although he had a sudden urge to kick him off his horse, he thought better of it at the moment, since he had been stripped of his guns. He felt a surge of disappointment. He sure was looking forward to gettinng home to his wife and daughter. He brushed the thought away. "This will be over in no time. These people can't hold me for anything. I haven't committed a crime. I'll just go into town, see what's going on and prove to these people where I've been. It should be a pretty simple thing. I can have them wire Mr. Kingston in Kentucky."

It turned out not to be such a simple thing for Brent though. It was almost dark before they got back into town. The sheriff took the key off the hook it was hanging on, escorted Brent to the cell and went to his desk.

Brent knew there wouldn't be anything he could do until morning. He took his hat off, lay down on the small, dirty cot and tried to get some sleep. Sleep didn't come easily, especially with the ruckus going on outside. At first, he thought it was the usual drunken cowboys, but then he realized, the commotion was all about the animal in jail. Since he was the only one locked up, he figured real quick, he might be the animal. He stood up. Putting his hands on the bars, he tried to see outside, but it was already too dark. He moved toward the front of the small cell and called for the sheriff. No one answered. Brent was beginning to think he should have let Ben come with him. It was beginning to sound like a mob outside.

By morning Brent knew he was in serious trouble. There would be no talking or reasoning with these people. The strange thing was, Brent didn't even know what he was being accused of. He could hear the mob, clearly. "Let's hang him. He doesn't deserve to live." The sun was just peeking over the mountain to the east and beginning to light up the small cell. With the light, came more people and more voices.

"Sheriff, Sheriff, I need to talk to you," He called out. The sheriff finally came into the small hallway just outside the cell. "What am I being accused of?" Brent could still hear the incessant sound of the angry voices outside the jail. He asked the sheriff again, "What am I being accused of, Sheriff?"

The sheriff looked at Brent in a puzzled way, as if it surprised him that the man behind bars was even asking. "You know I could almost be misguided into believing you really don't know, if it wasn't for the credibility of the eye witness."

"Well, why don't you just humor me and tell me what I did?"

"It's too disgusting to even talk about, but since you are the one that's going to be hanged, I guess I will humor you. The little Henson girl, do you remember her?"

"Sorry, never heard of her."

"Now, I figured you would say that. About a year or so ago, well it still makes me want to puke. I guess on second thought I won't humor you. The sheriff turned and left the hallway.

Hours passed and nothing seemed to be changing. If anything, the crowd was getting louder and more angry. Brent tried to close his eyes and sleep. It was a long time about coming, but finally Brent fell into a slumber that lasted only a few minutes. He heard the front door of the jail come crashing in. The mob was overtaking the sheriff. To the prisoner's surprise the sheriff did try to fight them off and wound up in the unoccupied cell next to him.

Two angry faces peered through the bars at Brent. "You are going to hang." One of them was unlocking the door while the other was cramming a shotgun in Brent's gut. "Head on out. It's time for you to meet your Maker. Brent almost doubled over with the force of the blow. Holding his belly he moved out of the cell and across the rough wood planks of the office to the doorway. The hair bristled on the back of his neck when he saw the crowd. He thought of Penny and Maggie. The thought of never seeing the two of them again, was almost unimaginable. It was clear to Brent that his misery was not likely to last very long. A half a dozen men grabbed him. Pulling and pushing they got him on a horse and had a noose around his neck. The mob was shouting and chanting. "Hang him. Hang him high."

The last thoughts entering Brent's mind before he heard the shot ring out was of his beloved wife and child. The rope tightened around his neck before he fell in a heap to the ground. The second shot startled him, but he knew he was still alive. It was only seconds before he figured out someone had shot the rope in two, just before it broke his neck. Scrambling to get to his feet, he looked up to find two riders, with black hoods completely covering their heads and faces.

Shotguns were aimed at the hearts of the two ruffians in charge of the mob. Brent was again amazed when one of the riders cut the ropes from his hands and handed Pacer's reins to him. The other rider, looked toward the mob and said, "If I were you, I would let the sheriff out of jail." You almost hanged an innocent man." Dust flew into the air when the riders rode out of town. They didn't slow until they were well out of harm's way. The rider in the lead pulled his horse to a sliding stop. Brent and the other rider did like wise. Brent smiled as he pulled the black hood off the man's head. He was in a state of shock when he saw it wasn't Ben's face looking back at him. He looked at the other rider. His mouth was open but no words came out. A hand slowly reached up and the hood of the masked rider was pulled off. Her long, dark hair fell around her face. The dark eyes looking into Brent's blue eyes were unfamiliar. He was further flabbergasted when he realized, it was a woman staring at him instead of a man.

The words finally came. "Jason Reynolds, what are you doing here?"

Jason answered. "This was not suppose to happen. There are things you didn't need to know."

"I was almost hanged. I need to know a lot of things. "And, who is she?" Brent looked again at the woman.

"I'm Ema, Ema Griffith."

Jason spoke again. Looking at Ema, "We might as well tell him. It's too late to hide everything now. I think after all of this, we can trust him."

"We are federal agents. We have been trying to put a stop to Chandler and people like him. Legally, right now, there isn't anything we can do to stop slavery, but there is a law against going into people's homes, kidnapping them and selling them as slaves. We have been tracking Chandler for months."

"Why should I believe you? You bought Penny and held her as your own slave for almost a year."

"At the time, she was going to be sold anyway. Penny was the only girl being auctioned off that day, who was brave enough to do any talking." Jason laughed, "She was telling everything, right there on the auction block. I knew if there was any way I could obtain any information about all of this illegal activity, it would be through her. You can tell her I'm sorry for any disrespect I may have shown her, but I had to put up a good front. I couldn't let anyone know about my work as an agent."

Ema spoke up, "Jason is telling the truth. I was taken prisoner by Chandler, too. I too, was sold on the auction block that day. It took Jason months to gain my trust. When he did, I was recruited as an agent. Please tell Penny hello for me."

Jason and Ema mounted their horses. "We better get out of here or that crowd will be after all of us. I don't know if they would be willing to listen to our stories. The sheriff knows about us, but you saw what they did to him back there. He will come up with some story to get them off our trail for a while, but I don't know how long he can stall them."

The three parted ways and Brent was on his way home. The events of the past two days had left him shaken. He lost no time heading for Alder. He rode hard and fast, but was careful not to leave a trail for the posse to follow. He needed Penny more than ever now. Pacer moved quickly and steadily across the wooded, hilly terrain. A lesser horse would have faltered, but Pacer was sure footed and strong. He was making good time. He proved to have an innate ability to find his way in the dark, but Brent knew they would both need rest soon. The stars were shining brightly and the moon was full. That allowed a little more riding time for Brent.

After hours of riding, both man and horse were worn down. Brent heard the splattering of water. He reined Pacer in and led him to the creek. The cool, branch water was a relief to them both. After they quenched their thirst, Brent tied Pacer out, unsaddled him and had a dip in the creek. He figured this might be the last chance he got to rid himself of the grime before getting back home. He was cold when he stepped out of the water and on to the bank. The thought of a nice warm camp fire sounded good, but not the thought of having a noose around his neck again. He wrapped himself in the blanket he took from his saddle bag and fell asleep.

He felt refreshed when he awoke to warm sunshine the following morning. Wasting no time, he gulped down a tin of coffee and left over beans. Pacer was ready to go too. He pranced and pulled at the bit, as if knowing he was on his way back to the ranch. Brent thought Pacer probably did know exactly where he was, after all he was no stranger to the area.

Brent chose not to take the same trail the men had followed with the herd of horses. He took the rougher but shorter pathway. He figured he would be able, not only, to loose a posses, but he could get home sooner too. By mid day he was out of the hills and back in the valley. Riding would be smoother and faster now. An even gait was kept in order not to break Pacer's stamina. Brent didn't intend to let anything or anyone interfere with his jouney home. The land was becoming more familiar, but there was still some ground to be covered. Brent could almost smell Penny's sweet scent as he rode. He could almost feel her soft skin beneath his finger tips. He could see the green of her eyes and hear her whispery voice. He gritted his teeth and breathed in a deep breath. Life filled his whole being at the thought of being back in his wife's arms. He said a silent prayer of thanks, for he knew it was a miracle that he was still alive. He thought of all that had happened in their time together and imagined much to come as he rode toward Alder. Brent was careful to stay as far away from any town as he could. He didn't want any attention at this point. He was a good hunter and game was plentiful in Missouri. He knew he could survive off the land long enough to get home.

Chapter
49

Penny had worked diligently for the past few days to get all done that she wanted to do for Brent's return. The house was immaculate. She had made new dresses for both herself and Maggie. Jars of apple butter were in the pantry. She would surprise Brent with that, for his breakfast when he got home. Not only did she have the woman's work done, as everyone called it, but she had also helped with the ranch work. Penny had always loved to work outside, even as a child. She had helped her mother and then later, she had worked with Brent. She again, thought of all he had done for her when she was growing up. She was safe with Brent. She knew she had always been safe with him and that she would continue to be, as long as they both lived.

Maggie ran through the leaves that had fallen off the apple trees. She fell and Penny ran, scooped her up in her arms and twirled her around. Maggie threw her head back and giggled until she could barely catch her breath.

"Just wait until your daddy gets home. He will be so happy to see you. Setting Maggie back down on the ground, Penny took her small hand in her own and walked back toward the ranch house. They stopped at the water well. Maggie drank the cool water from the dipper. Small droplets ran down her chin and fell on the front of her dress. Penny wiped it off with her hand. "We don't want to get you wet, little lady. It is just a bit chilly out here for that." The sun was shining brightly, but to the far west dark clouds could be spotted. It looked like a fall rain might be coming in. Penny was hoping Brent would make it home before dark. Maybe he wouldn't be caught out in a downpour.

The potatoes and fried chicken were filling for both Penny and Maggie. After lunch, instead of putting the baby down for her usual nap, Penny decided to go to her mother's for a visit. It took more time than usual to get there. Too many stops were made along the way for a look at a squirrel running up a tree, a whirlwind of colorful leaves or a flock of birds flying south. Penny had decided at a young age that she would learn to live a day at a time and to enjoy life to its fullest.

As they neared their destination, Penny could see her mother and step father sitting on the front porch. Julia and George had not been expecting company, but were very glad to see Penny and Maggie.

"It looks like we could be getting a bit of rain later, " George said as he looked toward the west.

"Yes, I noticed those dark clouds earlier. I'm hoping Brent can make it in before the rain gets here. We could get some pretty cool weather with an autumn rain.

"Are you expecting him home tonight?"

"I'm expecting him very soon. From what his telegram said the other day, it could be any time now. I have everything ready for his home coming." Penny smiled as she said the words.

Julia also smiled. It filled her heart with joy to see her daughter so in love. The three sat on the porch and talked for a long while, before George excused himself and went to the horse corral to do the evening feeding.

The women went into the kitchen and Penny helped her mother with supper. By the time George was finished with the work, a hot meal was on the table. They ate and after the dishes were washed, Penny decided she better hurry home just in case a rain hit.

"Why don't you let Maggie spend the night, Penny? We would love to have her."

"I will miss her, but I think she would probably like that, Mama."

After several hugs and kisses, Penny slid into her saddle and headed toward home. The sun was still warm, but the clouds to the west were, by no means, vanishing. Penny took the long way around on her way home. She wanted to see what horses were being worked. She rode to the newly built corrals. One of the new hands was on a huge black horse.

Penny tied Dolly to the hitching post and walked to the corral. Grabbing the wooden post, she climbed to sit on the fence. After watching for a while, she thought she would like to try the horse. He seemed to be safe enough. The men were leery of letting the boss's wife on such a spirited animal, but they didn't know how to refuse, when she insisted she would be fine. They were surprised. Not only did she stay on the horse, before long she had him doing everything she wanted.

Time had passed quickly and Penny realized she had done more work than she had intended. She rode home. By the time she got her horse unsaddled and taken care of, it was near dark. The wind picked up and she could hear distant thunder. The heavy wood door going into the house felt a little heavy tonight. Penny stepped inside and lit the nearest lamp. She took off her jacket and laid it across the back of the sofa. There was a sudden chill in the air. The tap of her boots on the floor was the only sound that could be heard. She missed Maggie and Shadow, and at the same time had a deep longing and hope that Brent would be coming through the door at any time. Before long a fire was rolling in the fireplace and Penny was warming her cold hands. Moving to the stairway she made the climb slowly and carefully so as not to fall. The lamp she carried flickered, allowing shadows to jump up and down on the walls. Penny pushed her bedroom door open. She lit another lamp in the bedroom. In no time at all she was cleaned up and dressed for bed. She brushed her long thick hair until it was shining. Tying it back with a ribbon, she went back down stairs. After going into the kitchen and making a cup of tea, she went back to sit by the fireplace. The house was quiet now. Not a sound could be heard except the occasional pop of wood in the fire. Penny selected a book and tried to read, but soon found herself walking the floor instead. She stopped at the window. The wind had died down somewhat, but clouds were floating across the big orange moon. Penny stood watching.

"Brent, where are you? I need you so." She had stayed up as long as she could. She knew if she didn't make her way to bed she would surely fall asleep on her feet.

She set the remainder of her tea on the table beside the sofa and, again, climbed the stairs to her bedroom. The floor felt cold to her bare feet. She pulled the covers back and crawled into bed. She was out in moments. Penny fell into a deep and restful sleep.

Chapter
50

The moon continued to slip in and out of the shadows cast by the heavy clouds. He tied his horse to the post outside the ranch house and stepped upon the porch. He was weary, but so glad to be back at the ranch. He pushed the wood door open and listened for any sound within. He breathed in a deep breath as he walked into the familiar home. No one was in sight, and not a sound could be heard. He walked quietly into the study. The fireplace looked so inviting. As he passed the sofa, he cast a glance at the jacket Penny had left there earlier. He slowly picked it up, rubbing it with his large calloused hands. He sighed heavily. Pulling the material up to his nostrils, he breathed in deeply, savoring the scent of Penny. He almost shuddered with the wanting. He turned toward the staircase, his blue eyes lighting up as he put his hand on the sleek banister and started up, where Penny lay sleeping. With each step he took, there was a hesitancy, He was prolonging the deep feeling that filled up his innermost being. The door was slightly ajar. He pushed it open far enough to see Penny lying on the bed. The open window allowed the moon to cast just enough light for him to see her hair falling across the pillow. He moved slowly so as not to awaken her. Before he lay down beside her, he pulled something from his pocket, he could hardly contain his excitement when he let it fall into his palm and closed his hand over it.

Penny felt his strong arms slide around her. Still asleep, she snuggled closer pressing her back to him. The warmth from his body felt good to her as she began to wake up. She was so glad for him to be back in her bed. She felt his warm breath against her ear as he whispered, "I thought this time would never come." He opened her hand and dropped the cold stone into it. "I brought you a surprise." The clouds moved from across the moon again and as she opened her eyes she saw the jade necklace. At that moment she heard the words. "I think you will like it, Miss Brown."

A knot formed in the pit of her stomach. She felt sick. She knew the feeling well. She felt the vice like grip around her. She knew she was trapped, once again. She began to think, maybe she had lost her mind. He was suppose to be dead. Shadow had saved her. She thought to herself, "Am I having a nightmare?"

He spoke again. "You have no friend, this time to save you. She did go quickly though, didn't she?"

Penny's mind was frantic. She momentarily, wanted to give up, but Brent and Maggie, her mother and everyone else who loved her came to mind. She had too much to live for.

Frank moved his arm from around her. He pulled her to face him, and then, taking her hand in his he put it on his chest. She could feel the scars. Suddenly, the light from the lantern was shining in her eyes She couldn't see for the light. Then he moved the lantern and she realized she was not dreaming, but what she was seeing was far too real. She remembered, Frank's body had never been found. He lived through it. At that moment she thought of Maggie being safe at her grandmother's house. She was thankfull for that.

Without warning Frank was standing. Grabbing Penny by the wrist, he yanked her out of the bed. Had he not been holding to her so tightly, she would have fallen to the floor.

"Take off your gown." His words were evil.

With her hesitation, came his knife at her throat. He tore the material from her shoulders.

"Pull it off." A small trickle of blood oozed from Penny's neck.

Penny let the gown fall to the floor. Her heart raced and her legs felt strangely weak. The room was beginning to spin. It was all she could do to keep from falling. She felt the pressure of the cold steel slip from her neck to the hollow between her bare breasts. His low, sinister laugh echoed in her ears. She was cold and numb, now. The warmth had drained from her body. Where once, her beautiful face held the flush of life giving blood, there was only the chalky, white look of death.

She stared into his eyes. She saw the satisfaction of his evil deed. She was no longer afraid. She heard her own voice from a distance. "You can drive your cold blade of steel into my heart, but you can't kill the love that will live on. His lips curled into another evil grin.

Suddenly, just as swiftly as Penny's courage had dwindled, it returned. She could feel the heat in her face and neck, from the blood pumping through her veins. Her heart raced, but this time, she felt the strength surge through her body. She dove for the chair in the corner of the room. Grabbing the pistol that hung in the holster, she spun around. She brought the gun up to shoot, but Frank was there. He hit her wrist as she fired, but not soon enough to keep from taking a bullet in his shoulder. He flinched, the smirking grin coming back to his face. He wrenched the gun from her hands. Blood ran down his arm and on to the floor. Penny knew the shot was not lethal.

Opening the cedar chest, Frank grabbed clothes and threw them at Penny. Put these on. She did as she was told. Frank motioned toward the corner of the room, where Penny had set her boots, earlier in the night. She hurriedly put them on and walked back to the bed. She noticed the jade necklace and blood stained gown. She hoped Brent would be home soon.

Frank grabbed her roughly, by the arm and led her out of the bedroom and down the stairway. He opened the door. Before stepping outside, he looked in all directions. He pulled Penny out with him. With one grip around her waist he pratically threw her on the waiting horse. The clouds hovered above them, but the moon still threw enough light on the pathway for Frank to find his way.

Chapter
51

When he reached the ranch, Brent was tired to the point of exhaustion. It was late, and he didn't think Penny to be awake. He slipped up the stairs, halfway expecting Shadow to meet him. When he pushed the bedroom door open, he saw the bed was empty. He walked on to Maggie's room, thinking Penny was probably up with their young daughter. He was surprised to find that room empty too. He walked back to the bed, and then he saw it. His eyes, first fell, to the torn and bloody gown lying on the floor, and then to the jade pendant.

His heart missed a beat as all his senses were suddenly brought to the most basic form of intensity. He was no longer tired. His body and mind were on edge. He was sensitive to every sound, from the slight rustle of the wind to every creek of the floor to his own ragged breathing pattern. He knew. It all hit him at once. "Frank is alive." He said the words with a deep anger. He took the lantern. He started tracking them where Frank had tied his horse. Brent followed the tracks. It soon became obvious. They were headed to the falls. With a gut instinct, he spent no more time tracking. He rode at a neck breaking speed to the falls.

When he was almost there he got off Pacer and tied him to a tree. He wouldn't take any chances with Penny's life. He could hear their voices. He walked in that direction. When he was near enough to make out the words, he waited. He could barely see Penny in the moonlight. She was hidden behind the huge boulders, dangerously close to the falls. He could hear Frank. "I have dreamed about this time for so long. No one could ever create the excitement for me that, even the thought, of you does. Not even Mary. Sweet Mary, with the golden blond hair and baby blue eyes. You know I didn't push her down the stairs, intentionally. If she only hadn't fought. She could still be alive."

Penny had known Frank was a sick man, and she had thought she knew how sick, but she realized she didn't know the completeness of his insanity until now. There was no end to it. He talked about all he had been doing at the ranch.

"So, it never was the rustlers. It was you, taunting me. It was you who killed Shadow. It was you!" Her voice was getting louder and angrier. "At least this time, I have the peace of mind that it is you and not my beloved, Brent." The words sent the demented man into a rage. He moved closer to her. Grabbing her, he covered her lips with his, crushing the soft skin and leaving her mouth bleeding.

"Forget him! You are mine, now. You will be mine forever." He looked toward the water gushing over the edge of the falls.

Penny knew she was in a fatal position. She knew this would be her only chance. She pushed him as hard as she could and ran. She cried out in the darkness as she ran. "Brent!"

Brent jumped and ran for her. She collapsed in his arms. There was no time for him to hold her for Frank was right behind her. The two men struggled. They fell into the water. Penny could no longer see them. She waited, her heart beating in her throat. They were under the water and out of sight. She saw no one, and then out of the water came a large figure. She couldn't see who it was. She scrambled to her feet and ran. Penny again heard a struggle and then a sound she would never forget: a pain filled scream.

She could hear the pounding of flesh and bones against the boulders. She again heard the sound of footsteps hitting the earth behind her. She felt the vice like grip around her waist. She struggled, her heart pounding in her ears. She felt the rough skin against hers, felt the warm breath against her face. She heard the voice whispering in her ear. "Penny, it's alright. Penny, I love you. I'm here, my Darling. I love you."

She looked into his eyes. The eyes that she had stared into when she was only thirteen years old. Her struggle ceased. She knew she was safe.